# LUST

## *The untold story*

**Jiwan Shukla**

PG PUBLICATION

Rohini, Delhi - 110089

Edition : 2020
ISBN : 978-93-89984-03-3

**Lust...The untold story**
By : Jiwan Shukla

Cost : 300/-



Published by
**Prakhar Goonj Publication**
H-3/2, Sector - 18,
Rohini, Delhi - 110089
Contact : 7982710571, 7838505899, 011-27851059

Email : prakhargoonj@gmail.com
sinha.neelu123@gmail.com



This is a work of fiction. Names, Characters, Organisations, Places, Events and Incidents are either products of the author's imagination or used fictitiously.

*Love is the breaking point*

*of the aspiration of an ideal union.*

*Love is a feeling of the heart, union its embodiment.*

*Is a feeling with involvement of bodies*

*true or bodily union?*

## This edition

I am handing over the first edition of 'Lust: The untold story' (English version, of my Hindi novell 'Paye Un Paye' was first published in 1973), in the hands of the readers of the twenty-first century. The century has changed, but the characters of the novel, even today, are trying to forget about the pain with renewed assurance, looking back at the feelings of their sorrow and living with the hope of getting rid of it.

A popular story writer Shri Rajendra Rao's brief but peeking into the story commentary is this new edition's present. It was a coincidence that when Razia's character was engraved in the form of a female IPS officer, there was no female officer in this cadre. But when the plan of its release was being made, then Kiran Bedi came into discussion as the first female IPS officer.

One of the novel's misfortune has been that it did become a choice for a new film producer Mohan Sahab and he even invited me to Mumbai (then Bambai) to converse about it. Until I decided to go, he suffered a sudden cardiac arrest. In 1950, I was in Kanpur as well when I was chosen to play the role of a supporting actor in Ranjeet Film Company, but at that time, my father reprimanded me and stopped me from going, calling cinema against the dignity of our lineage. For years, I kept those papers close to my heart and dreamt of Mumbai. In 1957,when I was working for the central government in Allahabad, I met film actor Prithviraj Kapoor, Raj Kapoor's mother and actor Premnath at Nirala ji's house. He had come to act at the 'Prithvi Theatre'. He also asked me to go to Mumbai, but then my wife said, 'You've got this job with great difficulty, don't take any risk.' And I couldn't gather the courage to go with him. I extensively appeared in international journals like Bharti, Navneet (Bhartiya Vidya Bhawan), Dharmyug and Parag published in Mumbai and in the current journals as well. But till date, Mumbai is like the Persian proverb to me - 'Hanuz----Dilli Dur ast.'

At the programme organised under the aegis of 'DAV College Old boys Association', when the president of the Constituent Council Dr. Virendra Swaroop and Hindi writer former parliamentarian Naresh Chandra Chaturvedi redempted it, till then the body of the senior novelist Bhagwati Prasad Vajpayee had also fallen silent. This work was dedicated to him only. He was the one who stressed on getting this published after hearing an excerpt saying, it's an unbeatable novel of its kind.

The first edition of English version is reiterating the memories of all these, with my first role 'Autobiography of stories' and the entire piece of the opinion of Professor Suhail Parmar on the first edition, in your hands, on the occasion of my 90 th birthday, it is not unnatural to feel a bit emotional presenting this.

**Jiwan Shukla**

## Lust:The untold story, a plotless novel

Lust, The untold story, doesn't fall under the category of traditional novels. It can be called Professor Raju's autobiography in one way and researcher Yashpal's dissertation. The title 'Human's family relations, sex and culture' brought Yashpal to Professor Raju. This novel comes close to Sigmund Freud's theory that most of the mental activities of a human are creations of his subconscious mind. Sex plays a crucial part at its core. For which, Freud has used the word Libido, which means sexual desire.

The central character of this novel Professor Raju is a Nobel Prize winner. Yashpal is his friend's son. If the efforts to explain this is on the basis of Indian mythological beliefs, then this work is a erotic creation. Freud also considers sexual desires to be the main source of human actions.

In the pre-novel time of 'Lust, an untold story', Ilachandra Joshi was established as the originator of the Hindi psychological novels. When the discussion of Marx, Darwin and Freud was there between the elite scholars as well as the middle-class degree holders, this novel seems like the creation of the same thought. Jiwan ji is famous as a poet but with this work he tries to knock at the world of novels too. But the way he stands apart in the crowd of poets, in the same way with 'Lust, an untold story' in the field of novels he isn't seen standing beside Ilachandra Joshi, Bhagwati Prasad Vajpayee or Agyaya.

The way Nirala has given direction to romanticism through wishing for the ebb and flow, probably Jiwan Shukla is the pioneer of the same consciousness of novelty. But to read the works of such people or to comment on it, one has to come out of the established contemplation camps. Before forming an opinion on 'Lust, an untold story', it is imperative to glance upon this statement from the act whose title is 'Autobiography of stories':

'I have met the characters of Lust:an untold story in some way or the other. Their sentimental circumstances have shaken me, their weaknesses have given me a new perspective towards life. The life that I have seen or seen others living, that will be found in my works, here and there, organised, systematic or scattered. This life, habitual of drinking bitter truth sips, is surrounded by the ruins of collapsing beliefs on one side and on the other side, looks forward to get drenched in the meager showers of the moonlight of Shri Chandi civilization. But the legs carrying the struggling breaths are trapped in the swamp that we have got in the absence of God's infinite compassion, due to the actions of previous births and for our disabilities. So society, government and the contractors selling opium of consolation are not at fault in this. I have taken birth in the courtyard of hard working culture of a fortunate country, where what is found sometimes remains lost and the loss is suffered, carried, lived the entire life and probably for ages.'

This tells that whether the experience is truthful or that which is seen, writer's euphemism is based on reality. That is what was seen being experienced by others or experienced by self, that reality isn't the reality woven by the fibers of imagination.

All of us live in the same neighborhood. We often met in the evening or on the holiday. Intense discussions on literature, art and politics would also happen. One day, I asked Jiwan, 'You've written that you have met the characters of Lust:The untold story in some way, so is this novel an autobiography of those characters, or a story of what they experienced?' Then he said, 'Suhail Sahab, I'm not a Professor of philosophy like you, nor a journalist who would report incidents. I descend into the souls of my characters and look at the reason behind the nonexistent elements coming into action and their reaction with a neutral approach. If I had to support my statement by taking an example of a character's dialogue from Shakespeare, it would be 'I try to establish a sequence between his different actions.' When Prince Hamlet's uncle takes a deep look at Prince's behaviour, then he sees Prince Hamlet who isn't mad like Prince Hamlet. His uncle says to his mother, 'There is a sequence in his madness...' He senses that the madness of Prince is an attempt to explore an invisible reality. He looks mad, he behaves like a mad person, but he isn't mad in reality. The exact same situation is of the person of the society who is a character for a writer. Literature isn't about serving reality, but about its expression. I'm a lifeist, not realist or imaginative. It will be clear on seeing deeply. Here, madness is only a condition to be seen or understood, but expression of literature is in sequence. Similarly, the characters that are there in this novel, I have tried to give a voice to the consciousness of their outfit. It's the responsibility of the reviewer to find sequence in it, not that of the writer. So, you should meet our characters and try to find what's intriguing in them and their behaviour. Yes, a great reviewer is one who enters the characters and the writer and on coming out gives that expression of reality a meaningful context.'

The reality of 'Lust,The untold story' is the time lived by Raju in his lifetime. Asha is his first love interest and Rekha his first sexual partner. Baarin Bhabhi is a young widow hungry for sex, Saavri an easily available alternative to Rekha. Razia the flame burning in the fire of love. In the autobiography of Raju, neither the effect of the flow of consciousness is seen, that is found in the stream of consciousness in the novels of James Joyce or Virginia Woolf,nor like the Agyaya's novel 'Shekhar ek jivani', the plot of this novel cannot even be seen on the basis of the theories of Marx or Freud. In this context, I would like to rest on this statement of Virginia Woolf, 'Look within and life it seems, is very far from being 'like this'. Examine for a moment an ordinary mind on an ordinary day.' This is probably what Jiwan ji means through his statement. The work of peeking inside the person and his behaviour. Man is the perfect entity of meaning and sex. But a new vision was required to see Professor Raju. In fact, this is a story of the consciousness of connecting unimaginable circumstances, struggling and colliding with unorganized planning, that is associated with the ascent and descent of events rather than a script. Therefore, I have reached the conclusion that in this novel by Jiwan Ji there is no ordered plot, that is it does have a start, a middle and an end. In the words of field theory, this novel is a historical one and in the ancient language of Buddha, this reiterates his call - 'Keeping aside the question of beginning and end, I talk about every religion or process.' Process is important, not character or story. That is why, there is no overwhelming character like Shekhar from Agyeya in this. Because this story doesn't belong to anyone; similar to how the electrons and protons of Einstein's physics are forms of activity, but it's nobody in particular's activity. The characters of this novel moving people and situations, character and plot, events all come in rhythm with each other. People and objects are all forms of action. It does not mean that this work comes under the tradition of those foreign novels, which is called the school of 'stream of consciousness'. Because the reality presented in this is not individual oriented, or status oriented, it is action oriented. The person is in some situation and the situation is in action. So, action has only one form and the entire novel is a series of new forms of action.

I hope that this novel from Shri Jiwan will give a new social 'space' to accelerate the blind frustrations of today's life and constricted forces of personality.

**Professor Suhail Parmar**

## An intense saga of the breaking and newly created dreams

Senior writer Dr. Jiwan Shukla through his long-standing practice in the strenuous field of poetic creation achieved fame and recognition. In the vast world of his creations, there is a novel as well, that has disappeared in the glitter of his poetic works. The Hindi version of this novel was written in the '60s of the last decade and published in 1973. Now its copies are nowhere to be found. The only available copy is planned to be republished as a manuscript so that justice could be done with this realistic and readable work.

When I got the opportunity to read it, then upon reading some pages, drifting in the fast-paced flow, it felt as if we have reached almost half a century back, into the post-independence Era of Nehru, due to the clock ticking backwards, sitting in a time machine. In a unique era of unprecedented expansion in socialism, five year plans and the public sector, in which the general public suffering from food insecurity, inflation and unemployment, dreamt with open eyes about nation building and a golden future. It had been 20 years since independence, but the majority of the population was drowning in the darkness of poverty and backwardness. The slow pace with which economic and social transformation was happening and the way corruption was spreading its legs in the rule of Quota-Permit-License, it was only natural for the younger generation to feel disillusioned. The heart wrenching narrative of the intense struggle of the families of the lower middle class of North India goes on in this novel from beginning to end. Jiwan Shukla has portrayed with great honesty the story of the continuous emerging resistance of the hardworking and sincere workers against injustice, exploitation and corruption and the rise of leftist ideas. The struggle of the education section of the lower middle class was on both social and economic fronts. On one hand, there was a desire to break the bonds of rotten traditions, the trade union movement was gaining momentum against institutional injustice and Freud was being looked upon to redefine human relations. While on the other hand, through aspirations of the egalitarian society Marxism was being spread. In this novel, a very realistic depiction of the superficial culture of the middle class has been made. In the absence of family planning, most of the families experience the hard blows of insufficiency, illiteracy, drinking the bitter drinks of life, becoming languid, meaningless and aimless. For them, life has become a model of 'a body of fire and one has to drown in it to cross it'. In this background, the subtle and accurate description of the undercurrent of resistance gaining pace in the intellectual society is characteristic of this novel.

This is an autobiographical novel. The life story of the Nobel Prize winner Professor Raju, as heard from his friend's son (research student). The background is the same as that of Dr. Jiwan Shukla. The lanes of Kanpur, the house of in-laws in Kannauj and the intellectual splendor of Allahabad. This story's female characters seem to be stronger, powerful and rational. The writer has penned down a very deep shaded female character as the mother of the main character. During the creation of the Hindi version of this novel (65-70), the silent portrayal of sexual relations in hindi novels had almost received the silent approval of the readers. But despite some fairly deafening episodes here, Laxman Rekha remains intact- as the self narrative stories hold, this novel has an open ended flat plot. There is no high point in the plot. The narrative progresses at a slow pace in spite of sudden serial events. As soon as there is scope for a discussion at any point, the ideological dimensions of the narrative begin to open up and such great blossoming. I'm not able to stop myself from vocal quoting. Please mind the following -

(1) 'The country was getting divided into linguistic states. America, Russia, Japan, Germany, every place had India's moustache hair mortgaged at their doors. Nehru had dreamt of socialism. Laid foundation of schemes for prosperity of socialism. The constitution of the country assured protection of the interests of all. Dams were built, factories were built and the planned way to eat every time by asking for it. Inflation broke the backs of the public. The glut of taxes flared the prices of the breath of man.'

(2) Ghasita said, chewing tobacco, 'Sir, but till when

will the darkness of ration remain?'

'Hey, why do you worry? It's not famine in America. The drought is in the fields of the less fortunate. Poor American people that have opened the godowns and treasure doors. People might say whatever, but only the money lenders feel pity for the poor. Debt will be paid by those whose ancestors had donated. Long live America and long live the government of the pair of two bulls. Hey, Kallu? Did you filter it less today?'

Overall, Lust The untold story is a serious intervention in a concomitant literary genre by a well known poet. You might agree with my accreditation on reading this book.

**Rajendra Rao**

## Publication

Dr Jiwan Shukla is basically a poet who is amongst pioneers of neolyric and post sixty poetry movement of Hindi. Eighty eight plus age appears to have no restriction in his creative voyage. So far he has given elevin poetry collections, one Urdu gazal compilation, two epics, one novel, one book of critical articles and three other books in prose belonging to different genre of prose writings. "LUST "is english version of his famous Hindi novel "paye un paye "which has created a new space between stream of consciousness and autobiographical way of novel writings. We hope this will enjoy wider favour of english readers.

## Autobiography of stories

The Hindi version of the book 'Lust:The untold story', like my other works, is a creation not published timely. Its typed manuscript was lying for many years. If laziness comes in the way, it is in the system of publication. Although its role is also very important prior to that, and that would be preparing a press copy of the written material. This work seems like a much bigger work than creative planning. The manuscript of 'Vanshi tum dhar do' wouldn't have been prepared if it hadn't been for great soul Nirala's rebuke. The period of one and a half years between the creation of 'Singhdwar' and its publication, the glory of the same laziness and inconvenience prevailed then. It sometimes results in the reviewer and the reader becoming incompatible with the author's writing process. There comes a difference between the analysis of the creation. But excellent and fundamental works don't live at the boundary of the years counted on fingers. This is evident not only with many great texts, my own creations have also given me this confidence.

The motivational statements of Pandit Bhagwati Prasad Vajpayee have played a significant role in completing this incomplete work. I have met the characters of Lust:The untold story in some way or the other. Their sentimental circumstances have shaken me, their weaknesses have given me a new perspective towards life. The life that I have seen or seen others living, that will be found in my works, here and there, organised, systematic or scattered. This life, habitual of drinking bitter sips of truth, is surrounded by the ruins of collapsing beliefs on one side and on the other side, looks forward to getting drenched in the meager showers of the moonlight of Shri Chandi civilization. But the legs carrying the struggling breaths are trapped in the swamp that we have got in the absence of God's infinite compassion, due to the actions of previous births and for our disabilities. So, society, government and the contractors selling opium of consolation are not at fault in this. I have taken birth in the courtyard of the hard working culture of a fortunate country, where what is found sometimes remains lost and the loss is suffered, carried, lived for the entire life and probably for ages.

What does Hindi have, answering that would be like praising your own self. But what it doesn't have, that I'd surely like to say. We may publicize Hindi as 'national language', that is, as a raw material of democracy, by shouting it out, by agitating for it, or by translating the Indian constitution into Hindi, but probably we wouldn't be able to make the language used by the 'Prime Minister' for his everyday work. The readers of which language's great works are less, that cannot just give birth to age transforming ideas but nor can its writers remain standing on the sticks for a long time. The writer, publisher and distributor of a cheap book earn black money, whereas the creator of the literary works does countless things in lack of funding.

Though this statement of mine will like a bone in the meat for those people who wish to keep our future accustomed to mental slavery for centuries by making us drink false drinks of the right knowledge like socialism. You know, the entire life of Vajpayee ji is a spoiled form of an independent text. The fact that he could love seeing his words isn't less of a proof of his greatness. But if he wouldn't have got the sympathetic shoulder of the courses of Universities, then his peace wouldn't have been stable in this old age. So, this is my great wish that those readers of Hindi that can practice reading such literature books should be encouraged. If you want your language to be the national language in real sense and become the official language of the world, then you should yourself start a revolution of reading creative writings, works of the poets and thinkers. The desire to get signed copies from the writers as gifts and the habit of decorating them in your cupboards, both are dangerous. To keep the language alive, it's important for its writer to be alive and the writer will only live when the number of people buying and reading his works increases. In our own country, Bengali language is its living proof.

Last year, I met Swedish writer Cigarette Khaale at the Afroasia Writers Conference. She told me that in her country, every writer doesn't just get the royalty out of his sold books but each time his book gets read through a library, he gets a fixed amount of royalty. That is the reason, the writers, poets there are entitled to greater respect than any capitalist or Government Political leader. Whereas in our country, perhaps an eligible member of the municipality receives more respect in the eyes of the public than a great poet. This is not just a fault of the social system, but who is responsible for it? We should start a movement against it. Today's writers should rise above the temptations of the government beliefs and demand for social justice.

If 'Lust:The untold story' shakes you up with your shortcomings and manages to inspire you towards artistic creations, then I'll regard my efforts to be fruitful. But I'm curious to. Know about your reactions personally, that could reach me through a postcard or an envelope. I hope to receive love from readers, their suggestions and whatever is left unfulfilled will be found in this work.

**Jiwan Shukla**
**Dharm Dham**
**Gwalmaidan**
**Kannauj -209725**
**(M) 9415471813**

# LUST

*The untold story*

**A** peepal tree in its infant stage ripping through the gaps between the bricks, sloping like an aureb cut vest, moved like the braid of a girl with the gust of wind rising upwards. At some distance from the tree, green moss on the wall looked like the ashes from a stove of sawdust. The house whose wall had this tree growing, that wasn't in ruins and nor was it the subject of negligence for the people who lived there. If it was something, then it was an ancient result of the autobiographies of a very long old history, where people came, lived and left blurring the evening of their stories of memories. Today, a family lives there, with three young boys, two wives, and a mature girl, lives two old husband and wife.

I kept watching for a few more minutes at that small creeper. At its courage to grow in this stony region, at the underlying motive behind its birth. I started thinking. Amidst several questions, a thing suddenly lights up like the lightning in the sky covered with clouds, do the elite people living here not know that a peepal tree is sprouting in their wall. Are they living by restricting their boundaries of curiosity, vigilance and responsibilities to their courtyard, rooms and terrace? They should know about their walls.

There was a ruin beside the wall, of which everything was destroyed, but a shabby door fastened with a lock. I even looked at this door with a question mark and decided in my mind, whose neighbourhood is deserted, he doesn't know about the peepal tree and the moss growing on his wall.

There is a reason behind what happens, what is to happen, and there is a motive behind what is happening. On this basis, I gathered my sight on these walls. I wasn't an officer at the department of archaeology, who earned by giving voice to the mute glorifying symbols of the past and their extinct personalities. I moved ahead of this house.

This big mansion standing on the elephant outpost, it was written 'Shanti Kunj'. Whether or not this mansion of two blocks is a bower, is known only to the people living the house, but if a person spreads his arms standing on the hut talking to constellations made on the terrace of second floor, then it's not impossible that milky white moon fell down in his arms.

I had come to this city regarding my research. The topic of my research was- Sex and culture in human family. Instead of the word sex, I have used the words sexual desire. I have come to know that somewhere here Professor Raju spends his solitary social life. Solitary because he did not have relations in the city or neighbourhood. Social because he was a man of a particular society. His routine was limited to studying and writing books. His sons were burdened with their family lives. My guide hadn't given any more information on Professor Raju than this. However, he was also my father's old friend. My eyes, for some reason, after wandering through the various doors of this city, fixated on this particular door. There were two reasons for that; there was a crowd outside every door, here or there were incoherent noises coming from inside them or people wearing tehmat and thick janeyu who were rubbing tobacco in their palms or whining about their business of tobacco or screeching voices from a radio were heard or loud abuses from some places. This was the only door from whose face mildness was flowing. Which on being seen from outside, reflected the inner prosperity. But who were the residents or what happened at that time, it was not possible to estimate that. The population of the house was informed to me by a little boy from the neighbourhood. I did not consider it right to ask the owner's name from him, so I searched for the name plate. There must be a name plate outside the house of a country wide famous scholar. But it did not come to my mind that whose name is written in black letters gold plated in the books, his door will have his name in white letters, what use will be a wooden plank on this door then!

On looking carefully, I saw a button to call. Without giving any thought, I pressed the button. After some time, an old grey haired woman with spectacles wearing a terricot saree came to the door and said, 'Whom do you want to meet?' I answered, 'Is this Professor Raju's mansion?'

'Your good name?' asked the woman in a polite and sincere voice.

'I am called Yashpal; I am the son of Mr. Kant from Allahabad and am coming regarding some research to meet Professor Sahab.'

'Come, sit here in this room. I will just send him.' Saying this, her eyes from behind the spectacles spread her heart's gladness. That gentle lady pointed with her finger towards a well-furnished room. I sat there on a sofa.

The room was big. A small sofa set, a sofa bed, four armed chairs, two tables with trays without a sign of decoration. Yes, in one corner there was a statue of Gautama, in front of which there was a picture of the Russian Revolution and on its side there was a marquee picture under which it was written in English, Sigmund Freud.

After around a wait of five minutes, a gentle, healthy man wearing lungi and vest, hawai slippers in his feet and holding a book in his hand with two fingers between its pages entered the room. I touched his feet, with this conviction and I am meeting Professor Raju himself.

Professor Sahab smiled and blessed me. Picking me up, he said, 'Hey! You have grown so much, Yash. How is Kant? Is your mother well?' It seemed like he wanted to ask everything in one breath.

I answered every question. He called out from there, 'Rekha, bring some breakfast for Yash, he has come walking from very far.' Then he turned towards me and asked, 'Where is your luggage?'

'My luggage is in the waiting room. I had come to find the place.'

'Have some breakfast first and then bring your entire luggage inside.' Professor sahab said.

I had not imagined that I was coming to an idol of such

generosity.

Professor Raju has got the Nobel Prize for his book 'Individualistic voices of the Indian scenario' after five years. Even after getting the most prestigious award in the world, he was not considered more capable than Padma Vibhushan back home by the Indian government. Here, only the achievers in the field of politics are given Bharat Ratna. But Professor Raju did not look like a man of such a stature if not told. There were two reasons for it, his simple yet serious personality and gentle charm, that had the glory of a deity but it did not have the pride of its position. It did not have the business shine.

He was respected in the neighbourhood as a teacher. Yes, but a few people with university level education knew him as a Nobel laureate and a Padma Vibhushan awardee. But he was not counted among the famous people in the society because neither he did any business in tobacco or perfume, nor gave loans on interest. In addition, he wasn't even in a government position that could give anyone quota permits or could rescue someone on being arrested. Society worships that form of a person which benefits him in some way. By the way, his sons traversed in the opposite direction to him. They all indulged in such activities that made the people of the city consider them as rich. The beauty of the house was a reflection of their business minded personalities.

His elder son worked with the bulk of tobacco, the younger one had built a small factory of tin cans and the third one had a shop of clothes. Apparently, people in service are seen as inferior in the city of Kannauj, if he is not an executive level officer. The culture of the Harsha period had collapsed before the decline of the fort of Jaichand. Even its ruins were not left. There is a kingdom of Mahajani civilization here. The feet of the Pundits are touched, but if they themselves are not in business or not earn more than a lakh, then they are not respected more than a beggar. Even if I might not accept this truth. The business class here knows that the ultimate respect of a Brahmin is limited to the statement of 'touching his feet'.

Whatever felony has been committed from the beginning to the present day; it cut the Kshatriyas, exhorted the Brahmins, converted the Shudras and looted the Vanikas. The kingdoms were snatched from the kings, gurupada from the Brahmins, but business was not taken away from the Baniyas. They are polite so that the god doesn't take away their business; they donate, so that the Pundits don't consider them unrighteous. Today, if the people of the same capitalist society are bombing Vietnam, then they are also seen making the futile effort of filling the trench between the poor and the rich by erecting the ghost of socialism.

I told Professor sahab the topic of my research and also that I will prepare a report on the aspects of the sex and culture in the personal lives of the individuals selected from different areas. Its results will be an important expression in my research thesis. Probably this will be a scientific endeavour to prepare the ground for creating a new document in today's changing perspectives. I also want to record your observations. I went quiet after saying so. I did not dare to fix my eyes on his face, let alone know his thoughts.

Social decency, personal obsolescence, knowledge of sin and virtue, influence on the young, thoughts of the peers gathered in a crowd in the courtyard of Professor Raju's mind. The helplessness of the Professor and the solitary evening of his past peeked from the edge of his eyes; sex is an entirely different topic. There is a life between the drawing room and the bedroom. Even I will not accept the social fabric in my personal life, but I am asking the same question from a prostitute, lady minister, labourer, Professor and a mill owner.

Professor Raju said, 'I should clarify one thing, without knowing what you think of sex, I would say that the word has dynamic meaning. Although its biological meaning is prevalent in the society, it is not just aesthetic but cultural. It covers everything from the desire to live to the plea for death. Not just in my life, but its meaning that is hidden in the society in others' lives, is sensual only. I am also thinking that when my son or daughter will read your thesis, then which form of me they will see. But there is a difference between Mr. Raju and Professor Raju. If every person goes on gathering the solitude of life into him, then how will the language of solitude and its grammar be understood? It does not mean that it is imperative to bring out the stains for the believers of realism. You have come to me in this desolate age to remind me of a vase of flowers. The forms of sex that I have lived, I will tell you all about them even if you or your society considers them unacceptable. When the prime solitary moments, their translation and their social environment of the life of a Nobel laureate will be uncovered in front of the youth that hate the opium ideals, they will spit on the picture of that great man.' Professor sahab continued speaking passionately, 'Though they should bow their heads before all my weaknesses because I have drawn lotuses from every swamp. The person who pretends to live his life according to Ram's ideals didn't write the Ramayana. Tulsi who brought the purity of Ramayana to every house was also a symbol of human weakness for sex, not a lord. Sexual relation is a sin as well as a virtue.'

'So would you also want to use the words of definitive translation of ethology here?' I asked.

'The context and meaning in which a word is said means the same. A word can have different meanings at different places, which you know.' He said quenching the curiosity of a student.

I asked respecting the decorum of the class, 'Sir, I would also want to know the reason and circumstances of you entering the academic life. My father told me that you were in government service before.'

He said, 'Yes, that's right. I should answer that in one sentence. Separation from Razia inspired me to write something and the upsetting life of office made me a Professor.'

'Sir, who is Razia?'

'I'll tell you when it's time.' He went quiet after saying this.

He continued, 'Yashpal, I will tell you some unsaid events of my life. From them you may sort the things of use. Although everyone's life can have moments like these that can be used for the time to come. I probably would have remained a clerk all my life or the pride of a leader of a trade union or died being a minister, if Razia wouldn't have shaken me so much that night. She was an IPS officer and I was her Raju, a mere clerk! The corruption, immorality in the worker class and the lack of meaning prevailing in the society has made me sorrowful in every way. I even considered migrating from the workplace sometimes. There is a strange story of the family relations lived by people who are called genius by the society. Had it not been for your aunt, this flow of life that wandered to several corners would have succumbed to join some stream. The corners that wish to be fastened by the excitement of youth mostly end being unstable brinks. Today, I think if I would've spent my life with Asha, Saavri or Razia then it wouldn't have been a worthy life. Every woman tied in marital bliss isn't the housewife to gauge happiness and sorrow in a household equally.'

Professor sahab said, seeing Rekha come, 'Barkhurdar is doing his PhD.'

'Obviously, unlike your sons, my Yash doesn't shy away from studying.'

Rekha said, smiling while keeping the breakfast on the table.

There was also a servant in that house but this was their sincerity that they would serve cordially to close people. Aunt Rekha's sentence filled me with so much affection that it reminded me of my mother.

Whatever Professor sahab had told me, I was writing it down today. He had read the unread pages of his life in front of me, who was in every way like his son.

So, he was saying-

The inner tendencies had started coming out in the same way as a Neem sapling. The shivers of the night were being felt by the veins. The algae of age were sprouting on the shining face. I wished to see pretty faces. I naturally got attracted to the opposite sex. The matters that tickled the soul were being found attractive by me. Looking in the mirror several times, combing hair, keeping the coat, shoes and even collar in order. The sense of loneliness had spread its legs. Acne started weaving webs on my face like a spider. A layer of the colour of honey emerged on the forehead. But the ropes of the cot hadn't started making noise in the night yet. The light switch wasn't forced to remain on. The mind didn't wander off from books. Sex was not anything more than a part of character.

I wished that the girl who was filling water at the terrace wearing underwear would talk to me. Sometimes I thought, now underwear doesn't suit her. Beauty arises in the knees. Then I thought, when she laughs, why do whirlpools form at her polite cheeks? Why do I like them?

Union. That hunger was being felt. Several times a day, I would go to the terrace with excuse or without, and look at the face of the pipe with a question mark. Eyes would question, 'Where is Asha?'

She had seen me gauging her figure a few times. Her eyes had also come with an answer. As long as she stayed at the terrace, her eyes wandered at the staircase turning from the terrace.

Now the eyes had started talking. The lips had learnt to express. The pipe was decorated like a marriage tent. The language wanted to come to the lips crossing the teeth.

Now Asha had started wearing dhoti. She made apparent efforts to keep the hair tidy. She ate paan. Rising-blood. Consciousness would fly away, very far away like birds. We were proceeding rapidly. Now one bucket would get washed by rinsing it ten times. People were noticing. And our eyes were getting blinded.

Gradually, the medium of expression of the mind was plain innocent paper and flawless ink. Asha would throw a crumpled piece of paper towards me. I would pick it up and even hide it from God, read it once, twice, five times, ten times. The ink of my pen would also heat up and I would also crumple a paper and throw it towards her. I would unbutton my shirt anxious from the heart's warmth and she would slide her saree over her shoulder. One had blinded eyes and the other had bowed eyelids.

Now we met at the terrace playing hide and seek with the world. We talked while roaming and keeping a distance. I would say, 'Asha, in which class do you study?' She would answer, 'Sixth.' When I saw Asha passing by or talking like this, the warmth of my blood shook the stage of veins. I couldn't think how or what I should do. How should I start talking? As if I didn't possess the language of love, the feeling of meeting alone, the craft of expression! Not just me, probably Asha's heart also sinked and emerged in this colour.

The mute bond of expression, the turmoil of emotions, the stagnation of shattered patience, the sweltering roof of summer, our naked innocent feet, the staring avenging sunlight and the love nurturing of age. ..... I wished to fill Asha in my arms. ....... Clear the silence of expression; give the stagnation of patience the bangle of the flowing river. Let the feet burn, the sun rays take revenge and the heartbeats breathe in the pain of heart. I could bang the chest of time and say, a sunflower has emerged in the sweltering heat in the garden of our lap.

Suddenly, Asha's aunt called for her, 'What are you doing at the terrace in this sweltering afternoon?' Asha climbed down rapidly as she spoke these words. She heard her aunt's last word at the door of her room itself.

The tide wanted to pluck the moon but the blind waves had pointed at the burning sun. And the nail burnt as soon as it got pointed. The haziness cleared. The feet were staring at the director like a beaten up producer. Beneath the feet was an unknown, uneven way and an antelope in front of the eyes.

Union is the end of love. This is the same affection where the humanness of love accepts sex.

Love is the breaking point of the aspiration of an ideal union. Love is a feeling of the heart, union its embodiment. Is a feeling with involvement of bodies true or bodily union?

.......And then I thought even the feelings need expression. Only feeling is self sufficient. Love is joy, union, a sibling of ultimate pleasure. But a feeling can arise irrespective, whereas the urns of beauty once bow cannot rise again. ..... Feelings are constant and union a coincidence. .... No, nothing of this sort, I will embody feelings. Idol worship is an aspiration of emotions. An idol is emotional, and its worship should also be done with emotions.

Now conversations had started happening with Asha unhesitant. We met far from the eyes of the world, away from the ears of the walls, we talked. While filling the bucket, she would sometimes sprinkle some water on me. Sometimes I would grab her while she passed by. If the eyes had hands; Asha would have been abducted the very first day. If the eyelashes had teeth ....... If it was that way, then something would have happened. Why fly in vanity?

That day it was very hot on the pipe. Babu Satyanarayana, Deshraj Singh, Doctor Aunt and the children everyone gathered. I had returned after studying. Master Sahab's house was in Rambagh only, at some distance. Mother had no idea about the commotion at the pipe. I had only just stood in the room, when Babu Deshraj called out in a serious tone, 'Raju, come here.' I traced back my steps to the pipe. My legs had the same titillation as every other time I would get touching the way to the meeting place. But on seeing the crowd all of a sudden, I got goosebumps.

'Raju, how dare you?' Babu Satyanarayana said with blood red eyes. My eyes felt his soldering gaze and the sharpness of his words. I shuddered from head to toe. I gathered courage to say, 'What happened?'

Deshraj extended his hand to Satyanarayana to ask for something. He handed him a piece of paper. Deshraj said, 'Read this, have you written this?' I looked at that paper turning it over a few times and involuntarily a smile spread on my face. The pupils of people's eyes dilated at my face.

'Yes. I have written this. It was a translation piece. Don't you see I have left two lines after every sentence?' I said I would return the letter to Deshraj.

On that, Babu Satyanarayana asked gravely, "I love you, why fear love?' Is this the kind of translation taught to you?'

Now I got a little taken aback. The reason for this shock was the atmosphere rife with fear.

The eyes of all those who were standing on the terrace were pawing at my face. There was a crowd gathered in my eyes as well. Like the upward facing neck of an Orient table fan, the people wanted to see a predetermined form of tragedy in a drama. I then challenged their patience.

'That isn't taught, but I wanted to see their English. But who has given you this paper?'

'You had given this to Asha and she has given it to me.' Babu Satyanarayana answered.

'This is wrong.' This paper was surely thrown away at the terrace, being torn from the notebook, after fairing it. This is someone's planning.

'So have you done these translations?'

'Yes.'

'Show me the notebook.' Babu Satyanarayana said in a strict tone, waving his hand.

I ran to get the notebook. Mother asked, 'What happened?' 'Nothing' I only muttered this much and fanned out with the notebook. Opening that page, I kept the notebook in front of Babu Satyanarayana. Many people bowed to see it. Master looked at the date and signature very carefully.

The revelation of the situation was strange. People

thought Raju would be beaten up. But hail the unwavering strength of love. The risk in love gives meaning to life's essence. Somehow I gave a new meaning to a truth in regard with time!

The matter was solved, but there were discussions. Now there was a sharp barrier to me climbing the pipe. From the window, from the crevices of the door, from the balconies, and some from their lawns soaking the happiness of the open, all were vigilant towards me.

My eyes, the speed of my eyelids were watched. When the society realizes what they want, it becomes a problem. The name of completion is related to the partition of hair. Love is born at the door of bondage, but those shackles need to be broken for growth. The air surrounding the secrecy of meeting alone gets transferred like pollen...... And now even the bucket gets filled quickly. Eyes looked at the hope in the drop of water made by the water flowing from the tap into the bucket.

Asha gathered courage. The union of letters happened. The warmth of the heart was spilled on the paper. Asha was made to cease her studies after sixth class; the days of dhoti from underwear had come. Her letters had broken words. They had lines from songs that expressed her feelings. Even I had to gather phrases of famous singers from the cinema to express my feelings of love. A man walks on the road of religion with superstitions towards circumstances and feelings of revenge in love. Religion makes you fearful and love makes you independent.

The house that we lived in was filled with very different tenants. There was a lock on the door. They ran factories, and cooked and ate by themselves. One was a labourer, blacksmith by caste, and had no children. There were two families. One was Bajpai gharana. In the upper part, in the adjacent balcony was Deshraj Singh. To flaunt their caste, according to the rules of their caste, they wrote Rathore Thakur before their names. Towards the pipe, Babu Satyanarayana, Asha's uncle, doctor aunt, etc had their places fixed. My father was an older tenant than all others. All were middle class subsistence people.

They loved a woman on the lower floor. Mother of a child, a widow. My health was an example for others at that time. When I used to wear underwear or shorts, many eyes turned my way. The meaning of sexual pleasure couldn't be realised in my life. I did feel some stress in my veins sometimes. My heart would flutter, for some reason, seeing a pretty girl. I would wish to talk to some girl alone. She would look at me smiling and I would tease her by tickling. One day I had gone to the courtyard on being called by bhabhi. All ladies of that house were bhabhi for me. They would joke with me. I would also take pleasure in it. She called me and sat me beside her. She talked about silly things. She said, 'Raju, I have a fever. Will you not bring me medicine?' I replied out of habit, 'Surely.' At my answer, she looked at me, smiling and somehow I couldn't bear that smile.

The conversation went on. I stood up to leave, when she said, 'You must think I'm lying. See, how high a fever I have.' On saying this, bhabhi took my hand and kept it on her breast pressing it against them. I felt a surge of electricity run from my head to toe. I freed my hand and ran.

I was catching my breath on reaching my room. Mother asked, 'Where were you?' I only said, 'I was down.' But my mind was caught in the uproar that while getting checked by a doctor for fever, people show their pulse.

But bhabhi had.... But then I remembered that even the doctor uses a stethoscope and places it on the chest. Then another explanation clicked me. When my mother was ill, the doctor had told us to remove the blouse a little from the shoulder and he had placed the stethoscope on the back, a little lower from the shoulder. But bhabhi had.....

I couldn't reach a conclusion. But even on being called so many times, I never sat beside bhabhi for some reason. She started teasing me. She sometimes said you look innocent. You are crazy about Asha. And it went on like that. I always enjoyed the banter smiling. I had started taking interest in such playful teasing.

One day my mother was sitting and talking with a few friends. Mother said that it has only been one year since 'Rania' got married. She is going to be a mother. These days, ladies become pregnant as soon as they get married. I was sitting in my room studying. I kept my books away and sat at the edge of the balcony looking at the passersby. Suddenly mother's words about Rania started rambling in my mind. I started thinking, 'What does it mean to be pregnant in the ninth month after marriage?' I turned around and saw the ladies' meeting was over. Now mother got busy with the chores. It was time for Babu to return home from the shop. The wood was soaking. Mother was getting angry at Babu. The matter of getting pregnant formed a question mark inside my head like a mystery.

At last I couldn't wait. I finally asked mother, 'Ma, why does a woman get pregnant only after getting married? Why not before? Does God know that she is married?'

This question of mine makes mother break into a smile. Her eyes were red from the smoke from trying to light the wet wood. The balcony got filled with smoke. It looked like a smoke cell. I had trouble breathing. Mother answered with fake annoyance, 'You are sixteen now, you don't even know this. Nowadays boys learn in the womb itself.'

I was surprised. Choking from the smoke I said, 'What do they learn in the womb? You didn't answer my question even.'

Mother said, 'You are foolish. Yes, God gets to know that marriage has happened.' And then she smiled hiding her face. I came out from there fearing the smoke.

I am naturally inclined towards talking less. I was counted among the sincere boys of the neighbourhood. Never sitting anywhere for a long time. Remembering Asha throughout the day and studying was the routine. When I was rubbing my eyes while standing on the staircase, suddenly Asha passed from there; she jumped a little and then smiled. Seeing me rub my eyes she thought I had been scolded. She said, 'Raju, what happened? Has aunty beaten you?'

I had forgotten about the bitterness of the smoke. Mother was still fighting the battle with the smoke. Clouds of smoke were leaving from the windows and the doors of the room. Even then their unbreakable queue was reminiscent of Rakhtbeej. He must've been this way, that merciless demon. He took birth every time he was killed. I instantly spoke, 'No.' 'Then why are your eyes wet? What has happened? Tell me quickly, or somebody would come.'

'You are crazy. Do you not see the thousand arms of the smoke? They attacked altogether on my eyes which you love.' On saying this much, I moved forward a little and made an attempt to pull her towards me. She grabbed the wall tightly. I tickled her. The corner of the wall slipped from her hands and she fell in my arms. Along with laughter, shadows formed and faded on her fair cheeks. Now I had tightly embraced her in my arms. The more she tried to evade, the more her body collided with mine, and my heartbeat would get faster. I was feeling something that I have never felt before. Meanwhile, someone's footsteps were heard from downstairs. Asha said, 'Leave me, someone is coming. What if they see us?' And she bit my cheek with her teeth so hard that my embrace got loose. She slid away from my arms like a fish. While leaving, biting her saree she said, 'You are a big one.'

Keeping my hand on my wet cheek, I kept looking in her direction. There is so much excitement in these hide 'n' seek meetings, how intoxicating, how impulsive. In the proposal of love, this was the first step. For the first time today, I saw and felt the softness of Asha, her shapely body, her developed organs from up close. For the first time I was feeling that even the veins in our body have bellies, where there is a hunger whose sleep breaks at a certain age. It probably wakes up to never sleep again. To curse your sleep forever. I moved towards the room with tired feet. The warmth in my blood was intact. One eye of the mind was still enjoying attaining the ultimate happiness, smiling, and the other would cry in pain of separation. I stood in front of the mirror staring at the moon shaped mark on my cheek. My heart beat was now calming. The heat in the veins was reducing. As far as the mark was, blood had come flushing.

The sun had toppled the door of the west. Seeping in from the corners of the door, the sun rays were colouring the lips of doors red. The birds ran across the clouds on its chest as if they were afraid of the eyes of the sun. The birds separated from their families in the morning, rushed hurriedly picking up sticks on their way. That is when mother came and asked, 'Raju, what's the matter? Why are you upset?' I didn't say anything. I was thinking everyone wants a shield. Be it sun or the flying birds. Even the sky fears the eyes. I too am afraid of my family's look, even Asha. But if there is no shield, not even the fear of eyes, then what?

'Why don't you speak? Have you fought with anyone?' Mother asked in a striking tone.

'Nothing happened. I just don't feel that good.'

'Hm, ok, get up. One shouldn't lie down at this time of the day. Go, fetch two buckets of water.' She said this and left.

As if her instruction of fetching water filled a new enthusiasm, I quickly got up, picked up the buckets. It was like the buckets had hidden everything and I wanted to say, 'Tell me, will you give it back or not.'

At the pipe, there was a loud war of words going on between doctor chachi and Asha. Chachi was saying, 'Don't show us the vigour of youth. Our hair hasn't greyed under the sun. The children of today will tell us now.' Asha was saying, 'I have been standing for so long and your vessels are still empty. If I'd have said that even others need water; you would be ready to fight. If you ever talk to me like this again, it wouldn't be good for you.' Asha's face reddened with anger. She was shuddering.

I felt my hands getting fisted. My eyeballs perished. Suddenly the buckets slipped from my hand. Instantly, chachi and Asha's eyes turned towards me. The piercing arrow injured me badly and her eyes fluttered too. Asha had gone inside. My body was burning like the vessel heating up under the rays of the sun. I quietly stood there keeping the bucket under the pipe.

Smiling lips tickle the heart and sad face ignites sympathy. There was an immense wish of embracing moments gone and now to take her in my arms and drink her tears. Emotion resides in the eyes of time. She was more upset at that time because I also saw her getting insulted. Nobody wants anyone around when getting insulted, most of all, a lover.

I returned, filling the buckets and food was ready. Mother said, 'Eat, you must be hungry.' I washed my hands, changed clothes and sat down on the stool. I told my mother while eating, 'Today doctor chachi and Asha had a heated argument. Chachi insulted her with very mean words.' I started drinking water from my glass. Mother answered, 'That's how she is. Asha is sincere. If it would have been Kamla in her place, then she would have given a fitting reply. Asha already doesn't speak much to us. Yes but she talks sensibly.' She said while leaving, 'I will go to the pipe, bring whatever you want.'

Development. In the order of life, in the progress of development. Progress, symbol and development of change don't get changed within themselves. Time when heals old wounds on one hand, it also expands the thirst for new agonies on the other hand. Time is just a name for the present that we live in, and present is the staple of the migrating era in the life of a person and that of society. Sometimes the past smiles in the lap of the present, and at others drenches it with the tears of repentance. Not only that, those moments that we are entirely unaware of get nurtured in the eyes of the same present in the beauty of future dreams. Future, you are so patient!

Today a beloved from childhood, Asha, is the anklet of a foreign house. And the first alphabet of her life, Raju, that is me, is himself someone else's vermillion. What does foreign mean? One which is not the present of an imagined future. Yes, that's true. How could I make Asha my partner in life? She was from a lower caste and I was from a respectable Brahmin family.

One day I said to Asha, 'I want you to marry me. Marriage, yes, marriage is that acceptance of the society that gives us the right to call each other mine.'

She looked at me with astonishment and said, 'Marriage! What has happened to you? What are you saying?' At that time it felt like love doesn't want to cross the barrier of marriage. It cannot even be said out loud amidst it. Every girl falls in love without thinking about getting tied to a marital life. There is no kohl of marriage in the eyes of love. At that time the existence of the society is miles away from the shore of its aspirations. Love can only be felt, it cannot be lived. Only the bond of sexual cravings lives on.

Today, Asha's statement, 'Marriage? What happened to you? What are you saying' made me feel that love has no future; it only lives in the present. The future wishes for it, but doesn't. I told her to peek inside the door of imagination that stood at my shivering heart. I said, 'Asha, on getting married we can make today's love an unforgettable past and give it a future worth living. The society we hide from, to meet, we would walk on its chest tomorrow, Asha, love doesn't need society, but our lives do. I am talking about giving life to our love.'

She said, 'Why are you thinking of marriage today? I have loved you. I have already given you all the love of my heart, respect and the place in my life that isn't even attained by a husband roaming around with a marriage certificate. The monument that you wish to cage our love in, I haven't thought about it yet. I need time. ..... The present isn't less problematic, Raju.'

And on hearing someone approach, she picked up the dried clothes and went downstairs. I started analysing her last words..... the present isn't less problematic....

The mysteries of nature do not get inaugurated at once. The changing outfits of the environment changes and transforms the dimensions of the inside. Rekha's entrance in my life has made me come a long way from the psyche that was the basis of my growth.

A woman wasn't a bodily mystery anymore but her context was still hidden like nature. When I had asked Rekha at the time I first met her, 'Have you ever loved someone?' Her coy face turned red. My heart beat had also become faster and I started thinking, a human always tries to read another person's life based on the circumstances of his own life...... Man has an insecure nature.

'No.' And she stood there with her head bowed down.

I pulled her towards me with shaking arms. When a person gets the feeling of familiarity from a woman, at that time his ego gets satisfied. Knowing that I was the sole owner of her body and mind, I felt as if that in this whole wide world the creator has also kept something protected that I can call mine. Neither has anyone else claimed it, nor will do in future. The heart is hungry for consolation. But when Rekha while in my arms, halting, asked me, 'And you?' My embrace relaxed. My own life, smiling amidst my heart beats, became a satire.

A thief needs the assurance of money from the other. He wants that he may have robbed another's house but his own house shouldn't be robbed by someone. I told her about my past life clearly. Amidst the wait for their first union, Rekha floated on the waves of my sentences like a weightless stick.

The shudder of the embrace frosted. Her heart got filled with the chaos of several conflicts. She turned away and said, 'Why didn't you marry Asha? Did you not dare because she was from the Kalwar caste?' 'No, I wanted to break the barrier of caste. But she couldn't gather the courage to bind our love in a marriage.' I went quiet.

Now meeting Asha is an incident of the past. The last few days have been like that.....

Rekha didn't feel anything missing in my love for her. She is one of those best Hindu girls, for whom husband is like a lord and his happiness is the blessing of God.

I also remember the days when my mother used to dream about my marriage. Every woman weaves her dreams for the marriage of her first child. My mother had also weaved dreams from the girl's shadow to the sixth birthday of her grandchild.

When the marriage, cultural program accepted by the society ended, the shape of mother's dreams started deforming. Like others, my father had also sold me. But like the book that doesn't have its price printed clearly. The one who bought me paid a price according to his status in response to my father's mute price.

I was sold, but I stayed at my own house, but the one who bought me sent the one to me who he had nurtured for years with great care. The drama of action and response, the irony.... The mere shadow of life of middle class people is etched in the minds of society. Life is a shadow made from the symbols of several shadows. This world is the playground of abstract nouns. A detailed description of the reality. Rekha had not imagined the kind of marital life I was living that she saw. A big family. Destiny's fate in the name of income. Babu's job is unpredictable like the patient of asthma. Sometimes it is hundred and fifty rupees, sometimes not even one. Mother cooked at various homes to earn and feed the family. I was unemployed as well.

The entire day was spent but the pan didn't even come close to the stove. Our eyes lit up when she returned in the evening. Rekha was surprised to see all this. The bindi she was wearing slid with the drop of sweat. The dreams of the night shattered at the door of the reality of the day. She was thinking, what kind of house is this? What kind of people are these?...... Poor mother......

'Bahu, quickly light up the stove and cook for everyone and feed them, I've already eaten. Take these four cents and tell someone to bring wood. And listen, I've to go somewhere, I'll probably return tomorrow morning.' After giving so many instructions at once, mother picked up the sheet. Rekha said in an obedient tone, 'You haven't eaten yet. When you'll eat, Babu and everyone else eats, then I'll eat whatever is left. Wait for some time, I'll just cook.'

Mother's blankets got wet from the activities of the morning. She only said, the place I cook at doesn't allow me to leave without eating. This dough wouldn't even be sufficient for all of you. Mother left after saying this. Everyone's attention was on the stove. Rekha was still looking at my mother's blanket fading in the distance.

Babu was talking to a gentleman sitting on the platform outside. I was making a futile attempt to read the chaos inside Rekha and the tears churning from her eyes.

I shouldn't have married until I would have stood on my feet. I had no right to drag someone's life into this hellish suffering. If Rekha's father got to know about all this....he wouldn't send Rekha to me until I have a stable income. Until I become a man. Men who carry their own weight can become crutches for others. ..... Why did I leave a stable job at the central workshop for a temporary railway job?

Mirror. A piece of glass in which everything that is front if it can be seen as it is. I was looking at my image in it, combing my hair. Stomach was oily and the hair was getting oiled. The plan was to roam around to get relieved from the suffocation of the house. I was amidst a conflict between Raju in the mirror and myself. He said, 'Shame on your young arms that couldn't gather two ounces of dough to feed itself ...shame on your education that makes you oil your hair with your illiterate mother's income....shame on him who uses a woman, entertaining her hunger'... I was saying.... 'What to do, I don't get a job and no amount of connections work. Even for doing small business one needs money....the essence is money. I am not the culprit.

Even Babu keeps quiet in front of my mother's anger.

When she gets mad, she starts unreeling those parts of his life that weren't even part of history for us, that were stitches on a wound dumped in the insides of my mother with time. Yes, stitches of a wound. A strange theorem of comparison!

'You spent all your life like this, eating off women's jewellery and utensils of the house; you have even eaten our children's future. Whatever was left was lost in gambling. Broke my bones on being directed by others.' Mother went on blabbering. Rekha was trying to stop her from under her veil. But mother had started talking, to stop which even the entire Earth couldn't become a pan. Babu had married thrice. Mother was her third. She was around forty years old and Babu was around 54 years old. Since my birth the number of jobs that Babu had taken and left is as difficult for Babu to count as it would be for a rickshaw puller to tell how many lanes he had to cross to come to this turn.

Once Babu worked in Calcutta and we were all in Kanpur. The firm in which he was a lawyer also had a branch in Kanpur. I had gone there to ask for money as directed by Babu. When I introduced myself as Mr. Ramdas's son, an accountant said to the other, 'He is the son of the innocent accountant.'

He was famous for his sincerity, if you ask him, he'll even give his clothes to you. Even his anger wasn't any less. When the boss acted like a boss, the accountant put down the accounts book and asked for his settlement. He never thought about what'll happen tomorrow. Babu was a slave to the proverb – 'Aaj khaye aur Kal ki jheekhe, Uska gorakh sangh na kije' His life was like that of an orphan. He didn't remember his father. He would tear up remembering his mother. As an only child to his parents, he was raised on the crumbs of his uncles. One day Babua was beaten up harshly by them for not studying. He said, 'I yearn to teach you, that's why you don't study. I was eager to learn but I wasn't sent to school so that I don't get to study. You have no idea how I was raised.' Babu's eyes were moist. The anger disappeared in the compassion of the bygone childhood. He went on, 'My mother washed dishes at several houses, grinded grains into flour. That is when she earned the left-overs from the kitchen to eat. If I would sit on the stool to study, then my uncle would make me stand in the centre of the room and smash me with that stool like cotton. They said, 'Your father has left money for your studies, right?' Babu's throat choked up on the bitter sips of the past. He went out, wiping his eyes.

A father dreams of fulfilling his life's unfulfilled aspirations through his children. A child tries to develop in the environment around him. On seeing his life's weaknesses not getting fulfilled in his children, his heart cried. And the child rebels against the father's anger against his environment.

Life cherishes dreams, is spent in achieving them and ends in the head collapsing at its ruins. Our eyes often open after the time has passed. If one wakes up on time, then how we would get the chance to blame fate. There was a man inside me that wanted that when I walked all eyes filled with respect should bless my personality. Every word that I speak should bathe in the dignity that would leave an impact on others. And in the end, there was blood filled with rebellion in the personality, fake ego that would haunt me in the search of a job.

I was just a suppressed note between these two personalities. A suppressed voice needs to stumble. His 'self' wakes up on getting stumbled. Babu asked, 'Raju, you stay at home the entire day and then as soon as the sun sets you set out in pants and tie. This is not a hotel. You wouldn't get a job staying home. Don't you see me toiling at this old age....?' I had just taken the first bite. His words pierced my chest like a bullet. I left the plate and interrupted Babu's sentence to say, 'I tried from peon to an officer, what do I do if I don't get a job? Should I give my life for it?'

'Get out of my house.' These words shook the walls. Mother screamed saying, 'I earn the money to feed you and you get to order him to leave the house. Someone just got his labour card for admission in swadeshi but you aren't getting....' Mother couldn't continue. I didn't stop. Rekha's sincerity was forcing her to sit beside her in-laws and cry and I was ordering her to come with me. I left my house to earn bread for myself and feed others. I didn't have even a cent with me. I wasn't even sure 'where would I go'. It was my first time to leave my house. There wasn't anybody with whom I could stay the night. Going to some relative's house would mean an insult to my parents and my own ego would stop me from going to a friend's house.

The rickshaw was here. I was keeping Rekha's and mine boxes on it. Rekha was washing my mother's feet with her tears. Younger siblings held on to Rekha's dhoti trying to stop her. Mother mumbled in the tearful voice, 'Raju, stay. You shouldn't take to heart your father's statements. ...... Rekha, you make him understand. If he wants to go, then go alone, where will he go with you.' Mother held on to Rekha and then tried to pull me inside. Babu wasn't standing in the front. Rekha said crying, 'If he wouldn't be here, what will I do here?'

Mother kept on saying, 'Raju, come back. Hare ram! He hasn't lived alone ever, how will I live.... Come back Raju....' Rickshaw left behind the house. Mother's love echoing in the lap in the atmosphere knocked at my ear drum. It was a deafening noise. The sleeping man had woken up and the waking maternal love was dying.

The neighbourhood was now left far behind. The family relations and all the bonds of this birth were like they once were but are now not even remembered. All the ties of the past were dissolving in a moment, trying to open new pages of a new chapter of life. A festival crawled in my inside thinking about 'where to go'. .....I should leave Rekha at her house and go to Kaasganj that is the decision I could take in the context of those circumstances.

Rekha was silent like the faith of belief, was grave like the actress debuting on a new screen. Every scene of the play was feared for new roles. Apprehension was only because the end of the play was unknown. The circumstances of ultimate happiness were unimaginable.

I had told the rickshaw puller to take us to Azad market. Rekha looked at me once with eyes filled with questions of problems. 'What's there in Azad market? She asked, lowering her neck. She only wanted to hear the answer and didn't want to read the emotions crawling on my face.

'You have several earrings, I was thinking of selling one of those, so that I can arrange your visit to Kannauj. Do you mind?' I said poking her with my eyes.

'I don't mind selling the jewellery but you are sending

me to Kannauj. I consider it disrespectful to go to my house in this situation. Even for you, visiting my house wouldn't feel very welcoming. Rest, you can decide. I don't even want to leave you alone in such a situation. Don't worry about me. I wouldn't live like a burden, but support. You are now my support, not yours or my father.' Rekha was calm.

I tried to explain to her, 'Although it is against the notion of pride if you or I visit your house uninvited, but your father hasn't expelled you. And then if he gets to know that his daughter along with her husband is wandering around, in search of livelihood, house, will he feel less pained, then? In that case, probably the character of me and my parents would induce hatred in them and then I wouldn't be able to meet them ever. Life isn't just living by principles, but also a compromise.' I went quiet. Rekha was silent, gathering all conflicts inside her. The plan of Kaasganj was unknown to her.

Dropping Rekha at Kannauj, I took the express train to Kaasganj. Her father heard everything quietly and calmly blessed me to get a livelihood.

Those people beg, whose 'self' has died. People who don't trust their own actions do charity and people who can con others and disillusion them are revered. And god? He is called their Adam to give shelter to these con men.

Now those days were in the past. The days of unemployment spent in Kaasganj. The flames of the fire burnt with the money from tuitions and then on forgetting everything reuniting with the family. The pain of falling after reaching great heights in life was materializing in a new context. Now I was living an organized life. The days of living off other people's money were gone. But mother's days were getting frosted with each passing day. What could I have done alone?' Suddenly Professor sahab started thinking. Probably the past spent in Kaasganj was getting stuck in the throat. After a while, he said, 'An unemployed guy and a young unmarried girl both prick people's eyes like a needle. The world can point a finger, but cannot bring to the roads. Those days of unemployment were strange. Wherever I sat, the spot got heavier, whoever's door I knocked and gave my book, he'd decline. An unemployed guy is thought of as a thief, robber and what not and an unmarried poor woman isn't considered anything more than characterless.' The atmosphere had gone grave.

It was a time of interest in the gods. All the world's powers seemed to reside in the feet of the goddess. I wasn't just a husband now, I was also a father. The days weren't spent on enough salary. Babu and mother had divorced unofficially. The people of the society understood this on their own terms, discussing about it. The matters that touched the heart, stressed the mind now, gnawed at the body. The shine on the face got lost like the dreams of youth.

When the paralysis of efforts gets tired, the usefulness of other things starts to fade, the mind only knits more and more questions and the shore of solutions gets lost in the exasperation. He gets stressed. Even if they have it, those who don't, but those who actually have it, later they cease to exist.

Allahabad is my self-proclaimed home town. When the central government's workers' strike was announced at the national level, my mind got lost in the 1942 movement and reflections of satyagraha (heard of) by Gandhi ji since childhood.

That day came, when the impotent Babu section of the society stood tall with heads held high. From 12 o' clock tonight, the train wheel will cease movement, the mail, post, telegraph, flight services will be suspended, until the government bends the knee. To bring to bow another person's head, every bone's support is needed. After tea, Kant said, 'Come, let's go and see how the train wheel is doing.'

Dhar babu said, 'Section 144 is imposed.'

I agreed but didn't stop.

Near Civil Lines in Allahabad, the bridge for exiting the railways had Cannington police station near it and shared walls with the mail house. Near that, is the best built church of the state and Yusuf road with residences of railway officers. There were hundreds of people gathered at the mail house. Among my acquaintances, there were more from the AG office. As it is, the number of people was more in mail houses, railway and AG house.

As soon as Kant reached, he met a colleague from his office. We started gauging the atmosphere. It was crowded, but no chaos. It seemed like something was bound to happen. But thinking about getting arrested, a lot of people thought of backing out. It was crowded. Like the gallery of a film's screening, people were divided in groups, people who didn't even go near the pledge that could shake things up and throw them away. But there was heat in the blood vessels. Everyone at least had the spirit to face whatever came.

Even in this scenario, addiction kicked in. On seeing Kant being busy, Dhar babu and I proposed to drink water and eat paan respectively in front of each other.

I entered the crowd too. I had used all my strength. We talked to a few people and then informed Kant of leaving for outside to drink water. Paan was only available across the bridge. People couldn't present the strength of the slave minds even on gathering so many feet. Every democratic government, if it's with dollars, then every worker working under it will continue to get hunted for state feudalism. He, who hasn't been fed, how will he fight?

That same sentiment took India's golden age ages apart from it. The hands that snatch the crowns can only be those that are hungry to break down mountains for the treasure. Yes, those half-eaten hungry people know their worth. They possess a spirit to keep the fight alive.

As soon as we came to the bridge walking in search of water and paan, the water came. On seeing that the water was flowing with great speed and that the story of the train wheel will make it to tomorrow's newspaper, we hopped on a rickshaw to go back.

Dhar babu said, 'Although the mayhem of the strike is big, the government has prepared itself for the worst scenario.

If the storm of strike would build, it's like the exhale of rebellion but wouldn't stay like the clouds of monsoon. Which rule or government can see its servants' heads high?' It was right. The strength displayed in Calcutta and Pune does claim to be untoward, but all this will fail. But yes, if the strike is successful somewhere, the government will get switched.

'Governments aren't more than a pan on the stove that will get down at the behest of tongs. If there is a government, there are servants and also their stomachs. Nobody wants to die of hunger. Understood?'

'I do understand. But if the people on strike disrupt the train, mail services, then who is at loss? Why do we forget even if it's foolish, it is our own government? For instance, god forbid, if your father falls sick, what option will your mother have to quickly inform you about it? The trains are suspended, mail, telephone, post everything is suspended. And if you wouldn't have been able to see him, wouldn't your heart wish to strangle all these strikes?'

'Sure, I will surely wish like that. Not just that, I might hate the word strike all my life but that'll be my personal situation. Where there is a question of forty lakh people, there will be no value of forty thousand people. A strike isn't just a disobedience movement but a united protest. In order to bring down the government, subversive behaviour has to be done with the government tools. The government only understands the language of rebellion.' I talked about the desired release in strike.

Dhar babu was left speechless with my rapid reply. He said, after a while, 'As far as the spirit and zeal is considered, Raju babu, your statement will be supported. But do certain important incidents in a person's life not affect his personality and development of society? Even a saint wouldn't praise the police force when a policeman beats him. The events happening in a person's life have a usual cause, that is what you read from a scholar's text one day. Did the events from the lives of Socrates to Gandhi not affect the fabric of their social life? The robber Man Singh who looted the wealth of a rich man or kidnapped a boy, will he praise the generosity of the robber? Will he have an affinity towards this kind of person?'

Dhar had now become a little spirited. He was in favour of the strike but shuddered at the possible obstacles arising from the mayhem caused by it. His entire family was in Kanpur and he himself lived in Allahabad due to his job.

Giving the discussion a philosophical context and to give a new turn to the body getting drenched in showers and the mind puzzled with the conflicts of the seriousness of the strike, I didn't answer Dhar but presented a question that often comes to mind in such a situation, 'Which is that other option in the minds of workers, apart from strike, that would help them to convince the government of their demands?'

The cordial dialogue between the workers and the representatives of the government can find solutions to a lot of problems. Dhar answered.

'My little experience says such a dialogue doesn't ever help in giving a solution for serious issues like salary hike. Yes, this medium is a democratic way to get answers to a lot of problems. The government keeps its scores and the workers theirs. Both sides are adamant on respecting their own pleas. A decision is of two types, either of fulfilling the demands or finding a way to compromise.'

'But brother, how will the government give what it doesn't have. Suppose you succeed in getting the train wheel to cease through your organized power, and the government bows but from whose pocket will the government get the lost amount of crores of rupees? Suppose your demands get accepted but to meet the losses arising from the economic harm the government will levy direct or indirect taxes whose burden the entire country will have to bear. And the workers as well who get happy with the pride of their momentary organized victory and the next day experiencing a deficient income gathers new data to present in front of the government.'

Dhar babu was a student of economics. He has studied especially the effects of taxes on the common public during his student life.

'Brother, this is one side. One cannot deny this. But does the matter of the prices not getting stabilized and inability to stop inflation not define the shortcoming of the government system? When the entire responsibility is on the government, then who else will bear. As far as the burden of taxes is concerned, for that the public should demonstrate in front of the government in one voice that they are unable to bear the taxes. You are thinking like that because between the government and the public many other entities are part of the capital system. If this would have been socialist system and the government and the public would not have been on the ground of discrimination, these strikes wouldn't have been happening.'

Dhar babu's attention was also far from the limits of discussion due to heavy rains and towards home.

Now the rickshaw had halted at the loknath crossroads, passing from Johnson ganj, after turning from the roundabout towards Bharti Bhawan. It was about 12 o'clock. We departed half drenched.

Rekha was at her house. The house was deserted; I prepared to lie down lighting a lamp. Sleep had evaded somewhere.

I returned from Rekha's house last night itself. But upon reaching, her absence strangled me. It was midnight. Clouds, thunder and darkness. A parade of crickets and solitary dark night. I laid down on the bed. Beholding the body of a young man, I started staring at his face.

When a man is alone, he lives on the dreams of longing and translates them. He looks for satisfaction in his ego and solutions for his problems. That situation is sentimental and the tortures of the loss of a known are only known by people who have gauged the creases of folds. I started questioning myself. 'Why do I miss Rekha when I'm alone?'

'Because you want her for that time only. In the presence of others, you can and do forget her. Lie, absolute lie. Remember it's not always right to see someone. How can the entire life be spent remembering her? Yes, though it can be lived for her.'

'A woman completes the man. You only consider her as a material of pleasure.'

'You are forgetting a man is also an enjoyment for a woman. If she also spends all the time with him, she'll also get bored. She will want a change, will get aloof. Life isn't just a frame of bone and muscle, there's also the rite of love. Yes, love is the name of a hunger that is the product of culture.

Every hunger is naked. You may be indulged in Rekha's thoughts right now, but her attention would be on her kids and their health.....

'You are without a conclusion. It is possible that all of Rekha's moments of loneliness aren't mine anymore. She is tied up as a mother. I'm not that busy even after becoming a father.'

'You had accepted her only so that she becomes a mother, a house wife and loves you as well.' The bitterness of the answer slapped the question.

I turned away and tried to forget everything. There was sleep in my eyes and they were closed. But there was someone awake inside..... Oops, this rain...

I don't know whether the rain stopped or not. The one awake inside slept at some point. We don't even know ourselves completely but wish to know about the world. But if we couldn't open our eyes to see the world, fix our eyes on others' faces, then how would we know where we are, what and why we are. Everything is rubbish. Nobody sleeps or wakes inside. There's nothing inside, just like the light in the moon. If it hadn't been for the sun, there wouldn't be any web of light from the moon. Truth is never complete in itself. Its incompleteness gets completed on getting linked with the circumstances to cease being incomplete. Don't know when the eyes went sluggish.

Sleep comes unintentionally and even breaks without notice. We even know that which emerges from the subconscious to the conscious. The subconscious revolves like the ball bearing and isn't seen like the wings. The tourist collides with what isn't seen. Science translates the indirect on the experience of direct. Now I was awake.

The next day Saraswat knocked at the window on the wall by putting his hand through the cracks. Though there was enough distance between his house and mine but the fondness between the land ladies had broken down the wall between the houses. Through a window in the middle, the two families talked at lengths.

'Kant has been caught. We had gone to see the strike last night' Saraswat said. 'I was speechless, seriously..... Dhar babu and I had gone together. This is bad.'

Kant is caught. He paid his price. I ...... I am the corpse returning from the altar of sacrifice...Kant lived on. He can say, 'We were with those who lived lighting torches. He must spit on Dhar and my faces and say.... They talk about the nation, saying the earth will only cool down with a revolution. But they hid their faces and ran away leaving me....they came along and therefore were partners.'

The government didn't move. The throats of the hunger ridden people were cut off. Factories of the government were illuminating with new recruitments. What was given to one brother was smoked by another. Now this big debacle either results in burning down Lanka or becomes a reason to get comfortable in the bed and sleep.

We went to Naini jail to see Kant. The bridge on Yamuna, whose width was crossed by train and passengers whose feet went from one side to another. And Yamuna continues to flow.... The Krishna of Dwapar yug also crossed Yamuna. Several Nehru and Gandhi of the time of freedom struggle were given way through this bridge spanning the waves of the river. The flow of human sentiments was diving from one place to another and Yamuna kept on flowing. The convoys of boats floated on the unstable banks of Yamuna hovering disconnected and powerlessly. In the twinkling light of the clay lamps singing praises of the holy waves, the darkness of humanity gets sold. The feet of the watchmen of the law, the pundits praising the purity of Ganga-Yamuna turn their eyes away to the liquor dripping inside the alehouses opened at the boats. Salty snacks, paan and everything else was available there and the Yamuna kept on flowing towards its specified direction, relaxed, uninterested and innocent.

Across the Yamuna was the 'Naini Jail' associated with the history of the Indian freedom struggle. The cells residing in whose walls illuminated with the experiences of pages of several autobiographies. The cells partners of experiences of freedom lovers, savage humans, criminal legends and the prison smiled with the decorated chambers of the Krishna graha. Whose doors opened to be closed, whose rooms were cleaned, healthy transmission of a hellish life. That same Naini jail, protected by its strong walls, was chuckling in the welcome of all those guests whose fault, against humanity, was decided against the government by those courts which we have accepted after the justice of the almighty.

For the first time in life, I saw a prison gate. There was an enormous crowd outside the gate. Although a crowd of visitors would emerge almost every day but in today's crowd there were more women than men. Sometimes it felt like it was getting late in the opening of the temple of Naag Vasuki and the mob of devotees was anxious to see the deity.

We had got permission to meet the prisoners. Behind today's crowd was the arrests made yesterday. With a stamp of Naini jail on the palm, the window opened and we started moving inside in a queue. There was mayhem in the mind, curiosity in eyes and a map of the prison in memory, unclear, unorganized and at least Dhar babu and I had no idea which cell Kant would be in. We kept walking with the crowd, browsing around with our eyes. Even in that noiseless, pulseless crowd we felt the fragrant flower buds. The stolen fragrance of the snow powder from the cheeks of the youth forced us to forget for an instance that we were entering a prison.

The identity of a young woman from a well off house comprises a well adorned face in happiness and in sorrow. Youth is intoxicating even without adornments, intoxicates but.....but even then we accept them only in this period. Adornments are there to complete the lack of beauty of the youth, for stimulation of youth. When there are flames with enough scorching heat, then to give it more brilliance, the oil of cosmetics is given to it. And when love is needed for an extinguishing lamp, we call it grandiose and wrap the ashes. Ornamentation is the name of fulfilling what's missing, and stimulation of the fulfilment.

Someone's wife, someone's sister, someone's sister-in-law and someone's old widow mother were finding their own in the prisoners from yesterday. We had to turn right after walking some distance from the gate. There were many withering faces filling in the barracks like straw. All of these people were in their own clothes. It wasn't hard to understand that these were the faces of those revolutionaries that lacked the dignity of sacrifice, devoid of pride and only called prisoners?

There were also some people who lived in Allahabad alone, there was no one to bring food or fruits to their houses. Some teared up when their eyes met those of their wives. Some calmed their hearts on seeing women from other houses. The brutality of death becomes soft like a newborn if a woman's face is there in front. The lives of these captive babus lacked the joy of family union. The emptiness of the prison was reduced to a picnic. On receiving the food from their houses, the melancholy on their faces evaporated like camphor.

There were fewer questions, fewer than the words of consolation and what more did the prisoners have for assurance other than there wasn't anything to worry about, everyone is a friend. Our union will soon try to free us. Some were suggesting their family members to arrange for bail.

Kant had now worn a pyjama, removing his pants. A few minutes before us, his brother and sister-in-law had reached there. On seeing us he hugged us. There was no complaint from yesterday, only today's glee, the prankster inside him was trying to come to the surface.

'It was all fun and games for her all night. There is no problem, how's the strike going?' Kant said this probably to strike a conversation with the visitors.

'Krishna graha is the house of in-laws for the revolutionaries, if you don't have fun here, where will it be? The strike failed.' Upon saying the last sentence my head bowed down and Kant had the smile of torn eyes on his face and speechless lips.

Most of the people had returned home after apologizing. Whatever was taken from the people, money, watch, fountain pen etc before sending them inside the cell wasn't retrieved in the same condition. Someone's watch wasn't of the same brand, someone's money. This was the free inventory of the independent nation. There was no scope of complaint. Kant had been released on apologizing.

The evening had returned like the daughter in spring. Saavri was sitting with her kids thinking about something.

I satisfied my hunger for my Neena through her daughter. The sound of the speech of her unclear, scattered words helped me convert the stress of daughter-love into sweetness.

Saavri's height, her stature and her superficial nature resembled to a great extent with that of Rekha's. Gudiya was the string of our relationship. Seeing Saavri sitting, I instantly feel the presence of Rekha. I don't know since when is the rule of imitation from the change of origin. A man doesn't want the beauty of a woman to be beyond his ordinary reach. A woman has an attraction that is the flame of a man's lamp. A man wishes to play with this nature's liveliness, not only see beauty but also become an object of enjoyment. A man can die while being alive, but on enjoying it he lives, even to fulfil the desire to die.

Saavri was limited between the kitchen and the door of the house. The means for her recreation were the four children of the great grace Daridra Narayana and the fifth child in the womb with the blessings of the ancestors. Suddenly our hearts raced and for some reason we started smiling on looking at each other. Smiles danced on the lips with enthusiasm. Reasons for conversations started emerging, that too, initiated by me. This is where a man relaxes to adorn the dignity of a woman.

My loneliness started gaining completeness in the absence of a family.

Night. A vacant room. A shadow turning alone on the bed. The rise and fall of questions. The pulsating moments of psycho analysis. The entire house was engaged in dreaming in the lap of sleep. I ...... only me....Rekha.... Saavri. Saavri, Rekha and I. This very trail of thoughts was setting a sequence in its chaos.

What is the need of looking at Saavri even after having a wife like Rekha? The woman who sewed all her wishes in life with the happiness and sorrows of her husband, whose dreams didn't long for any other person's arms and to whom I.....yes, I myself have given her the love that is not attained by every wife from her husband. The same Rekha, whose sole treasure, I, was distraught at getting spilled in the feet of an unfamiliar, married woman. But why? One who isn't filled with lust, who never experienced a lack of love, he is ready to wander. Why? For what purpose? And that too for a woman, who had nothing left to induce new vibrations. These were questions or different forms of a moment's thirst that were splattering like colour on the lids.

Saavri who after crossing the difficult times of the unmarried life and having completed 9 years of marriage, what will her smile mean? Fulfilment of her unfulfilled bodily desires and a thirst for the lack of love.... Why will she want to break and fall into the ocean after having grown into a mountain?

Presently we taught the lessons of love through eyes only. It was unknown who affected the intent and how much.

'Gudiya, will you not feed me?' I shot an arrow through that poor girl to attract Saavri's attention towards me.

'Yes, I will.' Gudiya answered in her sweet voice.

While joking around with the kids, the moments of life become immortalized. In that innocent smile one can see the cure of life. A family's happiness includes two red cheeks, smiling lips and courtyard ruined on knees.

At last that day had come.

That absolute darkness of the month, black clouds swirling, a cold breeze blowing from the hills and that night yawning. Saavri's kids were asleep. The lights of the house also closed their eyes and seemed to smile to themselves.

Sleep wanted to keep me away from its arms. I didn't even want it to poke me.

There was only a courtyard's distance between Saavri's house and mine. The ears of the neighbour and her twelve years old daughter were like that of the walls. I looked towards Saavri. If there had been a piece of mirror instead of her mouth then it was possible that I would have been able to clearly see my thirsty eyes, cross examination of inner emotions and the feelings of muscular quivers in the extremities like the expression of a language of a pattern kept on the table.

'You haven't slept yet.' Saavri said reading my eyes.

'I'm not sleepy and even you're awake.' I said while going closer to her.

She shifted a little.

'Go and sleep. I'm sleepy.'

'You may be sleepy but even my dreams have been robbed by someone.'

'You should report to the police else maybe a heart that would praise them....'

And she smiled.

The wind blew on the leaves of the tree of jasmine in the courtyard. In order to fill Saavri in my arms, I extended them like the thirst of problems. She hesitated and retreated. Today for the first time I had touched her body. My entire body was shivering like the leaves of a jasmine tree. As much as I tried to embrace her, the more she tried to stop me. Though the pressure with which she was pressing on my palms, there was acceptance in it and feelings of complete surrender. But there was no surrender.

Now the moon was situated amidst the jet black clouds like the locket hanging from a conspiratorial height. Crippling tremor of inner consciousness at the gates of eyes.

'Shall I ask you a question?' Saavri asked, looking at my face.

This night has brought with it many questions. ...... 'Ask'

'How did you get lost here?' She had fixed her eyes on the floor.

I started searching for its answer on Saavri's face. In

the deep raised line of vermillion in her black hair, I started seeing Rekha's bowed forehead. And Saavri was someone's dream girl, an achievement of someone's bodily psyche. Rekha was in my questions and Saavri in their core.

'Why are you quiet?'

She dug her eyes on my face. She started stroking my hand softly.

'That is what I'm thinking, how did I get lost.'

'Yes, this isn't even the age of drifting. You are a responsible man.'

'I'm no stranger to you, don't treat me otherwise. This is a time to get closer, don't retreat.'

My guarded emotions spilled. But for some reason, the word 'responsible' touched a vein of my morality and I said, like someone who has been caught stealing, 'Truth be told, you refresh my memories of Rekha. I love her so much as well. This antagonism arises sharply in my mind that how did my heart turn towards you in this phase of life.' She looked at me very carefully. A similar question had risen in her eyes too. She also spoke in my vocabulary.

The dilemma regarding you was more rapid than these gathering clouds. The matter of loving someone never arose in my life. I don't even understand the language of its manifestation. Even before marriage, I wasn't in contact with anybody where love would emerge. After marriage, I understood that my husband has a legal right over my body and my mind would only attain his worship.

'Still, why did we get attracted towards each other?' I asked slightly, pulling her towards me.

'That is the dilemma.'

And we both held each other's hand and began diving in the ocean of calm. Saavri's statement wasn't like a rehearsed dialogue by a movie actress at the studio set. It was embedded with the sound of a married Indian woman.

My conscious was busy in searching for that string of suppressed desire that brought two creatures like us together at this point of life, where we didn't wish to come. Or maybe we were.

On one hand was this dilemma and on the other was the great desire of the union of the beloveds in the auspicious time.

'So will you just let this night, weather and this time go in vain?'

'I am not able to think. For one I met you at this point in life and two my routine life. What should I do? Tell me?'

'I have boundaries too. I am also standing on the verge of a routine life but I want both of us to accept each other within our limits.'

Her entire body shuddered. He started digging the earth with the thumb of her left foot.

'I wouldn't be able to uphold all this. Let me forget today's meeting as well. I don't deserve you. I understand that we should return to our own limits.' Saavri answered.

It may be wise to return to our boundaries after crossing them, but my heart doesn't allow me to do it.' I said.

'Can the heart not be controlled?' There was innocence on her face.

'It can be, but after catching a disease.'

Saavri was tired of standing. Even I wanted to sit down. She smiled and asked, 'Will you sit?'

'Talk ahead of this.' I said embracing her but she answered, retreating from me.

'No, not today, probably never. Why, has only your lust pulled you away from your family towards me?' She looked at me closely.

I was speechless. On analyzing it, I found her suspicion to be right. And then the dilemma got stronger. Can a man drift away in need for a woman so easily forgetting his moral obligation? And Saavri, whose entire body is still shaking with excitement from my touch, can be so steadfast on her decision of morally protecting a woman's patience? Is man a flowing stream of water from a cliff, not immovable as a mountain?

'Can you forget me?' I asked.

'How can I decide in a moment for my entire life and that too at a time, when I don't feel like myself.' Her answer wasn't superficial like my question.

'Then why are you putting a stone on the beats of your veins.....' My voice started shaking.

'You should sleep. My principles are looking forward to killing me by calling me treacherous. If the end of love is the attainment of the body, then I'll have to think.' Saavri was serious.

I now looked at her with reverence.

The night was climbing its stairs of youth. The moon, like a poet adding a new verse to the ghazal of the sweet night climbed the heights of the sky with the anxiety of reciting it. Our conversation continued.

The lust was now silent like a devoted prayer at the door of the heart. Suddenly, Saavri's husband's voice was heard on the door. The needle of the clock felt compelled to change the date. We returned to our courtyards.

Rameshwar worked as a trader at a big firm of farmers. After leaving the house in the morning at eight, he only returned in the night at 10. Saavri didn't wait for him, she would eat with the children and keep some aside for him. Rameshwar often returned late. When he would leave for work he would see all the children drinking and when he returned all of them would be sleeping. Yes, sometimes Gudiya would hamper his solitude by waking up at an odd time.

Rameshwar's children only knew that if something in the house gets finished, then the person they call their father would fill it back. They hadn't even walked ten steps in the garden holding their father's finger.

Even for Saavri Rameshwar was better valued for financial reasons. When her petticoat would tear, he'd bring a new one, when her children would get sick, he'd leave some money for medicines. Be it Sunday or Independence Day, Rameshwar would never stay home.

He earned to feed the body and to satisfy his body he would willingly or unwillingly made her the victim childbirth pains. Till today no one has ever seen them go anywhere together. Saavri didn't know how cinema was and Rameshwar had no idea that a wife wants more than just food and pain of childbirth. On entering the house Rameshwar would throw his shoes and clothes in such a way that he would never have anything to do with them again. After changing his clothes he'd sit down to have dinner without even washing his hands. Whatever conversations regarding the household would take place during serving the dinner were the only ones. That'd be their vocal conversation and rest would be vocal acquisition of silent business.

Today Rameshwar was in a romantic mood. He answered even a simple question by smiling sarcastically at Saavri. Moments like these have often come before today in Saavri's life in the form of precious moments of marital bliss. This ultimate gesture was considered as the purpose of the vermillion on her head by her. But today she didn't like Rameshwar's glee. She wasn't experiencing any fondness in his words.

Saavri felt as if it was a vulture that aimed to kill her with a smile in order to satisfy his carnal hunger. She felt like she was a mere piece of meat in the beak of an eagle. She's a woman, who isn't just a maid, a housewife, not a prostitute, she's a wife and a wife's boundary, her life isn't to be burned in the fire in the ugly moments of the night.

The time of the past moments..... her mind was somewhere else.

Perhaps what we call the matters of age, they are actually matters of perspective. Saavri seemed shaken like Asha today. The difference between the age of 16-17 and that of 40 is negligible. Emotions have an age of their own, that doesn't walk tied to a person's age. The circumstances have their own interests. Age selects them according to its fulfilment. This is also unsaid in meeting Saavri.

The new model of the Allahabad railway station was being given shape and the old station was being renovated. One day when the prime minister of India Pandit Jawaharlal Nehru visited his home town in his motherland, he was warmly welcomed at the railway station itself. The bills and vouchers that had come for approval to Accountant general, 'Police Establishment' section of Allahabad clearly show that when the prime minister of India comes for a visit, that time for his security arrangements, poor people's money gets wasted like the water of vast Ganga emerging from Gangotri. The blood flowing in the vessels of the Indian proletariat that is increasingly extorted each day in the form of taxes, in the name of schemes, and for border defence, the mute papers of the vouchers testify for the exploitation that are witness of the attractive amount and its expenditure on the security of nation's beloved leader.

I had once seen the new arch of the railway station at platform number 1. An unprecedented gift of Lal Bahadur Shastri's railway ministerial tenure. Radhe, Moti and Sukha gave their lives in bringing down the robust building of this old station. Like Shah Jahan our prime minister who was fond of new buildings was proving his wisdom of beauty by building new buildings and demolishing old steely buildings. In order to bring an ideal time, it had become imperative to spend money on the high rises. If the white wash on the exterior is maintained, then who cares about the torn mattresses and cold stoves inside?

A new palace of socialism was being constructed on the foundation of debt in dollars. On the desolate hair partitions of the widows of Radhe, Moti and Sukha.

Upon completion of the construction of the new buildings, the doors draw a line on the forehead of the schemes and smile. The income of the government officers and contractors doubled at that time.

The Allahabad railway station peeked through the cracks at the sky with open eyes like that of Radhe, Moti and Sukha. It wasn't too long before the train arrived. The signal for Howrah-Delhi Express was down. The porters had queued at the platform. The eyes of the passengers were fixed at the track leading to Mughal Sarai.

Journey. Platform. Train.

As soon as the train arrived, the passengers didn't wait for the train to stop entirely and hung by the train stepping on the pedestal. Except for public and passenger trains, every train has less class III coaches. In a country which has a fourth class in the list of government jobs, first and second class coaches adorning that country's express and mail trains is enough to incite doubt in the outsiders.

According to the government regulations, I beget second class but according to my financial condition, I belonged to the fifth class. Although I also had a ticket for the public coach that is the third class.

The way porters ruthlessly slam the parcels in the railway wagons, that scene can also be seen in passenger trains.

Today I was going to meet Rekha. If your wife goes away from you even for two days, it feels the longing of years reduced to a moment's palm.

I missed Saavri all the way. The pain of not attaining her fused in every vein of my body. Her attractive face and the false smile on her lips on being touched were engraved in my heart like a delicacy.

I had to change the train in Kanpur.

The night arrived. The train had halted at Kannauj station. Now the journey from the station to home had become more romantic. There wasn't much luggage. Even the horse cart driver knew where to go. One went ahead and took my handbag. A person is valued and has a persona in a small city. That's the reason the horse cart drivers here personally know the special people here and give them the respect they deserve.

Kannauj is the city of Jaichand whose name has started being used as a noun and adjective in the Indian life. Presently the population of Kannauj is around 25 thousand. Every fourth house is either the palace of perfumes or the courtyard of people working there.

Reading the description of Kannauj in the pages of history, the disappointing land of Kannauj that is visited by foreigners to see the antiquities is currently drowning in its personal upheaval. The Kannauj of Shree Harsh isn't even a tourist place for the students of history. The past that is forgotten, the present that is gathered in its selfishness and the future which is disappointing, I am talking of the same Kannauj.

Once a student of Indian history from Sweden came here to see the ancient idols etc and all she got to see were the severed roads like the broken idols. People ignorant of their history. Kannauj neglected in the context of history is only a centre for perfume merchants. Indian government's neglected historical city. At the station, the carts like that of the half covered bodies of the beggars, the cart drivers sucked by their loan sharks and feeble horses praying for their death from god stood there to welcome the passengers with the same devotion as that of the pundits standing at the banks of a holy river.

Salharu's cart always stood at the entrance of the station. He was one of those cart drivers, still is, who prefers to take rides in the night. The prices are doubled in the night, sometimes even quadrupled. The principle of 'supply and demand' is known to the horse cart drivers here as well. Salharu went on saying, 'Our pigeon isn't slow in movement. Yes, we don't want to tie the animal unnecessarily. We just need enough to eat which is dependent on the grace of people like you. Why fuss over it?'

Kannauj station is in Saraimeera. Kannauj city is two miles away from there. The straight road can even take a blind man home from the station. On turning towards the bridge of sandalwood mill, the cart drivers started quarrelling. In the night, this road with all its desertedness becomes a shed for thieves in the absence of any light. Thankfully now a few houses have been built. The cart drivers load up to six to eight people in place of four passengers. The riders who sit on the plank are called the upper side riders. From the station to the city and vice versa, this road is the food for these horses carrying the carts and the gold mine sustaining the families of these drivers. The support for the festivals at the liquor shops and the tool for respect of gambling riches.

The cart stopped at the dairy ground at the turn for English school. I paid him and moved on. Kannauj is my in-laws home. After the death of my father-in-law, in his respect and in order to tend to my mother-in-law, my family has to stay here. This is the home now.

I prefer coming from the night train. Neither the kids can stay awake and disturb at that time, nor the residents of other houses. Soon the reconciliation with Rekha happens.

Like always a wave arose in my heart upon stepping on the platform. I think only when I get old that is when I'll understand that I'm no longer young.

Rekha! A sound came, 'Coming' as reply.

Rekha was awake and it was about 1.30 in the night. How can a woman whose life is only mortgaged to one person sleep? After all, I had told her. I have a condition, as far as possible, when I arrive by any train in the night or day and the door is locked, and then you should open it.

'Why?'

Remember the conversation of the first night, one love.....

She would smile in glee over the intensity of her sweet love. To change clothes, she drew a new pair, handing it over, she said, 'From the time I got the letter about your arrival, bhabhi ji is making fun of me. She said sleep in the dacron petticoat only, made a bun and started humming a cinematic tune, someone is about to come...

Her face bowed with coyness. I thought even after becoming a mother to six children, she has the same glow on her face.

I started changing my clothes. The bhabhi who lives on the upper floor was given a place by Rekha's father. Her husband is at a high position in a bank and she is his beloved wife.

After finishing my dinner when I was going to sleep, Rekha was moving some stuff. After waiting for a while, I called out for her. She came inside the room, switching off the outside lights. Everyone slept in the same room. The glee that was on her face when she had opened the door didn't replicate in any way now. I couldn't understand anything.

The lights of the room were switched off.

Rekha's face like a flowering lotus turned serious like the stagnant sunlight. She was lost in the baseless ocean of her inner conflicts. Every love bearing sentence from my letters floated on the lids of her eyes. She was thinking. She was flowing in the current of indecisiveness. I was looking at her from a distance. She was looking more beautiful than usual. The bindi like budding kusum flower on her white forehead, the partition of her hair like the rainbow resting in the lap of clouds and the two curls that fixed on her cheek on getting messed up. Rekha broke her silence. She put her arms around my neck and said, 'How is your Gudiya?'

I was shocked. Her manner of questioning was intimidating. My heart shuddered. I had expressed my love towards Gudiya in my letters. I carefully answered, 'Why is she my Gudiya? She's Saavri's daughter.'

'Who's Saavri? Is that the name of her mother?' She asked.

I was going to tell Rekha everything myself. I have never had the courage to lie to Rekha. But such questions made me a criminal.

Ycs. That's the name of Rameshwar's wife. But what's the point of your questions?

Nothing..... I remembered someone saying.....she paused and said. That if you love a married woman, then you should start loving her children.

On saying this, Rekha got more serious. She said that sentence with such conviction that I was taken aback. Now whatever I say, would be like accepting my crime, not my explanation. Thinking about which, I got more agitated. The moments spent in the hustle and those in gathering courage had said and accepted everything, that I wanted to say.

Rekha hadn't seen Saavri. She had heard about her through me. She was new in our building. Overcoming the disdain and cowardice, I said, 'You have thought till afar alone. You didn't wait for me to say anything. Ranno! Your statement isn't right. Yes, I've transverse this distance with you and our children, not alone.' Saying this, I engraved her. 'When you yourself lost the patience Raj....' And she broke in tears.

How vigilant is a woman towards her monopoly? I only realized it today that she has such sharpness in reading the motives in the eyes of a man.

I thought Rekha is right in her place. The question arose, if Rekha would have pleased another man like this in my absence and I would have even doubted it, then would I have expressed my anguish crying and cursing my fate in the same way....? Probably not. Never. My manliness would have boiled and I would have remembered great Shree Ram's elite masculinity who could 'have escorted Sita to the forest after having walked through fire on a mere doubt. When the supreme god Ram's dignity was compromised, then who am I?

I held up Rekha's pure head with my slanderous hands. Wiped her tears. I, a progressive man having crossed the beliefs of boundaries of sex, had become baseless at this conservative state of character. I was wrong even after being right and right even after being wrong.

Rekha began weeping profusely leaping at my chest. I tried my best to calm her, but her patience had paid off.

The flow of every river ceases at a point. Rekha stopped crying. I told her everything in short quickly in broken language. She heard all of it while placing her head on my chest.

'So where am I now?' Rekha's soaking extremities said poking at my face.

'Rekha!' I couldn't speak further. I hugged her tightly. 'You are the same, my queen, and you'll stay the same.'

Rekha was now entirely satisfied. She said, 'Sorry, my everything. I hurt your feelings. Even if I have the right to your feet's dirt, then I can thrive in my life. My life's aim is your happiness, fulfilment of your wishes. I don't want anything more.' She loosened my embrace and said, 'A woman can only lighten her mood by crying.' And in order to end this discussion here she said, 'It is getting late. Come on, lie down.' We did lie down together but our minds were flying in different directions.

Rekha looked like the piece of wood resting peacefully in the cold full moon night.

That had the moisture of the dew and the history of the entire day's heat. I felt immersed in a bathtub.

This is the very definition of sin. Snatching away the rights from on and giving it to another! Shivering on what has been done. Faltering in accepting that has happened. What I did may be a small theft, but it was indeed a theft. One who is rich with the crippling resolve to impose new boundaries in violation of societal dignity is characterless, cowardly, and a sinner. Even after accepting Saavri within social dignity, I couldn't have given her any healthy boundaries. No argument of progressiveness could support this. The light of the room was off. The moonlight brought the warmth like that of the loo of summer.

I said to Rekha, touching her, 'Have you slept?'

'No.'

'Listen, forgive me. I have betrayed you, will you not forgive me?' I said pulling her towards me.

'What is there to forgive? Whatever you did, you did deliberately. And a crime committed deliberately isn't prosecuted.' Rekha said very gravely, turning towards me.

'Considering your argument, all cases of crimes like murder, theft or mugging would all get dismissed. Do you accept that I'm innocent?' I asked, stroking her hair.

'There will be no difference in the legal decision based on my acceptance or lack of it. Yes, but tonight and the days ahead will be lost somewhere. I cannot bring you back and can surely distance myself further by continuing to talk. ..... After all I'm a woman....' She was stroking my chest hair with her fingers. I tried to read her eyes, lifting her face by her chin. Some uneven tears in her eyes lashes fell down spreading a shivering silence on her cheeks. I considered it appropriate to leave the matter here.

The distance that resided in the hearts of father and mother, now the world looked at it with naked eyes. Mother had denied Babu's entry in the house. The sons who earned had already separated from getting fed up with his behaviour. Just like our ages the black spot behind the vermillion the mother's bindi on her forehead seemed to grow from the second day's moon to a wicked full moon. We never tired from talking about the sacrifices of a 'mother' and her painstaking efforts. But the days of blind faith had passed. We had come to learn what mother, who gathered the means to raise our futile bodies, father who was forced by his fate and this society are.

Many days passed..... When mother wouldn't get anything to cook on the stove, didn't get on asking, then she would ask for money from Trivedi Sarrafe Wale to feed us. Father himself pressurized her to arrange money. We were not capable enough to understand where the money came from. When does Babu give it back? How much does he owe like this? Are his debts more or is it just us who have no clue about human sympathy?

One day father and mother started arguing. Mother often repeated one thing at such times, 'everyone says, what do you lack, you are beautiful, youthful, go somewhere and you wouldn't be short on any meal. But I'm afraid of my brother's respect. Have you given me anything more than clawing on my body and breaking my bones?' The expressions on her face at this time would be of hatred for Babu and a glimpse of such eminence in her that wasn't unimportant even after being irreverent.

A woman's man isn't a male's robustness but his masculinity. One who cannot feed others isn't given the body by a woman. Yes the fate of exceptions is exclusive of the usual.

This marriage license prevailing in the Indian society these days has forced so many boundaries to be crossed. Does this Shankaracharya have the time to assess that number? Mother had two slogans to ask for sympathy - the man left me, the sons are under the control of their wives and don't help. Her aging body and the sympathy in eyes with tiring manliness had become a thing of the past.

Today bade Dada, which is my elder brother's letter, froze the blood running through the veins. He is the son of my former mother. A person lost in his own small world away from our happiness and sorrows. My eyes were running across the letters in his letter. Every letter was zeroing the consciousness like an electric shock. He had written-

Long live Raju

You have left the city but I cannot run away. I really want my mother to stay with me but she's ready to live with me or you. We have come to hear that she was caught with some girls from the school at the wrong place. When it came to her life, then she took yours and mine name. Come quickly or tell me what should I do?

Yours- Dada

It was obvious of Rekha to get agitated reading this. I used to get serious at such incidents and seeing my seriousness Rekha would always try to change the topic. But today she herself wasn't composed.

'Tea is ready, have it. Go to Dada, nothing will come out of worrying. Does a woman lose her chastity in search for food? Are suppressed sexual desires and discomposure of unquenchable desire for womanly sorrows not responsible for this? Is mother a culprit because her steps faltered and she couldn't permit Babu, who was handed over to her by his widow mother and only brother in front of the entire society to be together in happiness and sorrow, to kill her chastity throughout her life? Is that why she is degenerate? She's not my mother.'

I was dumbstruck listening to what Rekha said. Is her

sympathy with my helpless mother to this extent that societal boundaries and chastity of women can both be sidelined for a moment? Or has the mere passion of supporting a woman intensified?

When the mind thinks rapidly, criticized by the waves of logic, at that time if somebody's character is seen inside the circle of social personal relationships, it'll be called prone to presumptions. My real mother was no longer just considered as a mother. She was a woman who had fallen from a society built on the stilts of principles, for whose topple the same society is responsible that established the values for these pure ideals. That still aspires to attain those values! No society can live up to the prescribed values, but surely tries to pretend to do it.

Babu's innocence and his gentle face danced in front of my eyes. The wrinkles emerging on his face and the compassionate impure history of his life confined in them, everything materialized. After all, why did he make mother a medium in his helplessness that could never dwell on the line of morality? Whatever happened

He didn't want that to happen, but did mother not tell him anything. Yes, she mustn't have. A woman can keep the value of her sold dignity in the hands of her husband and kids, but will never let them know how she has sold herself.....

Isn't it communication?

I started hating Babu. Nobody sympathizes with the coward, even his wife doesn't want to see him.

There's no difference between a man and a woman's will to live. When man established his monopoly over the sources of economic gains and gave women the tag of dependant, then in that case why should a woman feed an animal that is gnawing at her body? Why would she gulp down her throat the mucus of others and mix vermillion in the redness of kumkum to create radiance? If it is imperative for her to be sold somewhere else to maintain the redness of her vermillion then why shouldn't she accept some other eligible person forever?

I had to respect my elder brother's letter at all costs. Rekha was right in convincing me to go. I decided to go to Kanpur.

Everyone stood with sticks of morality aimed at mother. And mother, stood alone challenging the hollow beliefs recognized by the society like Abhimanyu surrounded in chakravyuh. Her words reflected repentance of her actions and not their clear acceptance. Her voice, not burdened with self deprecation, cursed fate and circumstances.

She was answering to her younger brother's allegation of stooping so low and not worrying about the future of her children and family.

'I was a mother, I couldn't see my kids dying of hunger. Why don't you ask the same questions, you're asking me, from the society that wants to pay the price for my daughters, ignoring that of my labour? Why don't you slam the heads of those contractors who steal from the bread of their children, from the hunger of their wives, and satisfy their needs by paying the price for uncountable mothers and sisters like me? And.... Why don't you strangle this father of yours who sent me to beg for bread from the dogs? Could your immaculate father not indulge in this system of borrowing money?

I could bring some bread by working at other houses and he couldn't even save his house's dignity from becoming some other's servant by doing some menial work. When his knot didn't have the strength, why did he use to carry that big bundle of self respect on his head? One who is in a situation to earn some other way should have the courage to resign from job. When he cannot earn to feed his wife, or raise his kids, why did he even get married? I haven't done anything wrong till date.' Mother was in full charge. Her arguments weren't meaningless. We had a big weak flexible axe to cut them. The violations of dignity of home, family and society would have been saved. But mother could have managed herself and left us insects to fate. Everyone was silent. Nobody had any word on their lips, not even a vibration. I couldn't wait and said, 'Your words may be flames of truth but you cannot call yourself guilt free. When all of us started earning and thinking for ourselves, why did you leave the house at that time? Why didn't you spend your life somewhere else while we still had milk teeth? It wasn't like Babu never had anything. Why didn't you smash your own brother's head for having thrown you, his crown at such a place? It is still not too late you can live with whichever man you want. After all, if it's not your fault for running away from us, then it's Babu's.

'I can get sold outside, eat left-overs, do slavery but at home, I'm just a mother! I cannot stand the daughters-in-law and your panache. Don't get after me. Look after your own houses. God will make my decision, not you.' Saying which, she went quiet.

When the elder brother started talking about the incident about the girls, she got furious- I am not despicable. Yes, I want to maintain the respect of the heinous ...... And she was quiet again.

We also hit our heads on the stone getting lost in our pain.

In the end, she said, 'You all are happy, I don't even need the vermillion on my head, and don't wish to be called a mother. You don't even recall me as a wicked woman. Go away, I'm no one to you.' Tears choked out my throat and everybody came out blabbering. Nobody even talked to each other.

A woman can be a wanton in the eyes of the entire society, she can be a beggar but for her children, she is only a mother.

The world isn't devoid of such women. The dilemma of Manu's situation, the genius of the commune of Marx, mockery of the laws of communication of independent life and the victim of all this, woman! Nature's sensitive creation. Today, suddenly, such a woman tried to enter my life, and didn't know what her name was. She had come as a guest at Saavri's home. She wanted to invite me when she was herself in transit. A stranger's letter in my hand... stranger.....

Dark embossed complexion, fiery red eyes filled with the strong intoxication of alcohol and in those eyes, a determined resolve to pierce someone. She knew the essence created by a veil. As if the haphazard alcoholic cloud rose in her life sometime, and the lightning, wind she met on her way ravaged her to sing the songs of the tavern. Now it was just the habit of scattering on being gathered. Powder, snow, lipstick and kajal and the dacron saree that calmed after being swept off. This was the identity of that stranger. She was the mother of many small and big kids. But not a wife. Probably couldn't remain one. Maybe she can't even remain one... she couldn't have been kept.

After all, how did she throw a letter to me in the eyes of my house using the magic of Professor Sarkar? What did she think? What did she want?

'You are sick. I cannot see your suffering. You know, I have committed a crime. I want....'

'What crime did she commit...? No, no, why did she do it? Life partner cannot be changed like the rented house/'

'Marriage? Is it important to tie the flow of life originating from the Gangotri of life to the brinks? For how long will the lotus be veiled? But....boundaries... everything will fall apart without them. Is drowning life? Then what is the wish to sail through....?

'When she had thrown the letter, my heart had started racing. Why did I start sweating? Why did I get angry thinking about something? Why was the blood rushing through my veins? Why did I get furious like a sincere woman?'

'The stranger was staying at some place. Why did she turn towards me? Why did the desires get trampled with her turn? She had asked for a promise. It was written in the letter, 'Tear it after reading. And do reply.' I made others read it. Called her promiscuous on not replying. She was defamed in the eyes of people. Her new support also got shaken. Have I not committed this betrayal?

Even a prostitute wouldn't like to hear someone call her promiscuous. Even she probably has a character. The stranger had started mumbling.... 'Says, who is she to give me a letter? Has he never looked at a woman with greed? Does he not want a woman? Thinks of himself as a very handsome man. Typical man...' She said whatever she felt like. Even her tongue had no right to stop her, nor her brain... Who heard whatever she said? She didn't even want others to listen to what she said to me. She quietly accepted everything in the first instance like a culprit. After all, why did she respect my boundaries when I left no stone unturned in unmasking her?

The landlord, his wife had swore in to never open the doors of this house for her. She had to leave the house.

This incident left me at the shore of conflicts. I could have expressed my disapproval by not replying to her letter as well. But if Rekha would have got to or Saavri would've heard, then? If the stranger who needed a regular salaried man would have hung on me, then? She wasn't even that young.

Character building is hidden in denial of wealth and beauty. The stranger wasn't lesser than me in condition. I didn't hit the jackpot by denying her, even then the notions about my character sparkled like marble. It affected Rekha's mind and Saavri's heart. I could dare to hold my head high for the first time.

On being turned down, a person gets lifted like a crane and even on attaining every opportunity, falls in his own eyes.

Rekha had read that letter many times hiding it from the children. My letter. Her husband's letter. A radio song is her favourite and she often hums it while holding the letter-

'Write it in the Leaf, the clouds have gathered,
Whose debts we had, have wandered untimely.'

That which is not accepted by the society, is sin. But it's not a sin. Absolute acceptance of the society to fall in love. Irony. I found completion of my entity with Rekha. She is the phrase of my life song in which the tip of the soul is immersed. But why did I falter?

Rekha was reading the letter and seemed to express her opinion on every sentence. 'It seems like you're angry at me. Aren't you? Don't be angry, my queen. I'm not bad at heart, my words maybe.' And she was thinking- He loves me so much. Why don't I love what he likes? It was further written- 'When I didn't get your letter until evening, I got more worried. Are you not well?' She was thinking how much he worries about me. And read on further sentences.

You must have received two letters till now. I am writing this letter to relieve the tension in my head, but wait on the night of 20-10-66. We'll meet.

'Smile a little, be shy a little, that's what I come to get. Where my life's garden is locked, what else will you come to get there? Stay happy always. In illness, in problems. In union and in separation. Idiot! This is life.' She got lost in herself again, but why does that happen? I want to embrace her and cry when he comes. The crying of the routine life, separation.

Crying like the actress of a drama who isn't just a part, but also a character. She was lost in the context of a letter concerning her and me and the festival of past and present. And she went in reading the letter and also mumbling.

-He is great, writes- I'll probably bring wool for a sweater. Will you knit? You must think, this man is great. He's an idiot. But it's alright, you're everything to me. Idiocy and happiness. Oh lord! What does he even write? What did he see in me? Why does he write, promise me you won't go to anyone else? Even if you do, wouldn't you forget me?' All these talks are foolish. No?' Must be. Let them be. You are mine, that's enough for me. There's excitement in this separation as well. Probably more than union.' How do I read further...? 'When I write the letter, you are with me. Just like when a person hides to seek, and on not finding him around, tries to find. And then when he's found?

Do you know what he'll do when that happens? Lessen his smile showing an excited set of teeth.'

The tickles originating in Rekha's heart were swaying on her cheeks. 'It feels like I haven't been able to love as much for a long time. I haven't gossiped with you all night. Haven't stroked your hair with my fingers in the moonlight. Tell me, am I wrong?' Her eyes danced like an excited deer in the forest at the letter.

Rekha had a stir of questions in her mind's province.... What's there in the world that I can call mine, all mine... But if it doesn't make a difference in his love or feelings, then who cares?... He can do whatever he wants. But Saavri. Can any court equally distribute the wealth of love... And then she got serious.

Rekha was pressing the ropes of the cot with her pulsating chest. The pillow, who was her companion, was getting pressed, not pressing. The bhabhi from upstairs came and snatched the letter. Said, 'You are enjoying this by yourself. I won't return it without reading.' Bhabhi pinched Rekha's cheeks with two fingers.

There's a bigger practice of snatching love letters and reading them among women. In reading others' love letters, one experiences satisfaction of mental confluence. A thirst arises in mind. A thirst that burns all life.

The relation between two sisters-in-law and with brother-in-law, in medicinal terms is a destroyer of 'fatigue fever'. If humans didn't have language, they'd have remained animals. If there wasn't language, then there wouldn't have been love letters, then the relation between a man and woman wouldn't have been any more than a mechanical one. Such letters should be written by every partner to each other. In the absence of the ideological land of love, a man only tolerates a woman, not lives. To flee from the corpse like faces of household chores, the voice of the language of love is imperative. That has been my ideology.

I made it a habit to write in my diary sometimes. The habit never got followed, but when it did, the mind got great peace. Creating a history. Today in self confessions I was suffering from the question of Rekha and Saavri. The pages of the diary fluttered in solving those questions. I start diving into the depths of the past. I was looking at an old diary, reading it to myself. Can sex not be removed from the definition of character? Why did this question arise in mind today? This was also an incident of a teenager.

It was the first time in the span of my memory that I met the family of my mother's sister at my uncle's place. Aunt had three daughters and two sons. One daughter was six to 12 months older than me.

When I was bathing alone at the well inside the house, why did you smile seeing me, Kanta? Why did she come there? When a man cannot see a woman bathing, what right does a woman have to see a man's body while bathing? I used to tease her. Probably she would have smiled at some mistake I made in my bathing order. No, but she also smiled with her eyes. If she smiled why did my extremities welcome her smile? But why did my eyes understand the language of her smiling lashes? What was the meaning of that melody....?

On my last night there, I was sitting with my mother. Like the coach of a train, that room also had my aunt, bhabhi, and Kanta. In one corner of the room, a lamp of bitter oil was burning in a slow flame. I was sitting with my aunt. Kanta was lying beside me.

Why did she invoke a shiver by touching my hand? There wasn't light on everyone's bodies. She was stroking my hand, against my will, in this bitter darkness in order to express some darkness. Why did I shudder like the petals of lotus in the cold wind? Why did the sister's touch induce the vibration of a beloved? Why didn't I jerk my hand off? I should've said, you're pinching me, sister. But why did my opposition go mute?

Her copper ring is kept somewhere even today. Kanta's pick seems to emerge in the right palm today.

Every memory was taking out its debt on me. The debts cannot be paid, but yes, their contexts can be tickled. Nobody's price can be paid. One dead with debts must take birth repeatedly, in search of those memories in whose accounts his name was written. But they also get lost. They don't live until their next birth.

The bee wandering the orchards of memories has to spend its life in the fragrance of the past. Every age cannot become history, historical are only those moments that are played with in the lap of papers stealing some time and there isn't always a basis for all words and expressions. The flow of the present sometimes opens the mouth of the shell of the past.

I still remember Kanta like the tickle of an evening of the entire life. It seems like today's night of memories, histories, words and experiences. The night of sleeping in the present to be awake in the past. Enclosed within the pages of my diary was my playful past. Today, reading which epochs of situations emerged and disappeared in my sleepy eyes.

Light is the companion of wakefulness. Be it the light of sun, lamp or memories. I was awake like the sparkling atmosphere of the glorious light of a wax mountain on a dark night. Like the outside light was locked at someone's door. It was forbidden to even peek at doused memories residing inside.

Every present evaluates the past. That is why people live in the past, to live in the present. To make the present past this page was named after Roopa.

Roopa's memories looked with hatred. She looked at

me, I didn't even gather a smile and she turned around. Her memories are immersed in the sea of questions.

She was from a poor family. 18 years old. I got to know from Rekha that she was infertile. She couldn't get married. I was shook. Her cheeks were also pale. She had great interests in comedy. One day she came to study with me. Rekha had also recommended her. She had confirmed something I told her from some other teacher, learning which I felt insulted. To seek revenge for my insult, I lashed out at her. If you didn't trust me, you shouldn't have come to me. Don't come to me for studies, understood? I'm not a useless person.'

Roopa fell at my feet. Which I hadn't anticipated at all. It is frightening to get your feet touched by another woman or girl other than your wife. I trembled with tears on my feet from the dedication and that praise. Before this, I hadn't seen her in any other way. But then why, on that day picking her up with my shaking hands, I say, I felt bad, so I scolded you. I love you, Roopa.' Rekha was cooking in the kitchen. I was in the room. And she was in my arms. Was this love also enlivened by the same feeling?

Has she considered me something?

I had longer for her for a few days. Rekha had cursed her fate. She had also fought with her. I used to forget, she is an incomplete toy at the hands of nature. Which thirst of mine can she quench-infertile Roopa? But why did I longed to see her even for once? Today memories have come into existence. Action forms of the abstract nouns were seen. Roopa's memory turned, she aimed at me and said, 'Raju, had you loved me? I couldn't quench only one thirst of yours. But I was a woman. A woman who doesn't marry. After all she's a vortex at the statue of Shiva. I cannot become a mother. Nobody will even love me. Because society gives love to that part of a woman that can bear kids. Raju! I don't have the right to be mad at you. That day when you said, 'I love you, Roopa.' My compassion melted. I had realized this life's dream. I started living... The girls of my age had become mothers. Raju, the Roopa you gave your love to, started dancing, why did you leave sleeping like Damyanti? You didn't even try to return to meet. Did you not miss Roopa...? Alright. You were an outsider, no? But I'm wind wandering in the heat of the past, which has been left here by the one who weaved the dreams of gardens.' The memory halted. There were tears in her eyes. The vermillion on her head looked like the forgotten memories. There wasn't satisfaction on her face, only a heart that probably couldn't be someone else's.

Now I wasn't at that house, not that city where I met Roopa. Today her memories were ready to strangle me like a ghost.

Why did I fall in love with someone, who couldn't be a woman, but was, who was considered to be a bad omen by her own society? Why had I forgotten Rekha's rights for her? I was hating the man sitting inside me who looks as ravishing in the facade of principles as he is deceptive.

Is a woman's frame itself sufficient to shake the flame of the wax mountain of the patience of a man?

My head started spinning. I was turning in my bed. Suddenly I remembered a song by Sehgal- when health declines, your mind has to get diverted. But the question was- How? I started staring at the sky with blank eyes with conflicts inside and questions in my eyes.

An elaborate group of black clouds seems to float outside like the pair of swans in a lake. I was lying on my cot in my personal courtyard. The fruitless branch of a lemon tree bowing down in my courtyard would flutter due to the wind. It was probably a frown of the memories of the passage of wind. Gradually the bits of clouds scattered. There were constellations and the moon in the vastness. The milky way was more clearly visible amidst the night of stars. The view like that of imagining Upveet on the shoulder of dark Ram, freed me from the memories of the strangling past.

Whatever there is, it's outside, there is only it's translation inside. When a person gets tangled in the translations away from the object, he suffocates. In that suffocation, there's an enjoyment, an experience, that the mind cannot provide even if it wants, the mind gets relieved even after getting bored from it. Alcohol is a poison. We drink poison, keeping aside ambrosia. Shankara drank poison even in the presence of ambrosia, why? Maybe there's more power in the development of the throat, more belief in faith, prayer of becoming something on getting vanished. That is why maybe I kept burning in the logs of the past, I didn't like the soft cheeks of the clouds, they didn't even catch my attention.

The present of the truth was standing outside and I was caught in its past.

The constant opposing circumstances of the inside and outside had taken away my sleep. I lit a cigarette and started walking in the courtyard. I was running. After new emerging clouds, but my shadow was being trampled by Kanta, Roopa, Rekha, Saavri and Asha.

Now it was late. I turned closing my heavy eyelids and made the atmosphere of putting to sleep the exhaustion of the day.

After an entire day, the queen of the house had returned. When a woman carries the burden of the entire house living away from a man, old age grips him before its time. The worry of the kids, the arrangement of the household and the burden of raising eight men was on Rekha.

When she was with me, she wasn't alone even after being in the yard of problems. Half of the pain of a woman gets lessened on being with a man. Now in the name of a man, there was only vermillion on her head, toe rings in her feet, glass bangles in her arms, the wait for money order and sometimes I myself.

That day, Saavri had seen Rekha for the first time. The kind of beauty Rekha had imagined for Saavri, the reflection she gathered of her behaviour, she was looking at her with those eyes. There was a picture of Rekha in Saavri's mind as well. Both were meeting each other, reduced within their dissatisfaction.

Humans think of his actions, repent for them, and consider them wrong. Even then, when he does something, the question arises that he's serving the situation or a slave of his repressed desires. I always think- I took away Rekha's rights for petty people, but for some reason I cannot go back on the floor of the inferences of my repentance.

Saavri's loved freedom wilted on seeing Rekha. Rekha felt as if the only person she called her own Raju, wasn't his anymore. She laughed, with Saavri as well as me. I also welcomed the queen of my house like queen Victoria as per my stature. But Rekha was a little upset since the evening. I was entertaining Saavri through secretive conversations through my eyes and with the same enthusiasm gave my love to Rekha. An actor with two actresses in the same role. This is the dilemma of destiny!

We always ate from the same plate. Rekha had come to me after a long time. Otherwise I was the one to visit her always. We both were sitting together to eat. On finishing the meal, I sent Bade to fetch four paans. Cautioned me to bring tobacco separately.

Rekha stopped Bade from being paan for her. 'I'm not used to eating paan, don't waste the money.' Her words weren't sharp, but there sure was a cold remark of opposition. This denial by her touched my weak spot. I felt as if it was my insult, that of my love, and of my welcoming feelings. I got scarred.

When the depth of love lacks legs and its request is denied like a registered post, its feedback seems to cross the difficult road. In such a time, the inner difference dissolves in the blood and begins to cut the edges of the vessels like paddy.

I was overwhelmed by the compassion of love. Language didn't have the courage to come close. I had gone and lay down on the cot. Even Kaikeyi wouldn't have turned anxiously. I wasn't able to understand her reason for sadness till now.

People search for upper class in the capitalists, but no one checks in the revenue farmers that how the man called husband and that too of Indian origin exploits the helplessness of the woman married to him. How confident he is about his faith in lowliness. He keeps confidence in what he does. What he does himself. To find arguments to satisfy the hunger of eyes and convince his poor wife, be it an Indian husband or someone raised in another culture, he is a very great patron. A woman's devotion, her tolerance don't satisfy her cruel antics.

The entire house got to know. We were lying down in the same room separately facing in different directions. When Bade brought the paan, he didn't dare to come to me. I didn't even eat the paan. Rekha herself brought the paan, I rebuffed her. She tried her best to talk to me, but I was at the height of revenge. I was a man who wasn't a culprit even after loving another woman and she was a culprit of being upset with my behaviour, she was a criminal!

The night passed. Someone cried, someone turned. The curse of silence was spilled like light in such a happy and fun loving house. Even the walls were intimidated. But several nights like these had come in our lives. We were capable of grieving in the moments of fun.

Love is the name of pain given in the process of recreation. Hatred, a noun given to the suppressed emotion in love. In one's reaction dynamics is the other's development.

It was morning. Along with ego, frustration, love and hatred, the claim brought peace of mind to the edge of alteration like the repatriated person at a court case. I, with the ferocity and sorrowful motives reprimanded the woman at night, who had given all her life's happiness to me, tried searching for opportunities to talk to her.

As if the torture of last night that melted both ends of the wax mountain, inspired to build a new hill with the melted wax in the morning. Lust for love reaching the boundaries of destruction finds the way to create new.

Rekha was replaying the things scattered in the room. My heart couldn't take it, I pulled her into my arms. She sat without opposition. Even her mind wanted to clean the inner suffocation with revelation. I asked, why did you say no to paan yesterday? 'I didn't want to, but why did you get upset?' She asked.

'Because you insulted my love. But you were acting differently since last evening. After all what was the matter, that you didn't even sit happily to eat?'

'You can revolt but cannot the mind of a woman. You decipher the public's suffering without them saying it, but you didn't try to understand the origin of my suffering.' Rekha couldn't say further.

Rekha's wilting face filled with cracks of anger. I kept on speaking. 'Since the day you've come, I've spread all the happiness in my capacity under your feet. I was so happy when you came. I wish you had experienced it!'

'You have experienced. Experience isn't irreversible

like the date of birth. But now I feel it was a waste to come. My arrival has disturbed someone's freedom.' She answered. Her voice had more anger than satire.'

'Why don't you tell clearly whatever you felt bad about? I don't understand the mystic language.'

Rekha's resentment fired up on her pale face.

'A person blind in his own intentions will find other's expression of anguish as mystic. It's not your fault, it's actually my destiny's fault. I couldn't keep you happy even after giving you everything.'

Someone opened the pipe from across, but suddenly the flow of the tap reduced. As if the one who opened it, turned off the tap as soon as he opened. The water was flowing slowly.

'Say clearly, Rekha. What are you even pointing at?'

My tone was bitter. A sentiment of a husband's natural right.

'Saavri, the ball of your eyes... Probably the boundaries of love, its pain you had with Asha must have been with Saavri too. When the family of love was hopping in glee in your courtyard, why did you write such a letter to me that made me come here even in shortage of money? This isn't your fault, but my bad luck.' Her eyes welled up.

There weren't any tears left to shed in Rekha's eyes. It was an open attack on truth, I couldn't even think of surrender. 'Rekha, your allegation is right. There are many stagnant and disintegrating steps in the path of life. Did you consider them home?' I said accepting her allegation.

'If you had to live in stages, you shouldn't have settled in a house. If I would have been in your place and you in mine, would you still have smiled witnessing the stages in my life?' Rekha said looking towards me.

Suddenly a tingling sensation ran through my veins.

'Principles are created when their symptoms are prevalent in the society. What you think, happens and what I'm doing is also not new.' I said simplifying things.

'You've always used me as a shield. Here, it's the turn of the nexus of family through me. Not just today, the day I came here marrying you, what was wrong with me then? Even then, you pricked my chest with Kamla's arrow, and played the act of loving Roopa. Whenever such thoughts even rose in my mind, your artificial love didn't let them materialize. Now the ailments of worry have shredded me. Death is the only cure for me.'.... I'll say that you're a husband now, you haven't understood the heart of a woman. Burdened with your useless lust, you've been picking on the worms like a chicken living a despicable life. And these women are such bitches... Rekha said without any inhibitions.

I found it appropriate to keep quiet.

I was broken. And she was tired. I kept quiet and lied down, turning away from her. She kept sitting in that same pose. Now she was lighter. Even after using a harsher language when she found me quiet, her eyes filled with feelings of gratitude. She shook me and said, 'Listen, are you angry?' There was a smile on her lips desiccated like winter. My wounded eyes were opening in the coolness of forgiveness, with excitement of reunion in revert.

Clarifying my situation, I began speaking, taking courage from her changed behaviour. She speeded up my silent moments with the vibrations of her love. We're not physical partners but for the intellect. I don't consider physical relation as a sin though. That feeling is a sin whose glasses we wear to see the object of truth. I accept that those principles are still alive in me, which if you'd have been in my place.... Even I would have thought the same way. But I understand that if it'd have been you, I'd have won over my principles and lived on. Even you have endured. I didn't chase any woman, but in whose eyes I saw a place for me, I didn't hesitate to halt for some time and talk, I didn't think of sinning. I've never been or am involved in physical relations with anyone but you. Can a woman not be my friend that I could talk to occasionally? That isn't a sin.'

'People like you don't have a character, as per what I've heard, but I've also seen that after marriage.' Rekha looked like a budding lotus and lightened like a petal. I was serious. She was in a natural lively mood.

Life is an evening of stories. Hyphen, comma, dash. Whatever happens, gets added. The liver might get treated without medicines but this life cannot be lived without love. Transcendence and love cannot be weighed on the same scale, that's the mistake. Love is a cumulative feeling of those desires that make us different from animals. We fall in love, that's how we love.

Rekha had dozed off making the children sleep. On getting some alone time, Saavri and I were standing in the darkness of the night and talking. I was saying, 'Saavri, you've taken control over my mind and heart in such a way that even on being close to her, I'm away from Rekha.. Only you can take away my sorrows.' She put her arms around my neck, pressed her lips on my cheek and took me for a walk. I embraced her tightly. She said, 'Why don't you understand my limits, my body cannot be yours.'

Where every man and woman's love ends, where there's ultimate satisfaction of love, she considered it a sin. A woman yearns to live the journey of love, but shivers even at the moment of surrender. Bodily surrender was the limit of morality for her.

Saavri's part of the room was on another side of the big courtyard. Away from our part. We were talking standing in the gallery leading to the outside. The light of the courtyard didn't reach this part. She didn't ask even if she wanted to, did Rekha say anything? And I deliberately didn't talk about yesterday's incident to her. Telling Saavri about yesterday's incident would be like making fun of Rekha, disrespecting her in comparison to Saavri. Whatever it may be, Rekha was an extension from the past to present for me, and Saavri a savoury of the present.

The deviation from the attainment of sexual satisfaction from Saavri was one important reason for my anxiousness. I was probably engaged in laying the foundation stonc of the localized centre of the fulfilment of needs. Like Roopa, Asha and Kanta, she will also remain a story connected to my life, only to be remembered sometime.

I tried to pull her towards me, she would try to ward me off by pressing her hands in mine. Her hands felt lukewarm sometimes, and I'd feel my heart beating rapidly. I said trying to melt her, 'What is the purpose of these moments of solitude, after all?'

'I like all this, that's it.' Saavri answered with a smile.

'Why not more?'

'That is not required.' Saavri said, freeing her hands.

'But I do.'

'You shouldn't even require this much but I cannot understand why you even need this much.' After sighing, she said, 'It seems like someone's coming, now you go.' She left like a breeze without waiting for an answer from me. I was shaken by Saavri's answer.

I was returning to my room. The neighbour's daughter was taken aback seeing me at that end of the gallery at this time. She didn't stop but I was dumbstruck.

Rekha was in deep sleep. I stooped to the bed and lied down. 'You don't even need this much', Saavri was right. Why don't I have on being with Rekha?..... Maybe a wife cannot give the vibrations of a lover!

Rekha will leave tomorrow. The house will get deserted. Neena's chirps would drown in the quietness of the room. Bade will also leave, I'll be left like the actor of the playlet 'Parkiya'.

How would it feel? My books, my clothes, other things in the house will once again live in disorder. 'Without a homemaker, home is the den of ghosts, that's it.... Witches dance in the den of ghosts only.

I'll have to give at least two hundred rupees to Rekha to go home. In addition to monthly expenses, there's money to be given to the doctor and clothing person. What if I don't get money from the cooperative tomorrow? Everything will be in vain. I'll have to beg the secretary, serving him at least one cup of tea.

I was thinking what a life the service profession has; be it for monthly expenses or needs for principles, one always has to look up to debts to meet them. The country whose government's schemes run in debt, if the worker of that government lives in debt why should that be surprising. GP Fund advance or loan from Cooperative, that's the support for the respect for the working class. This is his life, his support. There is that date of the month as well, when the paycheck gets autographed and what do we get, the fund gets cut, cooperative gets cut, festival advance is cut, cycle advance is cut, what's left! Whatever is left is spent on the external give and take. Superficial life!

I had reached almost 1.5 hours before the time for the

train's arrival to drop Rekha. The passengers of Delhi Express had not started pouring in. Rekha's heart always cried in moments of separation from me. Today she was saying, 'To evade the suffocation for which I came to Allahabad from Kannauj, I'm taking back double of that. When you talked about Saavri, it hadn't pinched me so hard. But on seeing it, my self-respect and rights had been struck so hard, that my body wouldn't be able to take any further.' The tears acknowledged the crowd at the platform. Even my heart welled up. I had fallen in my own eyes. But for some reason, there was no feeling of detachment with Saavri. And there was no lack of love for Rekha too. If I wouldn't have told her, she wouldn't have assumed it even after seeing it. And when she wouldn't have known all this, would she have said ' you are lowly', no, never. One who gets saved from the society's sight, he has a character. Probably the definition of character and the principles of morality don't go where such attachments don't exist.

I wished dearly to lighten Rekha's mood, but I failed.

Her health and happiness were more important for my life than Saavri's love. Anyway my children's future is imagined for the progress of the country, if anything happens to Rekha, my life will be a big mess. I will die like a cow tied to a peg. The children touched her feet. Both of us had tears in our eyes. She only said, you should go now. I said while walking away, 'Write to me when you reach. Don't stay in Kanpur.'

I took a rickshaw for Chowk on coming out. The rickshaw puller went on saving from the crowd, ringing the bell and scolding the shop owners. The rickshaw went on in its speed, I was lost in the suffocation of the humidity of my tears that didn't fall. How can a man be so degenerate. Women are still a source of entertainment for men in the age of science. When will these meaningless love stories end that have been going on behind the curtains? I wasn't finding myself any higher than the nominal level of that lowly man who drank alcohol when on being short on money for the house. Who goes elsewhere even on having a beautiful wife at home. For a moment, I hated the community of men.

He is wrong who is considered such by the progressive

society, one who is considered right by the court isn't always considered so by the society. Saavri thought, even said sometimes, 'What have we got ourselves into?' Her husband's image was in front of her eyes as well, questions of another woman's husband on her mind. She was thinking, why should a woman surrender herself to a man, apart from her own husband? I hadn't seen anyone through such eyes. Why did Raju fall into the vibrations of the mind? 'He' bears so much in worrying about my food, drink and health. He has so many aspirations in his heart for my kids. We were spending the days of poverty so happily, suddenly we are trapped now. In this small life, from where did Raju bring this catastrophe?

I felt suffocated. Raju on one side, and Gudiya's father on the other, am I not deceiving the lord this way? His lips have registered so many memories on my cheeks. When I think of it, I feel dizzy. When I look at it forgetting the reason and the end, I think, I wish I'd had met Raju before. Who filled a delight in my deserted life, an unimaginable and unspeakable love in my heart, I got drenched in the waves. I think, and even Raju says it.... A woman and man's love is a prayer of the body, and it's true. If I have surrendered my body to Guddu's father, whose witness is the society, then this Raju....

The light of the lamp is used to worship God. It's also for other gods, but specifically for the main deity in a temple. Is Raju one of the other deities of the temple...?

There is a limit to our thoughts. Even then she was getting deeper into the baseless sea of thinking, Rekha's behaviour is beautiful. There's unwavering love between the husband and wife. Raju sits beside Rekha to eat. Why did I praise Rekha's luck internally? Raju has said several times, 'Saavri, come, let's sit and eat together.'

Yes, when that day Raju was eating with us, I couldn't stop myself and sat with him for a moment. He took a piece and extended to my mouth....I stopped his hand and fed him that bite. When was I that lucky? But I'll have to return now. This is a flood, the rivers will get down. I looked in every way at Raju. Protected the periphery. He wouldn't be able to take it. I should meet less often with him. This love shouldn't and doesn't have a long life.

A woman can handle the staggering footsteps of a man, if she wants. A woman is like a shield for a man, he should get handled by this shield but he slips like a ball on it. A woman can express denial but cannot effectively provide a path to return the man to the same heights. Social tools of shame give rise to barriers, when it smiles in sacrificing those tools, then all peaks of conduct rise on being banished like the valleys. She presents the path, strangling the throats of her emotions, keeping a stone on her heart.

In comparison, one gets accepted and the other naturally gets eliminated. In that case, that which gets accepted is the one that's more useful. Similarly, two men can be accepted for a woman in different situations, but till when can they sustain that, that's the important question. Saavri's mind also had the same dilemma, I had the same struggle, and why are two women acceptable in the same situation?

If I say the situation is significant, then the question arises who is its originator? The human himself. Are these situations aren't just differences in perspectives? Perspectives can be changed as well. And they should be! Under the aegis of the union of a man and woman, even money plays a part in the context of sustenance. Can I not accept Saavri for ever taking the help of the law?

I can but where will the means to lift the burden of two women come from? And then an easily approachable woman seems to be bored as well. She isn't anything more than a cow tied in a shed, she cannot create new feelings. This can be done by hard earned things. Tempting are those things that aren't our own or cannot be. They lose their attraction on getting attained. This attraction is Saavri and that routine is Rekha.

Here I had become much indebted. Office salary was incapable of providing for the house. The problem of money has affected health. Although others didn't know about it. But I knew, that wasn't less. I knew so I was worried, suffering it so I felt it and feeling it so I started being sick. My sickness was a reason for Rekha's worries and a matter of regret for Saavri.

A lover had got a heart attack, that means I once got the opportunity to face death on the table at Hallett College. At that time, memories of Asha, Roopa and Kanta were like the names written on the torn off pages of a diary. Saavri hadn't entered my life yet. Even after being in a hospital, surrounded by 15-20 doctors, I couldn't get any help with my attack. I had gone there for a blood test and returned a heart patient.

How did I feel? I wish, somebody had told me because no one was there. Only the doctors and nurses there were the witnesses. But when I opened my eyes, I found myself lying on a table and a crowd of unknown faces around me. I asked them, what happened to me? I got the answer, nothing. I wanted to get up, but couldn't. After my failed attempt, even the doctors suggested I remain as it is. After resting for a while, I expressed my wish to go home and gathered courage to even get up. Upon washing my face and hands, I was about to call for a rickshaw, when somebody said, here, take this. The rickshaw was there, they probably had already arranged it for me.

When the rickshaw puller got me seated, he said, 'Babu, where will you go?' Without giving a thought, I said, '15 Naveen market' and he kept on turning around to look at me while riding. I only said, look ahead while peddling, I'm fine. I thought to myself, am I that sick?

I was feeling weak. I told the rickshaw puller to fetch some milk.

If on one side there will be my brother's dead body and on the other, my friend's, then my eyes will rain lamenting for my brother, and my shoulder carrying the platform for my friend. If the brother would be well off, he'll look with arrogance, wouldn't ever help and the friend will help being within defined limits. The brother's relationship is more formal. There's only blood claim in it and blood donation in the other. Anyone can claim but donations are rare. It's not like there's a lack of brothers ready to give their lives for the wrinkles on the forehead of a fellow brother, but they're so less than their existence is just enough to keep alive the pride of maternal love. The increasing heat of money has cooled the degree of affinity. That is why I went to 15, Naveen market, not home. That was a hangout for friends, they could arrange appropriately for me. They could run around, inform Rekha but on going home, Rekha could faint, cry or get worried. Poor Rekha....

I fainted for short durations many times there. They took me to the doctor and in the end when I could no more walk, they even dropped me home. Rekha froze seeing me faltering legs and friends giving me support to walk. The same father who had once ordered me to leave the house was now with me, turning his face around to wipe his tears on listening to everything from my friends. As long as Rekha was there in front of me, the calmness of the depths of the ocean reflected in her eyes. And for a while when she wasn't, the internal sea ripped the sand dunes of earth to flow out. She used to remember it was a bad omen to cry and she instantly wiped her tears. Babu was conducting a chant of Mahamrityunjaya with the pundit, Rekha sat there quietly.

The mother who had once said, 'How will I live?', today

everyone except that same mother had come to see me. From asking for tea from everyone who came and went to offering meals to whosoever stayed, everything was on Rekha's shoulder. Everyone asked about my health and left. But the colleagues of my office would ask even further, let us know if you need money. My own parents didn't help me, the brothers didn't even speak any assuring sentences of financial help amidst the expenditure. There was a friend of mine, from the office, who was arranging money for me from Cooperative and funds.

In today's monetary age, nobody can help each other with money even if they want to. Everyone has their income and their endless expenditures.

Even I wasn't able to give twenty rupees to Comrade Falgunan when he was suspended for the crime of holding a strike and he didn't have any ration even for another day. His daughter was ill and he was ready to mortgage his watch too. Money proved countless people's motherhood fruitless, denied countless relationships. We still expect others to help in our times of calamity like a skylark. A friend can give his life for another friend but not give twenty rupees in the absence of it, no matter his claim of sacrifice be wronged.

And since then, when Rekha gets the news of my condition, she would get distraught. My failing health had wilted her face. She used to write this in her letters, 'Worrying won't help, I still have a nose ring and bracelet that can be sold in stressful times. Everything is from a man. Your life is above every other ornament for me. If you're there, several ornaments can be made and after all, these are made to help in times of need.'

But Saavri wasn't this worried about me. She could, at most, cook a decoction for me or talk to me to take my mind off. The share held by any of them in the business dictated their will to take on risk accordingly. These are what we call relations.

The country was getting divided into linguistic states. America, Russia, Japan, Germany, every place had India's moustache hair indebted at their doors. Nehru had dreamt of socialism. Laid foundation of schemes for prosperity of socialism. The constitution of the country assured protection of the interests of all. Dams were built, factories were built and the planned way to eat every time by asking for it. Inflation broke the backs of the public. The glut of taxes flared the price of the breath of man.

When the fog of the resilient sky pressing the chest of agony roads outside, laughed with its beautiful smile. On the marks of the furrow used to plough the fields, like the child not being fed with his mother's milk, in the absence of irrigation like the patient of epilepsy, the straws were getting mistaken. Like the patient of asthma, the breath of the dwindling Indian economic system converted the pretty look of the floor into a barn of phlegm. The gold ring, the vermillion on the head, the bangles in her hands and the toe rings in her feet symbolic of the wife's husband, were all short of breath. When the epitome of the living symbols was experiencing hiccups, who was Saavri?

What was her love? That had suddenly started pouring water like a blocked source. And now wanted to return to its periphery with speed. She got aroused and she got stagnant, that was a result of her narrow principles. The meaning of this transit in the sequence of that speed where the entire meaning of my personal got transformed, was nothing. These days I was speeding awareness among the government workers towards their powers. Rising inflation, decreasing value of income, the future of our kids protected in the ancient books and the uncertain suffering of the tables laden with incessantly opening new files stared at me. There was a past devoid of the present in everyone's eyes that had fire, but not flames, blaze but not wish granted by Bhasmasur; but no, the fire was burning. Mother's drier than milk aanchal was wrapping around my waist, the crow of the state's system having run after injuring the youth of the wives challenged the insidious power of the women. The children for the parents who couldn't arrange the money for their fees filled the grounds of jail on getting bored of the college compounds.

The meaning of revolution will never be realized if the complementary entity of a man, woman, sits at home accepting her physical barriers. She is the history of the creases as well as the chaos of the catastrophe.

After attaining independence, Congress had got the opportunity to manage the state system and got that national and foreign policy that Nehru considered useful for the renovation of our society. Congress, the same congress after six years of whose death, Mahatma Gandhi gave his resignation letter not deeming it fit for his participation. In front of which Gandhi caps, the public of the nation bowed their heads with utmost purity, with the names of the leaders people tirelessly associated incidents of glorious stories, the Congress that ruled every heart, today that same Gandhi cap was more hateful than the red turbans of British bureaucracy. The same leaders were idols of deceit in the eyes of people ranging from the rickshaw pullers to the upper and middle class public and the same Congress and the policy of Nehru the reason for public anguish. The leading voice of our movement was also against such Gandhi cap wearers, these leaders and this Congress.

The present had gotten diseased. The basis of imagining the future was feeble. The past couldn't have been brought back, the future couldn't be brought and the present couldn't be lived.

I was the General secretary of my union. People had faith and trust in my leadership. My superiors were fed up with me, to the extent that they often dreamed about me. Not because my face was dreary but, they were terrorized, because their moral strength was merely a frustrated measure of the preconceived notions and common opinion. I hadn't just organized the workers against the officers but presented the ideals of discipline and moral strength. I believe that an undisciplined person can surely collapse the conservative society but cannot build a new society. I don't believe in building schemes upon destruction. I want to break the existing according to the concept of new creation. After every demolition, creation of new requires discipline. The meaning of discipline is anything but slavery.

I had raised a voice against inflation, for minimal salary according to the requirement. For sympathetic treatment of the workers. And therefore I was a problem for the officers.

Once I had gone to Jabalpur regarding the union's work. I met the head there. He was young, younger than me and a person with simplified thoughts. I had told him, 'What is this difference between you and me? You also earn the contractual value by selling your labour, like me. You are also related to a Middle class family like me but even then why do we roar at each other every possible time?' Sahab smiled and accepted our offer and said, 'Mr Raju, whatever we do is for the responsibility of the chair.'

Although the staff of Jabalpur was satisfied with their heads.

I had also said to him, 'I want to reduce the frustrations growing between the workers and the officers, because our joint responsibility is towards the country, not towards a particular person nor towards any government.' I also said to Mr Ramendram, the head there, 'How great it would be if both of us together fight the government for the welfare of the employees, their demands and their rights.' And he said, shaking my hand, 'Government isn't just the people sitting in the parliament or the legislative assemblies' and he smiled.

Then what is the government! The Indian government! Government is a mere suffix and the people sitting in the parliament and legislative assemblies the helmsmen? We are also government helmsman but to suffer and they are the sources of power that give pace to our lives according to their political ideologies. We get into fights with those people only. These officers who fulfil their orders are the arms of the goddess Surasa, that don't even allow a tiny object to cross the sky without their permission. These poor people are deployed to withstand the atrocities.

The most dangerous is the person who becomes an officer from Babu. Neither can he win over his old principles nor establish his parity with the older officers. He is like the dog that aims for his own tail on getting furious. The vacancy created by the officers getting promoted does create a path for the employees, but also teaches to bark on your peers for that piece of butter.

The greater the distance one traverses, the bigger a traveller he is. His experiences amount for a greater price. If a patient is made doctor, then we should hope that as having experienced the pain of the patient, he will treat the circumstances with sympathy that are, or can come or usually come in front of a patient. He shouldn't forget his part in the splendour of the present but not just past, in the greed for a promotion in the future, like a new Muslim becomes so staunchly conservative in following the hadiths, that he considers the pains of his nativeness superficial. And with a hollow future he starts floating like a balloon in the great abyss. He grows up in the manure of the dead bodies of his own people, he develops too with support from his old community. But he feels proud to eat his own eggs like a snake. He gets the title of headman only from the community which made him enter the office life, grew up but will die with others. But it's another thing, that the shoulders that'll carry his dead body to the crematorium won't be from another caste, rather from the shabby class of the same old generation. The people from. The new caste are aristocratic beings, they don't lend a shoulder but adorn the funeral procession. Those who lend a shoulder are probably from a lower class.

There was a double blow in the office- the colleagues disobeying their officer in the name of democracy and the officers showing their governance power. The situation cannot be misused by those at a lower level if the ones at higher levels are unbiased. When people vegetables aren't given special privileges but how can they not?

Human himself is a by-product of coincidence and contact. Nature is really born out of necessity, so whatever is compatible to whom gets adapted. Not just that, the environment affecting nature is also helpful in inheritance! Therefore, one feels the need to buy vegetables and another of revolt. That soil and air isn't enough in which elements are formed but also that tradition that makes them.

I was strolling in the courtyard anxious. In these nitty gritties. Carrying a problem bigger than all this - Rekha's illness. She was a patient of many severe female diseases. Her illness was a mess in my life and..... a catastrophe. It's not mine, but a test for my selfishness. I am myself a mere inspiration of references. A machine burdened with weight, an evening living the present in the past and the pages of a diary to be cherished, these are some names of that which I've known as life.

Suddenly my eyes fell on the bangles at the pipe, Saavri was fetching water. It was as if the inner suffocation found an excuse to be caressed in the outside environment, I felt relaxed in the stressed veins of my mind. In that moment, as if the eyes came around to test the security of character, the legs got the hint and they proceeded towards the pipe. I was stooping. The vibrations tickling my body rose and fell in my heart. I shut Saavri's eyes with my hands, on going from behind. She was surprised but didn't shout. She probably didn't expect this from Rameshwar even, in addition to me. That's why on getting surprised, she instantly knew whose heart was beating to the right of her back. She wanted to turn around in a whiff and I didn't want to give her the chance. 'What if someone sees, let go.' She turned around and stood opposite. I don't know what that statement had that my embrace got lighter and stood at a distance even. In the absence of any fear, nobody shall probably have anything.

On seeing me maintaining distance she went on inside her room. Like an eighteen year old uncontrollable young boy, I latched on the edge of her petticoat. In trying to free herself, she kept moving and it opened more. She said, grinding her teeth, 'Someone's coming, I don't like it as much.' But I felt as if everything was rubbish. I had forgotten that a woman can live the truth of the wedding night, not the reality of Draupadi.

She was busy covering her dignity, losing the courage to stop my shamelessness. Her dark face had reddened like a pan. Now I wasn't just inside her room, but was also embracing the Saavri who doubled up. There was nobody in her house. Both the neighbours had gone to the cinema. My heart beat was so fast that its pace could be measured and heard on seeing my bare chest. Saavri was sweating. Now she was only saying, 'You swear on me, you'll see my dead face, leave me.' And I kept on saying, this is not the time to leave, or to swear on each other, I want to see your bashful not dead face.'

She turned towards instantly, trying to find something in the cheeks. There was only a petticoat on her body and.... blouse. There wasn't love in her eyes, but hatred. I ignored even understanding it. As soon as she said, 'Raju, now go from here', I picked her up. In order to support her body, she grabbed my neck with her hands. She collapsed in my arms and left the pain of teeth on the doors of my cheeks. Suddenly her weight got too much for my hands and she landed on the floor picking up her petticoat from the floor. I had just come to the door to check for anyone, when I heard something. I didn't stop but continued in the same pace and form towards the pipe. I had hardly reached the pipe when I saw Rameshwar. My shuddering heart had snatched the shivers from my lips. Inside the room, Saavri had probably worn half the saree.

I was internally thanking the guards of time. Even if Rameshwar would have seen me inside the room alone, what would have happened? What other option Saavri and I would have been left with other than suicide? There is no difference between the condition of a thief caught red-handed and one proven as a culprit. One instantly gets punishment and the other needs to be guarded, hated.

I was washing with water the marks of Saavri's teeth.

‘Where were you, Bhua?’ Sushma asked the sixty year old woman who was panting. The oldie was short on breath. In order to get control over her feeble body, she was moving her bony face up and down. The veins hanging from her wrinkled skin, puffed like a balloon filled with air, like the immobile stance of a snake hung from her body.

The soiled dhoti having getting stuck at various places, a thick denim top and on her head, white tangled under the sun and messed up hair, eyes filled with cataract, the bent back of the lost youth in the market of time, in the right hand the support of the faltering legs, a piece of wood that cannot be called a stick. Bhua now said, resting the sack of wheat on the floor from her left hand, ‘Dear, I had gone to get ration. After standing in a queue from four in the morning to one in the afternoon, I got this tiny sack of grain. The beggars get more ration than this by begging for it, bloody ration.’

‘Bhua, there’s great trouble. Even our father had to return two days and take off from the school, then he could get ration for fifteen days. And sugar and rice are still left.’ Sushma said, answering.

‘Nobody asks, dear, this famine is there since the time of britishers. That Gandhi didn't know what kind of freedom, that we are indebted of a single grain. The stomach has to be fed, as long as we live. Now those days won't come back. Hail freedom.’ Bhua got up and started walking. Sushma kept on looking at her. The present of the past was an asthma patient and that of future hunger struck. Bhua had gone inside her cell.

Sushma was 25 years old. Her father was a teacher. There were three younger sisters, two brothers, mother and father, a total of eight people in the family. She was unmarried. On being from a vaishya family, she was only allowed to marry when her father would be able to give 100 grams gold, cash, and clothes for all family members as dowry. Inflation had also affected the demands of the dowry. The depreciation of Indian rupee had also affected the exchange rate of the body. The tree on the chest of a private school's teacher, night's sleep and sobriety - Sushma, was still sitting at home. Whereas her school friend Radha having studded her dress with four stars, decorating the poor evening of her youth, the early morning bread, the life of her children and the dignity of her husband was being asked by her from the unseen God who was regarded by Shankaracharya, known by Jesus and Moses had seen it on the horizon of earth.

Bhua was spreading the grains of rationed wheat. Sushma came and took it from her and said,

'Bhua, leave it, I'll do it.' Bhua had a cloth wound around her nose. She gets breathless on inhaling the husk.

'Girl, leave it. As long as I live, I'll do this. May God make your hands yellow. Who knows when I'll stop breathing.' Sushma speeded up the fall of the grains so much that she couldn't hear Bhua's prayers for her.

The landlord didn't talk to Sushma's father nicely. Whenever he spoke, it seemed, like. Satan was talking. Sushma had winnowed Bhua's wheat, now she was filling it in a sack to get it crushed. She heard someone known talking loudly to her father outside.

'It's been four months, master Sahab, there is a limit to patience. Every month you postpone it by saying, I will deal with it next month. I keep silent considering something. You have all grown up girls, little kids otherwise your things could be on the road long back.' The landlord was collecting rent.

A few husbands from the neighbourhood gathered at master Sahab's residence hearing the roar of their fellow. Now pandit Murarideen spoke facing them, 'Now you people should decide, I'm fed up of this master's image. Sir, four months' rent is unpaid, that is one hundred and twenty rupees. You only think, the person who cannot give rent every month, how will he pay so much money at once?'

'So master Sahab, what do you think?' Munshi Rambhajan asked strikingly.

'Master Sahab doesn't think about not giving the rent, yes, there could be some helplessness.' Another friend said scratching his lips.

'So master, do you plan to get your daughter married with the saved money of rent?' Ramkatha orator Pandey ji said, stroking his beard.

'Pandey ji, if my daughter could be married for a hundred and twenty rupees, then there wouldn't be a chance for your lectures, that too like the uninvited guests. You must enjoy making fun of someone's situation more than reciting Ram Katha.' Master Sahab was losing patience.

'Hey Master, keep quiet. How dare you teach me the importance of the story of supreme lord Ram?' Pandey ji shivered with anger. 'Story teller, be within your limits. And listen to me, pandit ji, until the time the debacle of my school's management committee gets resolved, new or old managers, nobody has the right to withdraw money from the bank and there's no hope of getting our salaries till that time as well. Your money hasn't stopped prior to this, nor I want to have even a penny for yours. Rest, you can do whatever you want. You have no right to gather a crowd at the door of a respected family and disrespect them.' Master's limit of tolerance was crossed.

'Well said. After all, the stove is lit up all day long, you leave the house all dressed up as well, only when it comes to giving our money, do you have the debacle excuse? I have also built this house taking a loan from the Board, I also have to pay my instalment. The board members wouldn't leave instalment heating about the debacle at your office or pitying you for your condition. The way you manage the expenses for your house, manage for the rent in the same way, otherwise one day that will happen, which I don't want to do to you as a family man myself. I give him another month's time in front of you all. What do I do? I'm a Brahmin, I get merciful on seeing his kids, and otherwise it's just one day's play.' Pandit Murarideen said, changing his tone.

Rambhajan spoke up, 'Awasthi ji, this is your house. If it would have been mine, I would have vacated it in a moment, it's just a matter of hinting my disciples.'

'You did the right, Awasthi ji. Every house has an earthen stove, though he is a good man, never talked to anyone disrespectfully. A private school's teacher is more vile than a rickshaw puller. At least the rickshaw puller earns 5-6 rupees daily but this poor man signs for 200 and gets 90.' Munshi ji turning the conversation towards sympathy, started praising Awasthi ji chronically.

When the landlord was storming out of the door mumbling something, Sushma had tears in her eyes. There was an empty stove in front of her mother and clenched fists of her brothers.

Pandit Murarideen had spent fifty years of his life living in a rented house. Whether or not his ancestors even had a hut, the historians have no clue. But now, pandit ji is a landlord. Including everything, the monthly rent comes to about one hundred and twenty five rupees, however, in the register of the Corporation, the annual income from rent is registered as just two hundred and forty rupees. His partner, the storyteller is married to a widowed water woman and Munshi ji is the owner of a ration shop. Often when Munshi ji is floating in happiness on straining the green brick, he says, 'Through artifice, I only have two hundred rupees as income in my business. Give it a thought, friends. Where is it written to earn two hundred rupees monthly after investing fifteen thousand rupees? The government says, whatever I do, you do the same, which means, friends, that which is said is not done, what's done is the right thing. Bam bam Shankar, drink bhang. Our lord Shankar, owing to this influence of this greenery, considered Brahma, Vishnu etc as mere insects. Before even the pellet dissolves in the stomach, the flight of the jet plane takes off. Bhangbhawani says, Munshi, use it wisely. The ration inspector, the Daroga, all the high profile people of ration are all customers. Understood. I give these pundits who celebrate my praise five hundred rupees each every month. That's why, due to the grace of the almighty, my name is on the list of honest dealers.

'Just think about it, Kalua, your father was a porter,

your uncle was a cloth hawker, and your brother has a stall. But 'Munshi Ration Wale', by the grace of God, eats after feeding everyone.'

'Bachhu, the lock of luck doesn't open by joining your hands but by artifice. Whosoever rowed against the wind, didn't see the shore ever again. There should be money in the bank, if there's a name on the register of names indebted to societies, then you're finished.'

'......why do you crawl, walk fast. It is said, 'Krishna went to Baikunth, Radha held his hand, of tobacco is eaten here, wouldn't be any at the other side. I am a poor man, I indulge in cheap intoxication. I give ration to the poor and return their bellies after heating it with my sweet tongue. Brother, you came late, whatever there was, got sold. I'm going to worry about you. If I get the quota, your work will also run.'

Ghasita said holding the tobacco, 'Sir, but for how long will this darkness of ration remain?'

'Hey, why do you worry? It's not famine in America. The drought is in the fields of the less fortunate. Poor American people that have opened the godowns and treasure doors. People might say whatever, but only the money lender feels pity for the poor. Debt will be paid by those whose ancestors had donated. Long live America and long live the government of the pair two bulls. So Kallu? Did you filter less today?'

'No, sir, when I spent the entire day harmonizing with you, how could I have worked? We snap the whip of charas and then sit calmly.'

'Well done, son, one who will not be felonious, how will he earn feloniously? And he, who does not earn for himself, how would he feed?' This is what our old boss Lala Ramratan used to say. What do you know, foolish Basant? Where did I bring fifteen thousand rupees at once when my father Lala Karam Chand worked tirelessly lifting sacks? Bless Lala Ramratan, his income tax debt and the office worker. When the ten lakh income tax file got passed, Bade Sahab got fifty thousand, the clerk got twenty thousand and Oh! Our majestic dear lord, I got fifteen thousand as well. All of this is a result of my service to God that the government continues to work as well as the court. Did the milk come to a boil yet, Mullu's mother?

'Yes it has, Mullu's grandpa!'

'You are a great example for all housewives, bringing everything in order before even asking. It's true that a house blessed by the almighty, is blessed altogether. If the doctor, washer men etc are happy, all pilgrimages are meaningful. Even the tenants don't seem to have a problem with us. When there is a profit, we pay back, when there's loss, we take debt.'

'Master?' said Ghasita.

'What now?' Munshi Rashanwale said, turning his eyes, shining like ruby, from the mountains down to the ground.

'Sir, now there is difficulty in talking.....it is slightly colder......if you allow, should I get double from single?'

'Go, but take care of your health.'

'Mullu's grandpa' Munshiyain called. She also used to enjoy sitting behind the door. They didn't need cinema.

'Coming, Mullu's grandma, axe of old age, my wife', saying which Munshi ji lifted his eyes and walked towards the house. The meeting was adjourned.

'Hey Ram, what will the kids think if they hear? You speak like that in old age as well.' Mullu's mother said while placing the turban on the frizzled hair on the head.

'What is old age? In the court of the followers of Bhole Bhandari, everyone is young, never gets old. Do you know why there are three colours in the flag of our country? Green leaves, saffron and milk, a drink mixing these makes our flag wave in the sky. And whether our prime minister is Chinese, or Pakistani , where there is debt of dollars or PL, it is all inconsequential. Now don't say Rano, Bhaang says maang, and there is the name of old age on the door of he who begs, yuck..........yuck yuck......

Shiv shiv shiv.......Hare hare hare'

Having strained the boiled milk, Munshi ji now resigned to his cot. While sleeping, his nostrils flared like a Canadian engine, piercing through the calm of the night.

I had come to stay at my sister's house, which was adjacent to Munshi Rashanwale's home. The block in the locality Kidwai Nagar of the city Kanpur, in which his house was, had residents who were well off on an average. If one person was being paid four hundred rupees per month, then the other earned as much as their rent. This was a display of economic communism.

‘ Our head is the only son of an Aristocrat father, who has a dream in his eyes, a photograph in his hand and plans in his pocket. He practices individualism and is the vision of socialism’, said Thakur Sundardin, taking the discussion further.

I had to stay there for two to four days. Society is necessary to kill time. When unable to do so, either initiate a discussion on a sensitive topic or delve into politics. It fares better at killing time than playing cards. At the end of discussion on a sensitive matter, one feels the lightness of the fresh breeze at the dawn in his heart; and a fatigue after a political debate.

Here, the robust Jana Sangh Party with Hindu ideology gave its full support in the movement to protect the Holy cow. Shankaracharya, who enjoyed the opulence of the hard work of being a religious leader, was also forced to suffer in life’s real struggle. Ramkatha narrator Pandey ji often told people, ‘Look when this non religious government is threatened by Akali Saint of self-immolation or pretends to hunger strike, then our secular government puts their ears under the minorities’ soles to listen. The entire government starts rotating like the searchlights of an Aerodrome.’

Chandraprakash, a great devotee of Pandey ji, blowing some cigarette puff, said, ‘Sir, it is useless for us to be Hindus. We are the ones being tortured. If Muslims are aggrieved, then namaz is read to please them, if Sikhs get offended, then Sat Sri Akal is called out. But if the Hindus even as much spoke loudly, they run after you with the reins of DIR.’

‘It doesn’t end here, Babu Chandraprakash, it is astonishing to note how the Muslims tear the pages of our Tulsidas in the court and pretend to follow the legalities while shining their eyes through the spectacles of legislation.’

It is the right of Pandit ji to say, this unreligious government is anti-Hindu,’ said Babu Chandraprakash shaking his head. ‘Actually, the fact is that until the government creates a national code of conduct for all castes, these classist assumptions cannot be ruled out. Although we are a secular state, when it comes to forming a government on the basis of votes, then the leaders of Muslims, Christians, Sikhs as well as the Untouchables start to gain reverence. As long as caste discrimination continues in the name of caste organisation, Jan Sangh, Muslim League and Akali Dal will continue to prosper', I said restraining myself.

This meeting was occasionally graced by Thakur Sundardin. He used to work in a mill and was a diligent worker of his union. Although he only knew to write his signature as far as his education was concerned, he learnt to converse under his peers' influence. Today when politics was being discussed, he sat there to disclose his opinion. He started grabbing eyeballs like spilling a trail of aces. He said, 'As Pandit ji said, what kind of government is this? It is not an enemy of the castes but intellect. Our chief has a dream in his eyes, a map to prosperity in his hand and plans in his pocket. He is a man of individualism and a vision of socialism.' He further said, 'Did you hear the Logistics Minister's suggestion? He suggested eating rats. Ask his one and a half metric hemispherical stomach, if it grew this big because of eating rats? Babu Chandraprakash, I say that they are not only enemies of intellect but even in matters of awareness, they neither fall at third nor at the thirteenth position. They roam like pure men having rescued the Untouchables.' A hair in Thakur Sahab's right moustache fluttered as he spoke. 'Now where should we take our troubles, these people were keepers of the power of the state earlier and even today they bark at government's directions. It is their tendency, Pandit ji, which is why I have turned my ears away from their voices. They will continue whining.' Thakur stopped on looking towards Chandra Prakash.

Babu Chandraprakash was the clerk at the Roadways Office. While a strike was going on, he was spending his time of unemployment at this place. But such was the condition, TB of inflation inside, a headache of the government's stern attitude and wrinkles of debt on cheeks. The strike was going on successfully for fifteen days. Neither the government nor the workers were ready to give in. It had been a long time since roadways buses or city buses wheeled on the roads.

Babu Chandraprakash put his perspective in a soulful way in the gathering. What should I tell you about Thakur Sahab? Whatever meagre I earned by changing the route of some conductor or driver has also ceased. Our hearts have started cursing the leaders of the Union. They talk about increasing our income, but end up taking away even what we earned.' Chandraprakash Babu said, rummaging his heart. 'Whether you are in his chair, Sir, or the one who is currently their eyes burn anyway. The cataracts of being in power, cascading responsibilities and burdening circumstances have a combined effect on the pace of its steps. If the problems of workers can elevate a small group to the sky, then the government responsible for the entire system can resist them if they want.

Now, Chandraprakash's eyes were fixed on Thakur Sahab.

'What do you say; does the relationship between a servant and owner not obey the socialist structure of the government? The government is ours, by us and for us. All government employees like us together run the system of the country. It is not like the government is a statue of Gautama Buddha, such that every person sitting near it will be called a Buddhist,' Thakur Sahab said explaining the government.

Although these stories did not seem to end soon, but in order to divert the topic, I said, 'The situation of the servant and that of the responsibility of the current government are both fair, the only unjustness is in the figures that feed the history. However, your strike was successful.'

'The government claims that the national income is not enough to meet the needs of the workers. The owner of the mill says the income is not enough to give raise bonuses. Then what should we do? Eat poison!' said Thakur Sahab.

'Look, I do not agree with this statement that the mill owners do not have money. If it were true, then the ratio in which the revenue of Birla, Tata, Dalmia etc. increased, why did the income of small farmers not increase with the same ratio,' I said.

'That is what I am saying', Thakur Sahab confirmed.

When the government is ours, it will work for us. What is the point in facilitating decrease in national revenue by holding strikes?' said Chandraprakash.

The gathering was entirely enjoying their conversations. Everyone sat quietly listening to them talk.

The newspapers said the strike was successful, the government thought the same, the people as well, even the corrupt head too, then on the stove said it was successful, the paan wala agreed to it, the dhoti sewn by the wife said the strike was successful. The record books of house owners said the strike was successful, someone's flowing unloved hair strands said the strike was successful.

Was the strike successful? A fight without a cause. False promises made by the government satisfied the hunger of the workers. Their tears were wiped, without asking the reason behind them. Daroga ji interacted with the striking workers' mothers and sisters, saying, 'These rascals did not let us sleep.'

Even today the meeting was held, but on a different topic. A girl had come to Munshi Rashanwale's shop to buy ration. She was around eighteen years old, dressed in a new style. She started looking around in confusion, when she spilled wheat grains. When Munshi told her to sit down and gather them, she did not say anything but looked annoyed. A few people around broke into smiles. She left the grains as they were and called a rickshaw puller to collect and fill it back.

'Brother, what use is a dress that deters your movement. This is Kalyug, their parents are blind to such things and the daughters are proactive. They will go to homes but showrooms. She is a cold daughter, not a hardworking daughter.' Munshi said, rubbing tobacco on his palm.

'That is true, Munshi ji,' said narrator Pandey ji. 'As you know, in our mythology women are considered strong and fierce, but today women like Sita or Anusuya do not exist. Rather daughters of Rati are seen roaming the streets in groups. Sahab, clothes are worn in accordance with the weather and terrain, not to put one's body on display.'

A typist at Reserve Bank Shankrit Babu was also present. Although he was a typist, he earned seven hundred and fifty rupees per month, which never used to satiate him and thus he was a regular at strikes. As a student of psychology and experience of rodeos, he had to speak up, 'Beauty is not a thing to be confined. Beauty is a gift of nature and ornaments of a civilised society. Do you want to strangle nature with the hands of civilization? The form of a mother or wife is equally pleasant to the eyes. However, a mother's beauty does not excite us in the same way due to social traditions.'

I had a question in my mind, 'Should I also order my daughter to adorn herself to come closer to nature and far from the parched society? Should I allow her to only exist as a stimulus for lustful motives? I understand that external beauty falls under civilisation, but is not synonymous with nature. I did not stop myself from putting across a question for Shankrit. Well, I partially agreed with him. I believe beauty is a thing of inspiration.'

And do you know Yashpal, what did that typist Babu said to me answering my query? He said, 'Raju, the transformation of the sacraments of societal traditions is not one day's dream. One has to make sacrifices in order to make it true. As long as a girl's purity and paternalism is under consideration, any father would not permit his daughter to spend time with a person who is not her husband.' I had only talked about psychologically disappointing failure of pleasure , not of political ethics.' Shankrit said, resolving my doubts.

'You are right. I often think, if humans are also permitted to satiate their senses like the chariots of God Bhairava, then what will become of the ethics of community life of humans? What will happen to the human who descended from a primitive life to a civilised one?'

Shankrit glanced upon his watch, and it had struck eight in the night. He asked to be permitted to leave. Even Munshi Rashanwale wanted to slip out, rising up he said, 'Brothers, you all have degrees like B.A., M.A. and are learned, and I am as related to the alphabet, as a prostitute is to faithfulness. However, if the trends in fashion continue this way, no policeman would be able to stop these girls from getting abducted from the streets. Everyone blames the man, because he gets tempted easily, but no one questions these girls who give birth to detachment instead of faith in the hearts of saints. Nobody is going to shut their eyes while walking on the streets and since they do see, bumps are inevitable.'

'Well said, Munshi ji, and so correctly, as long as there are temptations, events will take place!' And he walked away smiling.

Narrator Pandey ji considered our arguments to be propagating immorality and even then, he listened silently. He was getting the spice he needed for his stories. Thakur Sundardin was thinking, 'Yes, everyone is at least entitled to have knowledge of this aspect of nature. What kind of a woman would only set fire to the stove?'

The meeting got over. I was turning towards my brother-in-law's house while pondering over several conflicts in mind. I thought that if sensory oppression wouldn't have been a principle of society but conveyed by nature, there wouldn't be a problem in Saavri filling my arms. Animals wouldn't be free to indulge in sensual satiety, to the extent that there wouldn't be a difference between humans and animals. Is this not necessary? Does civility not owe anything to nature? Is nature the truth, reality and efforts and civility a fad of centuries?

Nature itself creates the conditions for emergence of civilisation. If there is a need to change the moral values with time, then the instruments of nature have to be consulted, the essence of its soul to be understood and new moral beliefs have to be developed. But a civilisation has to be built, without reversing nature's origin. Reversal is death. Culture is also the definition of intellect of the era and therefore civilisations keep changing and change is its morality. However, absence of civilization is the creation of darkness.

Since that day, Saavri has been afraid of my shadow. I, too, having crossed her couple of times, continue moving with my eyes looking down. The reason for her restrain could be to keep a distance from me but I don't know why, could meet her eyes. From that day on, I started feeling that she was too proud. She doesn't understand the value of my love and pretends to be a nun.

Rameshwar's actions did not feel like he knew anything. I was thinking Saavri did not tell him anything. Why did she give me the fervent affection of her lips on culminating disobedience? Is she also uneasy on the inside like me? Is she also thinking about getting lost in the free valleys? There were only questions, without any sight of answers.

Professor Raju, showing his usual sincerity, said further. Now, feelings of vengeance are arising in my heart. I started long at Saavri as a prey. Feels of jealousy arose in my heart. I started creating scenarios in my mind. She has evaded me twice. Even after being a man, I was not able to fulfil my desires through a woman. I was a petitioner returning after being despised. Nobody will even pity me. If Rekha discovers the extent of my hunger and vain efforts made by me for her, will she not start hating me? And if Rameshwar would have seen that day and I would have been embarrassed, then would Rekha not commit suicide? If a husband solemnly attempts to establish immoral relations with another woman in the presence of his wife, would it not be against the wife's dignity?

I spend less time at home now. But I surely looked out for opportunities to avenge my insults.

Evenings after returning home from office, started being spent at Nirmal tea-stall in Johnson Ganj. Kant and Dhar Babu used to regularly visit that place, but the main attraction was Guru ji. Guru's attire consisted of a dhoti past his knees and a shirt, a thickly spread out unbendable moustache. Teeth stained with the ever present paan gilori in his mouth. Dark complexion, fifty years of age and a habit of wearing glasses while reading. Meeting points were a few usual shops from Johnson Ganj to Zero Road or a Sarraf shop situated on the way from Jawahar Square to Mutthiganj. Guru was also fond of jewellery and was a small trader. Although he was a government servant, he was called Inspector Sahab. He used to drape himself in clothes like that of a retired soldier. If the dhoti was clean, the shirt would be a bit dirty and if the shirt would be washed, the dhoti would have been worn twice or thrice.

Although I did not get the opportunity to converse with Saavri before as well, I used to eagerly wait to meet. Merely looking at each other would do the job. She was a stone-hearted woman. She did not care much about her relationship with me. She valued my love for her in the same way that a labourer gives more importance to extra income earned by doing over time than to the regular salary. Even the labourer values only the earning, and forgets the value of the hard work after getting paid. He does not even remember the extra income he gets. But because I am emotional, lonely and burdened with problems, I am anxious to live that extra time.

Perhaps, she would have been more impatient than me, if her time wasn't mortgaged to her children and household. But this was the simple truth.

Truth can only be the name of an authenticated object or event, leaving no place for probability. Events on being unproven are rendered baseless. The truth was she sometimes danced on the waves and admired the ocean stirring from the shore. Whenever I used to say, 'How is your heart? You look stone-hearted. Do you not suffer the agony of separation? Do you not remember in seclusion?' She used to smile and say, 'He used to say the same thing- You are a strange woman. One can grow fond of the trading times, not with the roles played before and after. I consider these things to be rubbish. Even his requests make me feel bad, but I do not say anything. I do not have the courage to take away his right. Only he can possess my undue dedication, no one else. I cannot betray him, I do not want to.'

We were sitting at the Nirmal tea-stall. Everyone was waiting for Guru to arrive. Although all of us took care of ourselves, Guru used to take care of all his visitors. Tea and snacks would also do the rounds. In Guru's presence, tea for everyone would be arranged by him without any expectation. From children to old aged people, Badoa pundit was a Guru to all.

More people who had no connection with literature waited for Guru at that place. Guru himself had only two pastimes, having tea and snacks at our office and buying and selling Sapphire and Topaz. His association with literature was as much that of the people living in Daraganj had with the confluence. He has also written some poems, an article and a novel. Some poems have also been stored along with the compositions of other poets of the group. However, time was slowly licking the ink from the articles and novels. Guru personified the historical progress, be it Nirala or Firaaq, new poets or musicians. Today, he was already sitting there. Realising my arrival, he increased the order for tea by one.

'Say, what is all this mess?', asked Guru as soon as he sat down. I did not get the meaning of this statement from O Henry's story. I locked my eyes with his, and asked, 'I did not understand, Guru. Please speak clearly.' 'I have been thinking since morning about the importance of love and romance in a novel. Isn't all this mess a scam, a novel has to have love?' And Badoa Guru whilst sitting with a bent knee broke into laughter. Sometimes when he laughed, the paan gilori pressed in his mouth slipped out as if being disrespected, which would make us break into a bout of laughter. Guru did not mind this and said, 'This idiot found his exit and spoiled my shirt.' The same thing happened today, but since I was alone, I sat there smiling.

'I cannot say how this novel got your attention today, but if there is any relation between literature and our life, then all that happens in our life is important to be a part of it.' I tried understanding the reality by studying his face.

'I perused my novel today and there was nothing like this in it. If it were, then it would have been fit. Here, it was already white.' Guru was in a state of content today, and went on saying, 'I have a friend named Bataobay, around forty years old. He is currently having an affair with a thirty year old woman. I cannot even manage a sixty year old.' And then he burst into laughter. 'Ladke Chaarpan' He fixed his eyes on me after ordering paan. I started finding an accused one inside me. He said smiling, 'Raju, you have really lost it. You think I am kidding.'

' No, Guru, that is not true......................... I was about to say that Kant, Dhar, Narsingh, Tiwari all came. It changed the course of the conversation. For some time, even until the second round of tea, a narrative with no ebb and flow continued. But Kant was ahead in teasing and mocking Guru, he turned the heel in the same direction from where he turned before coming here. 'Guru, did you not ask Raju for the fun of old age romance? He is the most experienced of us all.' After saying so, he looked at me and smiled. He was naturally a rascal. Amidst his fumbles, tea sips and Guru's quick words, sometimes I felt a blow on my core.

Now I was entirely shocked. My face must have also looked pale, because inside I felt clamoured. ........But Kant and even my neighbour Rameshwar had no clue about the love affair going on for years. Telling other people would amount to immorality. I gathered courage. In order to conquer fear, one must face the horrific circumstances. Fear is a ghost born on the crest of weaknesses. Silence at the time of accusation, amounts to being guilty. A straw in the thief's beard.

'Why am I the expert?' I said with a natural grin.

'Because you are a victim' saying this, Guru chuckled. When Guru laughed, his big head moved like a drum of monkey charmer, lips spread and a crease is seen in his curly haired moustache. Teeth stained with betel, peeked their ugliness as the lips unmasked them. He didn't laugh loudly but chuckled with small bouts of laughter. If the laughter was uncontrollable, then he drew breaths neighing. Seeing him laugh, even the walls of the hotel would break into laughter. His laughter was a medicine to people like us who were accustomed to daily torture and perpetual anguish in their hearts. Crying is forceful and laughter a necessity. The greater the arrow pierced a heart, the greater the need to indulge in laughter. ...........Was guru so heartbroken that it necessitated interaction with people of his age and delving into laughter? It was a gathering of young people. People's income was his money to be spent on tea. He used to earn to spend it on tea to relieve his heart of the bereavement...there was something in him.

The bridge of thoughts being built in my mind about Guru's laughter and my weaknesses suddenly collapsed. My neighbour Malviya ji called me outside, to hand me a letter.

The arrival of a letter is a matter of suspicion for such families, a time of increasing heart beat, where external relations are traded. The purpose of sending a wire is fulfilled by sending a letter. Everyone started looking there astonished. I descended the hotel with heavy feet. I started reading the letter, it said that mother is ill, came soon and was signed by my younger brother.

Guru asked in a grave voice, 'Raju is everything alright?

On holding the letter in my hand, I shuddered while reading it. Everyone saw me calming down, but only the syllables on the letter saw the darkness in front of my eyes.

'It is alright. My mother is slightly ill.' I said while returning to the hotel.

Kant said, 'Which train will you take?'

Narsingh said, 'Brother, you should leave.' He choked

with emotions while saying this.

'I will only get a train after two hours. Okay Guru, now I'll leave,' I said this while turning around. Everyone said, 'Yes, reach the station soon.'

Guru climbed down the stairs with me. After some distance, asked me, 'You must have prepared to leave. I only have twenty rupees to give you right now. Keep them, you might need it. I denied, but he persistently kept the money in my pocket.'

Mother was spending her time of loneliness in a small house in Aryanagar. After working for a couple of houses and obtaining wheat flour for each day from Awasthi's mill, she was able to pay the rent as well as pay for other minor expenses. She was known as Raju's mother in the neighbourhood.

On the way, I was thinking, 'Why did I give so much importance to this letter? What is the importance of the illness of the mother who was dead to me forever?'

The train passing through some small stations, continued to run rapidly on the tracks. Many people had spread their sheets on the berths and lied down, some sat with their eyes closed. Those who sat with their eyes closed were stirred up when the train halted and then again they went back to their meditation. Some people were sitting on the floor of coaches, some stood erect as if in a meditative state. I was one of those people who sat with their eyes closed meditating. Kanpur was still 100 miles away.

I sat there thinking.

Mother is the name of that purity, saying which Bhagirathi got blessed, this earth got blessed, the cow who took birth in the animal kingdom got blessed.......kuptro jayte mata kwachdapi kumata na bhavet, is this right? Does not the Ganga who is called the mother takes the lives of many women, children by taking them all down in her flow? Does pregnant Vasundhara not become the reason for her children's death? Does a cow not throw its dead children taking them by its horns? Does a mother who gave birth to a human Karna, not become wicked by giving him to the flow of the river? Is, like my mother, taking a decision to do bad to her children not a mother's flaw? The mythology that propagates the wickedness of a son also wants the death of sons like Karna, chant the names of women like Draupadi. If Ganga that takes the lives of so many creatures every month, every year, can still be considered pure, the nun who reformed as someone who killed Karna by taking his shield and earring is considered memorable and the mother who has socially killed all of us brothers is pardonable, then what is wickedness, what is sin?

Even then I didn't think of returning from the middle. I could not disrespect the woman, who gave birth to me, suffered many problems keeping me in her womb for nine months, and raised me into a man that today even I could be a father, by protecting me from cold-cough, diseases and illness. At this time, her actions were not in front of me, only that diseased lap in which at some point I played. Maybe purity is considering the source as pure and best as impure. The feeling of worshipping the source relieving it of its responsibilities.

I wasn't clear on my role in reaching her house. I had got the mail I was indebted to, I wasn't a bad son, so I was going. He also doesn't earn, no?

Kanpur central station is about 4 miles from Aryanagar. The rickshaw puller in his own stride, passing the crossroads, turned, piercing through the pedestrians continued moving rapidly. His face clearly showed signs of ageing. I was going to meet my mother after about ten years. The rickshaw was opposite 'Madhur Bhawan'. My heart fluttered strangely. I wanted to leap a rooms' distance in one stride. Where did that hollowness go that resided in my heart for ten years?

With the bag in my hand, nostalgia filling my heart, I climbed one stair at a time. Mother's affection, the longing grown over the years, all swelled up at once and then subsided. My sinful steps lost their pace. I was like a car moving in neutral gear. I was only thinking, what name I should call out, who would be available at this time. I now climbed the last stair. Meanwhile I saw my younger brother climbing down.

Before I could say anything to him, he pounced to touch my feet and turned around gladly towards the room and informed mother about my arrival.

'Brother Raju has come', called out Karan overwhelmed.

My elder brother, younger sister and a neighbour we're sitting in that small room. There wasn't any cot in this house. My mother was lying on the rug spread on the floor itself. On hearing of my arrival, all eyes turned towards the door. My mother's eyes got emotional. Welling up, she said getting up, 'Oh! you came, where are you?' Elder brother told her to keep lying down. Though I had heard what she had asked. 'I am right here. How are you?' I said this as I bowed down to touch her feet when she quickly embraced me. Her tears touched my neck, mine drenching hér saree. No one can tell who accepted whom today.

For some time, the room remained grave. Nobody talked or looked at each other. Even my mother was clearing her spectacles while looking towards the wall. And I looked at the things untidily kept in the room. Wearing her spectacles, and wiping her tears, my mother looked at me intensely. My mother looked down and my mother pulled my hand towards her and said 'Look, how old you are now.' She patted my head while saying this. If I hadn't received the mail of her ill-health and these people wouldn't have been sitting around her, then I wouldn't have realised her illness.

I looked at my mother's frail body without her noticing. My younger sister was looking at me through the corner of her eyes, while my elder brother sat there thinking. I had forgotten to touch his feet. As soon as I touched his feet, he put his hand on my back and said, 'How many leaves have you applied for?' I answered briefly, 'I have requested for two days' leave.'

'Go and have a bath. Get relieved from the journey's tiredness,' my mother said as she turned away. I am glad you came. How are the kids and your wife?

'All of them are in Kannauj. Where is Babu?' I said the latter while turning towards elder brother.

'He is in Kanpur only', he replied.

'Why? Does he not know anything', I asked bewildered.

‘He knows everything. I had told him and even asked him to come.... ‘, the elder brother said as he looked away.

Alright’, I started thinking, whether Babu has no place for mother in his heart. Meanwhile mother shifted her head on the pillow and turned to the other side of the bed, she said, ‘I had myself told them not to come. There’s a difference between your visit and their visit. I wanted to see you in my last moments.. .’, saying which she silenced.

I asked my elder brother, ‘What is the illness?’ There’s nothing that cannot be cured. The doctor said that there is a problem with the heart beat. She gets a fit sometimes and starts blabbering.

I asked, ‘What does she say?’, while glancing at my elder brother and then at my mother.

‘She sometimes says- ‘Don’t even touch my dead body, Raju, if you even touch the soil surrounding me, I’ll find peace.’ Other times, she says, ‘I am as holy as Ahilya. I was a mother. Nobody can tell who she talks to when she murmurs. Probably, she debates with Babu only.’ elder brother said while looking at my facial expressions.

‘I am as holy as Ahilya.’ These words rang in my ears. What is unholy? Is society’s rejection unholy? Or is it her husband rejecting it? Even Gautama sacrificed his wife. He who was constrained by the circumstances had sacrificed his wife who was subjugated by them. But when did Babu, even after knowing everything,

Disowned mother? She only talked about forgetting the past. But can it be forgotten? ........ Its recurrence can be prevented.

I sent Karan to summon Babu. Mother resisted, but when I didn’t budge, she gave up.

Everyone in the family except Karan had misbehaved and betrayed me. My sister’s behaviour was unpardonable. Amongst my brother, I was only fond of Karan. I had cordial relations with him. Rekha was very fond of him as well. Therefore, he was the only one happy with my visit; others might have anticipated my arrival. Sister was unhappy with her own actions, having married on her will. Her husband used to beat her, drank alcohol, gambled and created ruckus. She used to cry, be sick, but did not tell anyone. She was at a place from where Hindu-Brahmin women cannot return.

There was no worry about food at my mother's place. A plate from the neighbour Gupta ji's house used to come for her. The doctor had advised her to drink fruit juices but she was not destined to get any more than the ghee in the dal. A country where eighty percent population does not even get dry chapati and dal, the doctors there advise their patients to drink pomegranate and orange juice. I thought it was decided for everyone to sleep at my elder brother's place. Although I had to stay there only, even if there was limited space, I experienced a new found uneasiness due to the presence of my sister. I had seen her only now after her marriage. She had the right to stay there as well. She has been occupied in her service before me. A daughter is more affectionate than a son. A daughter is more concerned for her mother than her husband or son. In addition to being a daughter and a mother, they are both women. A woman's plight is best understood by another woman.

We were waiting for Babu to come. Father said, 'Let us go back to our house for eating and sleeping after talking to Babu, as there is not enough space here.'

I did not answer. Mother said, 'For a son, his father's palace seems small but his mother's hut seems bigger. You should leave him here.'

'I will not be able to stay for other reasons.' I answered in a neutral tone. Mother was aware of this tone. She understood, but today it was as such she was determined to finish the unfinished history. She probably wanted to, once again,

Use her right but by then everyone turned towards the sound of someone's footsteps on the stairs. Little sister came out of the room to find out. She called out from there, 'Mother, Babu has arrived.'

Mother stood up carefully. She did not stop even after we advised her, but her heart beat rapidly rose while rising up. She fell instantly. I panicked. Nothing else happened; such things were common for her. I asked Kara to call a doctor. There was a T.B hospital just opposite, and a doctor working there was treating mother for free.

Doctor came and with a stethoscope heard her heart

beating, checked her pulse, blood pressure. He kept down his stethoscope and aid, 'If you want her to be healthy, then immediately give her medicines I prescribe.' Without waiting for an answer, he took his notepad and wrote them down.

I gave Karan twenty rupees and sent him by a rickshaw to fetch the medicines. He went ahead.

'Will she be saved? I asked the doctor.

'Although pulse rate and heart beat are not worrisome, but I can't declare her out of danger as well.' After saying, when the doctor got ready to leave, I proceeded to pick his bag. He stopped me and said, 'Leave all this here. Call me when Karan returns. This will be needed again.'

The doctor had gone. Babu was wiping his tears, saving everyone's eyes.

elder brother faced Babu and said, 'Mother is not well. She needs to be fed properly. It is not wise to leave her here alone. Even at this time, leaving her here to indulge in other things would be foolish. Somebody should keep her with him. If I would have been capable enough to do so, I wouldn't have to say this.'

Meanwhile, mother turned in an unconscious state. Younger sister sprinkled some water on her face. Babu tried to bring out her teeth by pressing her cheeks. Everyone's attention shifted there. elder brother's statement was left unanswered. Today, Babu had touched his mother's body after 15 years. I did not consider it impossible but significant news. Even at this time, was there an internal conflict in the mind of Shankar who spent his life silently?

Did this seventy four year old man remember thirty years back's time while sitting here? Did the pulsating history of living these twenty years shook the shabby present?

Is the entire life atonement and sacrifice?

Younger sister was now wiping the mother's face with her saree. Her eyes were teary, her saree contained the wetness of the water sprinkled on mother's face and her throat had the dryness of a desert. Her mouth had been opened. She was slightly in her senses but not conscious. She started murmuring, 'leave me.... go away from here, who called you here... I don't have anyone; I belong to no one... I was a mother.... I did not do anything wrong..... Go away....I do not even want to see your face....Coward...Selfish....... Traders of respect.' The last word was said so strongly that her teeth stuck again. Everyone kept quiet. Babu stood up to leave. We managed to stop him. He said while sitting down, 'Do you people want me to put my head at this wicked woman's feet? Do you not have any respect? It is as if she was the man and I the woman.'

Babu while looking at her elder brother and being hurt said, 'She used to tell me to get a loan, and when I asked about repaying it, she said I have paid from my salary. Don't worry. Today she is cursing me in her unconsciousness.' Babu shivered with fear. I did not dare to stop him. He talked carefully, 'There is a difference in yours and mine situation. She is your mother and will remain so despite your rejection but she was my wife, I do not want any kind of relation with her. She wouldn't even have the right to touch my soil.' Babu had made his statement.

Mother was now awake. She heard Babu's last words carefully, but kept quiet. She signalled to bring water. Sometime later, she had recovered from the effect of the seizure. Whenever she used to get a seizure like this, she used to get better after some change of air. That is what happened even now.

My heart was filled with questions regarding Babu and mother. They both stood their grounds. Who was the culprit then? ........circumstances!........ What gives rise to circumstances?..... the person himself!........ lie, an absolute lie. Society gives rise to circumstances, the person himself is a situation in it.

Situations give rise to circumstances and even these are mere societal influences. .....This is all escape, blaming others for their own deeds. ......In a society, the person is a partaker of fame or .... Even the court punishes the person. Punishment is given to improve the society. A person is made to serve the society. ....Who is the culprit?

'He who repeats his mistake is a coward. You have braved all your struggles in life, you are not a coward. Even mother has seen the crests and troughs of life. She has stood up, on falling and braved the mountains that can only be conquered by strong women. I do not see a child in either of the two. A man and a woman, both are animals. Animalism can be given up, not the person. One can disapprove of your wife, but not the truth. You can disapprove of your mother, but cannot disapprove of the fact that you are also responsible for her condition. This society is also. A son recognises his father on being told by her mother. He can survive without his father, but he weakens when he loses touch with her mother.' Everyone stood there silently, looking at me. I was unable to stop myself today.

Saavri, Rekha and I? Babu, mother and ...? scattered question marks.

I studied everyone's faces and proceeded, 'A wife's pride is only realised in front of her husband. A wife who lives apart from her husband, even if she is Queen Victoria, is not respected. An Indian woman with vermilion on her forehead and glass bangles on her arm, like Savitri, can sacrifice the entire state. Her life is only fulfilled in her husband's feet.'

'Have you come to teach me how to respect my husband? You have gathered all of us here to talk on the old-age traditions.' Mother asked me angrily.

'You will have to meet Sindhu like Ganga. An ocean is not obtained by the waiters spreading out in the plains. Your life is incomplete with Babu. At least in front of us, you are parents. A lone father or mother is a societal murder for us. You will have to live together for our future and for future generations. You will have to talk to each other. Will you not grant us this last wish?' I said.

'I can have a last wish because my time is ending. You are healthy, how can you have a last wish?' Mother was calm now.

Babu was silent like a criminal standing in a court. His ears were perhaps waiting for a decision. elder brother put forward a solution, 'If mother agrees to stay with one of us, then it will be alright. We would be able walk in society with our heads held high. Even in all her purity, her staying away from us is a reason for inadvertence for us.'

'Cowards! Society, whose society? One which considers women as mere toys to play with? A society that houses misdeeds like dowry, offering daughters. All of you are cowards. Insects that are hungry for society's acceptance and that beg for mercy in front of despicable beliefs. Should I water down my claim to seek persistent revenge because of your social dignity? I will continue to suffer till my breath the society whose side you have come to take. Mother said in a revolting tone.

'I have daughters, so does Raju. There are many stories floating around about you living separately. The society that you seek to avenge, we can make it stop talking. We cannot live after disregarding society. Even you are not able to live peacefully, but too proud to admit.' elder brother said angrily, mocking her false revolting tone.

'Yes, we are all cowards begging like insects in front of the unfair societal traditions....But even you did not establish any new decorum. It is easy to satire on the shabbiness of these beliefs, their degradation, but establishing new beliefs is difficult. One should abandon the clothes worn for new clothes, only because it is torn, resulting in nudity, not to materialise rebellion. If you wish, you can protect the beliefs by accepting us.' I said, waiting for an answer from my mother.

She had started feeling weak. A glass of milk brought from the neighbour was kept beside her. Younger sister handed over the glass to her. She resisted. But she did not resist when I touched her feet. She emptied the glass and kept it aside.

Babu was ready to leave. He was quiet the entire time as was his nature. I tried to ask him many times, but did not dare to. While he was leaving, he only said, a woman who makes fun of my misfortune after having enjoyed my splendour and who hides her actions under her own importance, cannot be accepted by me. I don't even want to see her face. While turning towards the staircase,

He even said, 'I am leaving, let me know whatever you decide. Even if I couldn't leave anything for you after me, I do not want to leave this dishonour to you. I have seen everything in this world and do not wish to see anymore. I wanted to end this story on a happy note...after all; all's well that ends well. Babu said this while sliding his feet in his shoe. This time nobody tried to stop him.

He went.

Karan had arrived with the medicines. Handing over the medicines, he went to call the doctor. The doctor gave her an injection and told her to gulp down a capsule. The rest of the medicines were advised to be taken after every three hours. While he was leaving, he said she requires complete rest; it will be good if you don't talk to her much.

We left the iron to heat in the heat of time. elder brother and I left. Only her younger sister and Karan remained there. Mother lay there blankly, not tensed by our debates but the peace of self realisation on her face.

Upon our departure, on finding a good time, younger sister to mother, 'Mother, I understand your inner anguish. A woman is not just a tool to satisfy a man's needs. She is also a mother. A mother can be everything, bear everything, but cannot stand with her foot on her children's neck. When you worked at another house, leaving you to raise us, can you not then be stubborn for us today? Why are you closing the in-laws' door for us? You said everything that another mother cannot. You suffered all that another wife cannot. You are anything but you are a mother. Raju bhai Sahab doesn't speak to me but I have no complaints from him. He wanted to send me to a good place and I thought I was going to one......but why think about it now. One has to live in the present.' Her eyes welled up.

Karan joined her as well, 'You can yourself see how far we have reached in the last 15 years. I regard the society above God. Please agree, my good mother. Please say that you will live with Babu.'

She had tears in her eyes and an indescribable smile on her face. She carefully turned and said, 'I was trying to seek revenge from your father and the society. But I realise now, that both of you are bigger victims of it than them. I do not have any qualms with my children. They have not done anything to hurt my soul. .....take care of your old father. A child is known through his father's name in a society. A mother can be the beauty of the turf, but a father is the light of the house. All of you should take care of him. My heart feels lighter now. Now I have anything to complain about. I pray to God to take me with him now. My death shall grant you something that cannot be given if I live with Babu.' She spoke these words calmly. The air of stillness after a storm floated on her face.

'So, will you not live with Babu?' Karan said with a turning voice.

'Actually, I am no longer worth living with your father. Even if I am innocent, even then I would not like to be with him again. He is a man away from the misdeeds and I....' she couldn't complete as she suffered a seizure again.

When she was in a semi-conscious state, the flame that burned her thoughts, scorched people's hearts once again. 'All of you are under this old man's influence. The day he dies, my soul will rest in peace that day. All of you are slaves to women. Disrespectful imposters, go away.' And she yelled loudly with her closed fists. Then she resigned on being worn out.

This time, she stayed like that for an hour. I had returned from my elder brother's house. Mother had regained consciousness, minutes before I entered.

I was aware of all her dialogues. All these years, I had tried so many times to wash off this dishonour. But when Dashrath, who was distinguished to be Ram's father, couldn't prevent Kaikayi's anger and Rama's exile, then how can ordinary people like us erase this disgrace from the destiny? There's a saying, elephant's protruding teeth cannot go back inside. Sarita does not flow towards Gangotri. An arrow released from a bow may not reach its aim, but does not return to the air. A prostitute even after becoming a saint cannot consider her husband as God. In this context, I remembered a sentence by Rahim Khaankhana, Rahiman's thread of love...

I started hating my mother. Despite being too much inside Babu, there were signs of compromise due to our pressure. That old man, who used to stay quiet, always had the power to bear the stroke of a corpse despite his social, physical, and economical shabbiness. Even if men compose a nature of living with overlooking ideals of centuries old traditional moral values, then it is not possible that he starts thinking about his masculinity being nude in front of femininity.

We all agreed with the fact that mother is an abnormal character and is on the other side of the border. With whom we could not even stand, let alone living with her.

Everyone left her to her fate.

A new culture was born from the real core of socialism, bars, and hotels. In Hotels, men of every caste, every class, drink from the same cup, and sit together. The ways to eat, sit, get up, and are taught in this school. At this moment, humans forget all grieves and drown in the sips of tea, and get lost in the discussions of their friend circle. That's why I thought Guru instead of spending time at home, spent time in the hotel.

There were no arrangements at Mother's place. Therefore, I thought I should go to a nearby restaurant for tea, etc.

Now, I was in front of such a restaurant, in which workers from mill, rickshaw pullers, motor-hand cart pullers, used to come. Sometimes Babu's like us also wandered at that restaurant. This restaurant seemed to be open a few days back. But, I did not stop even at that.

My feet stopped at such a restaurant, outside of which "Madhurima" was written. It was a simple restaurant. I turned towards it. After going inside, without looking at others, who were sitting inside, I too sat on a chair. After a while, a boy, around 15 years of age, kept a glass of water on my table. The boy was wearing a dirty pyjama along with a half sleeved untidy-worn out shirt. Hairs were combed as if cones over Howrah Bridge were rising on his head. His complexion was fair, and was in good shape. His lips were blackened, probably he used to smoke. There were not any special reactions on his face to welcome the customers. Perhaps he was taught this much only, whenever a customer arrives, immediately offer him a glass of water, so that he can quench his thirst, and after that when he puts back that glass of water back on the table, then he, with a special gesture and bowed head, could ask the customer- what to bring Sahab?

He asked me, what to bring Sahab?

'A cup of tea and cigarette', I said looking at him carefully

He kept the cup of tea, Panama cigarette, two match sticks, and an unsealed empty match box in a dish, and left. I lit the cigarette and took a sip of tea by taking my lips to the tea cup. Tea had flavour. I came here to stay away from near ones for a moment. Seeing that boy, I started missing my elder son. He was also of the same height and age. Whenever I see a child of my child's age anywhere, I suddenly miss my children's. Seeing this boy, I started imagining my elder one. If he had not attended school, he would have been the waiter of the hotel. Human's stomach takes a man wherever it wants, but he cannot take the stomach to wherever he wants to go. Is he also a child of a spoiled family/house, like Karana? From the age of eight, Karana's livelihood was to clean used plates to collect his two time bread. This was the result of our parent's relationship.

I no longer think that on the basis of low caste, he could not study. Today, caste was not as much of an obstacle to progress as his environment was. The environment is a social right that is to be created, their relation is just like water and lotus since birth.

When I start thinking, I keep thinking. This is my habit as well as weakness. I was engrossed in thinking......maybe he is also the son of an accountant?

Half the cigarette was burnt. Cup of tea was getting cold. Mind was also running around. Don't know why cigarette puffs with tea were not able to set up mood today. I finished the tea quickly. Until that time, I sat and kept looking at the empty cup, outside and at that boy, till the cigarette's money was recovered.

When I went to pay money at the counter, the owner of the restaurant kept talking to a gentleman, and was taking and giving money from other customers in between.

His line of thoughts sometimes breaks while dealing with the customers. When i reached the counter, she was saying, 'Sahab, what are you saying? My old lady owner has four sons, all of whom earn. A few of them earn high incomes but that poor woman earns for her bread with great difficulty. Now she has been sick for 15 days.....' All of a sudden he stopped talking and turned towards me, 'Yes sir, how much?'

'A cup of tea and a Panama cigarette', I said while looking at him and towards another man expectantly.

'Here, seventy five paisa', as he resumed his business.

She has four sons.....earning well....the poor woman earns with a lot of efforts....I thought as I left putting the change in my pants. His words rang in my ears, 'The world is blind and selfish. As long as the sons were unemployed, they must have depended on their mother for food, and now when they earn well, she has become a burden for them. Earlier she endured everyone, now the same people consider her an inconvenience.'

Both kinds of people, who have not been given justice and those did not do justice to anyone, live in the same society. Does the person asking for justice for that queen not know that justice is like the yield that is begged for, the rent that is procured? Justice is not dead but is not even easily available. We go to ask for justice but return with the judge's views. The right to justice is no more! Even some courts think similarly.

Who knows if the poor owner is Raju's mother?

It was six in the evening. The wind of the month of equinox was blowing. I wasn't even wearing a sweater. I hugged myself to evade the chills. My footsteps rapidly proceeded towards the house.

The light of the room was lit. Mother sat there eating something. Younger sister had gone to her elder brother's house. Even Karan wasn't there. At this time, only Babua was with his mother. He used to visit sometimes. This time, it was my first meeting with him. He stood up and touched my feet, the moment he saw me.

'How are you now?' I asked my mother.

'I am fine, just feeling weak. I won't die. I still have to seek revenge from your father.' Mother said in a grave tone.

Mother seemed healthy by way of her brilliant shape.

I stayed for two more days. Mother was doing better day by day. There was a calm reflecting from her face. On what stood endure the happiness and sorrow here itself, be it heaven or hell. There is no court of God beyond the clouds. Whether or not the pleasures get accumulated over the births, one has to sustain several births as long as he lives in this world. Being a partner in birth is different from a partner in actions. I am not Brahma to save mother from the torments of her indulgence. And even she is not Maya, destroyer of Shiva, who would take away from happiness. All of us are repenting our Karma.

I had returned by a night's train. Saavri opened the door. It was around 11 in the night. Everyone was sleeping in their rooms. Perhaps Saavri was still awake. I was surprised to see her, and then on gaining composure, I asked, 'Are you still awake?'

'I wasn't able to sleep.'

'Why? Is Rameshwar not here?' I asked.

'No' she said and turned to walk away. I held my bag in my left hand and pulled her braid from behind. She stopped. She turned around and looked at me from head to toe. I let go of her hair. She stood very near to me now.

'Where did he go?'

'To his village.'

'When will he be back?'

'Tomorrow night.'

I almost forgot about all my troubles from yesterday and my tiredness from the journey.

Both of us stood there silently. I kept my bag on the floor. I wanted to bring her closer to my breath, embracing her, but she resisted. There was warmth spreading through my veins. There was a vibration in her voice, 'Such nights have been less frequent in our lives... One love... That's all.' I succeeded in my attempt and she shuddered too. Freeing herself she said Is mother alright?

'Yes, she is fine now.'

'Bring her here; you'll also leave the hotel.' She said

'She will now live with me. She was not fit enough to have endured

Travelling in the train.' Every little thing cannot be expressed to everyone.

I started moving towards my room. She returned to lock the outside door. On unexpectedly finding her this way, all tiredness from the journey vanished. It was as if someone had put sandalwood on the wounds of my heart. I had even forgotten about the revenge on seeing her. But Rameshwar not being at home today surely gives me some motivation. I kept my bag in my room somehow, left the light on, and once again, returned to the big courtyard in the chilly night. Saavri was about to shut her door, when she saw me coming, she stood there holding the door. I was silently moving towards her, as she stood there watching me approach.

I heard the bell ring outside. The bright light of the full moon scattered like the grains of rice outside. There was increased chilliness in the air. I was wearing a sweater. Saavri was wearing the same clothes she was wearing the previous night. I stopped at her door. She looked at me and said, 'It is cold outside, come inside.' I felt as if the doctor and the patient wanted the same outcome. She slowly opened the door; the children were lying down with their faces covered. The light was on. She told me to sit on a bed. I sat and took her hand in mine. I asked her to sit down but kept standing. To strike a conversation, she started asking about her mother in detail. I only said, 'There is a time for everything, we can talk about this tomorrow as well in front of everyone......Come, sit near me for some time.'

'It is not safe to sit, it is the seventh month.....she smiled and said. But when her hand moved towards me, she moved a bit and sat on the same bed. Her doll was lying on the same bed. Picking up Gudiya, she said, 'It is too late and you have to go to the office tomorrow. Go and sleep now. If some kid wakes up to pee, what will he think of you being here this late in the night?....This is enough Raju, I don't want to understand even after knowing. I am a mother as well as a wife. .....She became serious. And lover? I asked. She looked at me and then turning her eyes down said, 'A beloved is there to inspire the lover, not to lead him to his downfall....... it is enough that we both belong with each other. Attainment is not the end of love. There is Rekha as well as Gudiya in front of me.' She got up and stood facing me. Her words neither stirred my mind nor erupt feelings of vengeance. I stood up and pressed her shoulders with my palms. She looked down and said, 'I not only love you, respect you as well. A man of your stature cannot fall in love with a woman like Saavri, but you did, and that is my honour. The history of this honour should not drown in the ink of lust; I have protected it by placing rocks on every bit of my body. Else whatever is mine is not liable for your mere look. By pleading with me, you can ruin this lovely night but you cannot attain me. If you want to sustain the moments of love, you can complete the courtship. And....the rest is just a decline in the flushed flow.' Saavri's stomach had gotten much bigger. The fruit of one night.

Gudiya was moving. Saavri went and lied down beside her. I looked at her for a second, and then returned to the room where Rekha lied down and fed Neena. Saavri always kept telling me the ways of life and I, like a foolish follower kept going to her and returned empty handed. This is the usual ending of a story. A woman who can come so far, breaking stereotypes, why doesn't she consider the outcome favourable?....She has always been told that the body belongs only to a husband. The woman who betrays him is impure, a prostitute, dishonourable. She did not want to lose those beliefs that were a joke, pretence, and a facade in the face of situations, even after loving me. I too started dividing entertainment into two categories, sensual and verbal. One is a halt in the pace, the other just a surge.

I lay down on my mattress, switching off the lights. I felt I would get sleepy, only on meeting someone. All matters of Kanpur started arriving in my mind. I had one question that kept rambling in my mind, 'What is the difference between offering a body out of love and devoting a body for a purpose? Probably, nothing. Yes, at least there is this much that in one, your heart lives after losing something, and in other, loses after gaining something.

Saavri's Gudiya was crying. She was trying to keep her quiet. My eyelids feel heavy, I was beginning to sleep.

As long as a woman is a personal possession, only then

her submission holds value

The day she becomes society's possession, that day the purity of love will land the shores. The right to authority gives rise to protection. ............? Then.....then I will realise the purity of my mother, like a calf. Neither the burden of Rekha nor the fondness for Saavri has been erupting for so long. .......A man is a machine, a framework to develop new machines. But machines are run by the government, they cannot build men.

Amidst this argument, I did not realise when I fell asleep. The next morning, everything shined like a clean washed cloth. Adding new references this new morning, sat on my parapet like a sparrow.

Today, on reaching the office, I was informed that I have been transferred to Lucknow. I could not have imagined this. I was given a week's time. My heart resided in Allahabad. I shuddered with the thought of all the difficulties I will face in shifting from Allahabad. The people who are employed in jobs that dictate being transferred as one of the conditions understand well, how tedious it is for a man to move all his belongings from one place to another.

Being the Union's General Secretary, I was a problem for the other officials. I did not conduct a strike, did not raise slogans, and did not create unrestrained propaganda to insult an officer. I despised the habit of leaving the office early, the tendency to delay work, and considered them against the interest of the person and the nation. Even then I was a problem for my fellow officials. Why?

I was not accustomed to beating my head on the medium. If an official did something or formulated a rule against the interest of the people, I complained to the highest officer in sharp words. In doing so, not only was the Code of Conduct Act of the institution created by the government violated, but the lower rank officers had immense difficulty in answering the streak of questions posed by their heads. My letters were not addressed to officials holding positions lower than highest department officer, financial assistant, ministries, military headquarters and president. Although all these people in the end defended the views of the departmental officers, but in the name of democracy, seek views from the officials at the lower levels. The lower rank officials had to face the wrath of letters like these. They felt humiliated in answering the questions. I was a headache for them for this reason. Another reason was, my boldness, candour and impartial nature had a good effect on the officials. Only those who lacked the power to accept the truth were afraid of the effect of morality. I was amber as well as nectar.

The news of my transfer spread to all the units in Allahabad in an instant. I started getting phone calls. I started wondering how I could free myself from this problem. Many people came to me and said, 'People older than you are still working at this station. Your transfer despite that is unfair.' Some people were also heard saying, 'He considered himself a big shot. He talked to the controller in a way as if he was under him. Now he will realise the politics.' One of my rivals went on to say even this, 'When Hazrat was elected the General Secretary, he said in his speech – You people should work fearlessly. There is great power in unity. During my tenure, nobody can spoil your report and nobody can send it to another place before time or without reason.' It is easy to carry the burden of protecting others, difficult to carry your own. Let us see now, how you stop your own transfer.' My supporters were shocked to hear such statements. They told me to devise a plan. It was a testing time for me too. I hadn't noted down the order yet. I only knew that 2-10-64 is my joining date. It was ten days for 1st.

When I asked for the transfer order to note, people gave many kinds of reactions. The officials were especially conversing with each other. The head's peon came and said, 'Sir wants to meet you.' When I was entering the Head's room, an accounts officer was saying, 'We will get a great party from Raju.'

After entering inside, the head officer said, 'Come on Raju, Have a seat.' I sat down pulling the front chair and asked, 'Tell me sir, what is the word?' so now you have reached closer to your parents. Lucknow is a locality in Kanpur only. Around 50 miles far.' elder brother said.

Shankaran Sahab went on and said, 'So Mr. Raju was ill, how is she now?' Now, you will not have to waste the same amount of time and money in going to Lucknow to meet your parents. So it is good. However we will lose the valuable support of a diligent, practical and qualified employee.' On understanding everything, I answered, 'I am not able to the same amount of importance to the transfer as you.' He was studying me, I was studying him. After giving some thought, he turned the course of the conversation, 'though it is a necessary condition in our department, transferring frequently from one place to another, packing all your belongings, is not only harmful but tedious. It mostly affects children's education. But your kids don't stay with you anyway. Consequently, from this perspective, this transfer is not bad for you.' He dug his eyes on my face.

'Mr. Raju, did you express your wish to CGDA sir to get transferred to Lucknow?' Shankaran sir asked deciphering the depth.

'Who is even going, sir? Who wants to go?' I said abruptly. Sir was surprised to see this unwarranted answer. Sir twisted his eyebrows and asked, 'What do you mean?'

'This transfer of mine is politically motivated. It is yet another technique to prevent me from being actively involved in the works of the union. How is my transfer justified when people who are senior to me are still working here? The way I put my statement, the Head looked towards Shankaran sir and then looking at me impressively said, 'this is not my order. This statement from him had a tone of authority.

At this time, a peon arrived and kept a sheet of paper on the Head's table.

'Take this; I reckon you haven't noticed it yet.' Shankaran sir said while handing me the order. 'Look carefully', I had written 'Noted' with my hand on it.

'It will be better if you give a copy of this letter. I will appeal to the finance assistant today itself. This order will be postponed surely.' After saying this, I got up and left.

Ever since the strike of the 60s took place, government officials had to follow a special formality in interacting with the heads of the employees. Incidentally, these great men, who grew up in the tradition of suppression, consider it an abuse of their generosity to speak directly to those who work in positions below them. the socialist government, Gandhi's principles made some improvements in office antagonism, but still some polishing was required. The manner of interaction of my colleagues with me was on par.

Many people were listening to our conversation from outside. Some began to discuss well-known cruelty with an exaggeration of a chronicle. Some just got serious and left after I left, towards their respective departments.

The office was big. The intercom telephone wires were bigger than that, and bigger than those was the conversation between Bade Sahab and me, being heard by everyone. Half a day had passed. Similar to the importance of the eagerness of the election result of the President of America, was the deliberation regarding my transfer for my colleagues. Everyone was curious to know what happens next.

I submitted a complaint application against the transfer order to the financial assistant. I called my transfer political retribution, inter alia, citing the safety of the union employees provided under the Joint Consultation Council. Fearing that our local officials may not delay forwarding this, I conveyed an advance copy to the Financial Assistant taking protection of a particular section of the General Body.

Nobody expected me to behave in such a way. I was certain now. It was a time of the officers being confused, a time of concern for my active opponents, an opportunity for my supporters to be satisfied. There was something for everyone, for me as well as for my rivals. There were also people who had no interest in these things. Some people who only did their jobs. An officer's order is God's command for them, nobody belongs to them, and they belong to no one. Some people consider them sincere, gentlemen, Mahatma and some consider them repulsive. They do not understand what the world thinks of them. They do not even want to understand.

From the time I gave the application, the hustle for the cautious clerk of the General section had increased. Bade Sahab had picked up the application from the postal tray itself. A red light was blinking outside the room. Books of law, books of departmental orders were carried to the room. One person assessed his duty against another. Poor confidential clerk. For the matters of the stomach, he too, was presenting efficiency and ability in creating the causes of our death.

When I returned, stars had started a gathering in the courtyard of the sky. It seemed like every star is a story, every story is a life to be sold in the market of darkness. This evening of stories is the achievement of the entire day. Like the pendant attached to the forehead of every ray, this evening of stories gives a sense of meaning to life. Had it not been for stories, life would remain a sigh. Today, these stories that bring us the history of life have brought us an evening to talk. An evening of new questions, a night of new environment.

I was parking my bicycle, when I saw Saavri walking towards the terrace. She questioned me while walking, 'You returned late today.'

I said without stopping, 'There was some work', and started opening the door.

The room was deserted; there were conflicts in my mind. There was a certainty in my vision, a stir in my thoughts.

I walked towards the hotel. There was no fear of transfer, anger or of that attack done to disturb my peace of mind. There was no question of fearing or loathing the crocodile unnecessarily while living in water. One servant should fear another servant, what for? Both officers and employees are servants of the same manager. If the crocodile has to live in water, then my life can also become impossible without water. He can be the lord of the river, I am the swimmer on its waves.

The date of transfer was extended until an answer from the senior officer.

I had to prepare to go to the All India meeting of the Union to be held in Khamaria. People were swift to make us of the Union, not to donate. It is not possible to go to every person but there was a hope to receive donations by sending someone. The member who donates for the union considers the Secretary as his slave. If the leader himself does not go and ask for donation, then people consider giving as much as a penny as deduction in their monthly budget. I call a person successful in collecting money worthy to be the Finance Minister of India. It is the work of a great man to generate even a penny from an outsider, even if it is not in public interest. To be the hero of a great revolution would be meaningless, if the art of collecting money is not known. A person who works in our departments is away from his home state, from his home for years. Currently, there is no unanimity in the field of education, social traditions. The need of mother tongue and caste categorisation for educating girls and boys and marrying them is not yet over. The feeling of considering every part of India as their home despite many variations had not developed in the hearts of the people living away from their homes, even after so many years of independence. Today, more than any ever, we are living and believing in provincialism. The question of transfer rose in each conversation. Officials citing government orders, expressing their inability, say that the country is short of money. This time as well this proposal came from all the units to Home province, an impact of the Home station transfer.

That day also came. I landed at Jabalpur station. I received an unprecedented welcome. Tempo is the means to go from Jabalpur to Khamaria. I rode the Tempo for the first time in my life.

The session hall was packed full. There were around a thousand people including representatives and members. When I stood up to speak, the people present greeted me with applause and shouted slogans of unity. I started speaking....

'Like the previous years, our caste fair has been organised this year as well. If last year, Kanpur was illuminated by the delegates from every far away town and city, then today, Khamaria is proud in the same way. Pride is rendered not by the attendee, but by the host. We will forever remain indebted to Khamaria for this heartfelt sincere welcome. Some people think such sessions, thoughts, and fairs of the branch units are wastage of money. I only want to convey to them that we cannot understand each other or even ourselves, without interacting frequently. Only after knowing, there is a vibration in the fibres of connection and unity prevails. Such fairs prove very meaningful in the trade union movement.

'Like the last time, our representatives have approved a list of proposals that are attractive. I am also glad for them being approved and for your final confirmation and the representatives who have come here are also satisfied. I believe that more than us, all of you will be happy to hear them. but the question is, do we gather only to frame and approve proposals? Will our colleagues' hard earned money continues being spent beautifying this platform for sessions only?

My last sentence permeated a strange kind of silence in the atmosphere.

'I do not mean to blame anyone or all of you. I ask, what steps did we ask you to take who would have helped in getting these proposals approved by the authorities? .....but when I look within for answers to these questions, i realise we are all lions made of paper. Brave to frame proposals. We are so weak from inside that without taking any risk, we want our sufferings to end, our proposals implemented. It is impossible...not possible. One, who has the courage to pass a proposal, should also have the ability to get them implemented. When we cannot get our proposals implemented by our government, we have no right to discredit the name of our union. Already, a railway employee Pundit N. T. looks with disgust towards a defence employee. Should we not pledge in this conference today itself, 'We will fight together, die together. Today, castes and geographical boundaries are not a barrier to unison. Unity is brought upon by the blood boiling in people with similar needs. Wherever, the interests of the working class are concerned, we will stand ahead. One has fallen out of the eyes of his class, never rises. We will have to earn the trust and gather support from our brothers.

'Considering all circumstances and understanding my powers, I want all of you to put your seal on all these proposals, but also get ready from today itself, to fight the battle for the verdict.' Decisive resistance would have been done against the proposal for transfer. We have to make sure a policy is made by the department in this regard.

The entire hall resonated with a thunderous applause.

'It will be a battle fought the entire year to be won. To get it implemented, we will have to throw a few brave men into the fire of 'Conduct Rule'. If a person is residing out of his home district for more than five years, his age is more than 48 years, any other validation is not required by the departmental officers, and then at that time that person shall take a written permission from the General Secretary to depart to the station of his choice informing the department. His monthly expenses should be managed by the Union, and his family still needs to be given financial support, then we should have his back at all times. Today's fight is dependent on the financial strength of the Union...our blood is one, our needs are one.........

Meanwhile, a Bengali gentleman stood like a commotion in the middle of the peacefully listening gathering. He interrupted me and said, 'What power does the Union have, that if we lose our job, it can successfully make it stop? This is not an institution providing jobs, but an organisation protecting the interests of the workers. When our leaders will take us on the wrong path, our welfare is impossible.'

The attention of the entire gathering was drawn towards that old man. All eyes fell on his face. Old Banerjee's statement changed the attitude of the entire assembly. I was not shocked, but a little angry.

'The power of the Union is scattered in the souls of its members. If you follow my instructions, then the bread of the people who took away your job will be snatched away. Otherwise I don't speak of providing jobs, but of the help from a few people to protect the jobs of thousands and their interests. If our thousand hands together cannot help with our body, mind and money, those brave men who sacrifice their future for the benefit of all, then our Union is of no use. The talk of fighting together is meaningless; the expression of 'Bahujan Hitay, Bahujan Sukhay' is false. ...... A leader only talks of rising above personal gains, gives direction. I do not talk about those who organise the public for their personal growth. ....perhaps, you did not understand the meaning of an organisation. I mean when one does not get what he wants by asking, he must fight for it. One or two people can lose their jobs, but the problem for the rest will be solved forever.'

Hearing my answer, people made a ruckus and made old Banerjee sit. I continued my speech, 'So, I was talking about solving the problem of transfer. Not only transfer, whatever is the problem, we will have to solve it together.'

'The call for a strike, that too country-wide may be justified to provide a solution to the problems of the working class, but in the present scenario, it does not seem useful. You all are familiar with the history of such failures. I think the failure of strikes is not only due to the government's persistent repression policy or our fascination with jobs, but the main reason for that is we do not have people's sympathy. In a democratic country, no movement can be run without the trust of the people. The government will kneel on the second day, if the people of the whole country stand with us.

'But the public could not support. When do we go to them to ask for their support? The people of India have poor as well as rich. The poor shed their blood to make these rich people even richer. How can the pain of one-tenth of the population of the country be the pain of the entire population? How will people who have to travel by car necessarily feel that the wheels of the train are blocked? How will the small traders, families living in villages waiting for money orders understand the strikes of the postal or telegram office? When the sorrow and happiness of one class becomes that of another class, only then they walk side by side, and be sympathetic.

'Therefore, try to match the steps before fighting. In order to match the steps, we will have to keep close interaction with the employees of the private sector. By impeding the strikes of the postal, telegram or electricity departments, we will have to obstruct the paths of those ministers, encircle them, those who are unable to allocate judiciously the income and expenditure of the country in the people of the country.'

'Speaking from the heart, I should say surround those ministers who are puppets in the hands of the capitalists. Those who had sown Gandhi's dream in barren land. The solution to all our problems is blood rebellion...... But we do not have time for that. Trade unions do not have a direct responsibility towards this. But a revolution is needed. Using the weapon of non-cooperation, developed is an advanced violence of that. The bullets of violence and non-violence are not in the soldier's box. The enemy's death is wrapped around his waist. Your enemies are inflation, cruel job wages, and feelings of hatred towards those working on lower positions. And the enemy of all this is the bullet fired by the Russian workers, farmers of China, which in time will have to be fired by the Indian working class as well, if the country's leaders do not try to eradicate the chaos of feudalism in the name of democracy.

'There is a lot to be said, can be said, but I would like to say that we should say as much as is necessary for inspiration and do more. If I could get your proper and timely support in every way, then I assure you that I will be able to succeed in fulfilling the key demands from the long list of demands. You will fight as well as win. I will act as a lawyer and keep making efforts in demanding complete justice for you.' The speech must have lasted a little longer, but the audience did not lack attachment or show disinterest. The next day, I had to speak at a meeting in Jabalpur, which was organised to honour me and I also wanted to see the marble rocks of Jabalpur.

Firstly, I considered it necessary to participate in the event. The program at Bedaghat was scheduled for the second day.

It was the month of February. Although it was eight in the morning, but Bedaghat was drowning in the dense fog. There was no smoke from the chimneys of the mills, but there was morning dew. The waterfalls were flowing cutting through the black and white marble rocks falling into the depths, forming pools of foam on the floor, clouds of fog in the sky. The fog touched the cheeks like someone's dew soaked hands. There was darkness at the peaks of expansive rocks, in front of my eyes, on the continuous flow of the waterfall itself, on the face of the rays of the sun. Amidst the darkness, the cold wind like the memory of someone said something in the ears, amusing the mind.

Man was born in the lap of nature, where he sat singing. 'Charaivat Charaivat'. Nature says keep moving, man keeps on repeating the same primitive shloka, moving on. Nature's son wants to know the secret of his mother, wants to possess her. He wants mother to serve her, mother opens up in hiding her secrets and he gets conquered resins to her lap. Conflict between attainment and efforts is a new creation.

On the roads of Bhedaghat, tempos were standing after dropping the riders. It is only possible to get those rickshaws or tempos that drop riders. Most of the people plan for pick-up and drop. Every day, crowds of locals and foreigners, rural and urban tourists come here on foot or on a ride, to witness the marble rocks. The way to the waterfall was also made of marble rocks. The white marble dust scattered around symbolises the sculpting of stone idols by the makers. These illiterate people carve marble into beautiful and artistic sculptures, introducing humans to a new human who does not know any language, only expresses. Whose expression of tones is understood by an artist, and resonates in heart. An idol carved out of stone or any other work is a centre of attraction for passersby. These artists who make and sell idols, artisans of chisels and hammers, do not understand the pain of their idols or the sentiment of the people buying them. They know only the money, earning which is the aim of their art, the bread for their children. The emotions of the heart that get expressed through the lifeless chisel, that will pay its price in the form of the speechless stone idol?

We were proceeding towards the waterfall. The rays of the sun continued to prevail over the over casting fog. Like history, the rocky peaks staring towards the left into the abyss, were saying – we fall after the struggle of centuries. The parts of our body, these blue-yellow, white-black stone artefacts which want to tell the map warped in history, in the carving of the chisel. And the human wrapped in emotions is left in the present and the future is like it doesn't exist.

I used to think, the inaccessible faces of the morning rocks from far left, all these entities would look different from different sections. But it flowed , bursting the rocks under my feet. It was a similar scene to when a pipe under the road burst and the water was rippling through the land crevices, flowing under our feet.

From far, beyond the boundaries of vision till some distance near, scattered a flowing, thoughtful, stirring water body. Nearby the trees lined up like tourists. Amidst the heavy rocks, the way the heat of the moisture made its way, it was a wonder. This was the origin of the skills of an artist and the essence of creation of nature's bliss. A sense of amazement was the speciality of the art here, but its aim was still an analysis of reality in nature. There was a creation of simplicity in nudity.

Now we were standing on the tip of that rock, which had covered the surrounding rocks like a bouquet. But in the middle was a pool of swirling water, deeper than a sinking elephant, that enclosed an unending water body hopping over the shoulders of the sloping black rock, scattering like the dance of tandava. There would be no sense to go there without going to the edge. The heart would not be convinced. But on going to the edge of the rock, when we saw the vibrant waterfall descending into the hole like a pearl oyster, the mind shuddered.... Oh, the smiling death. My friends Dubey and Mukherjee Dada stopped me from moving forward. I even stopped at a height.

When I was lost in the clamour of the waterfall, that time if someone's memory materialised and stood beside me, it was of, vermillion wearing, suapankhi bangles wearing, white brocade saree clad Rekha's memory.... I wish she was here. Which concern of the world, which sorrow, which questions came alive in front of me? Whose shadow was it? The man whose proud aristocrat, destroying the pride of the rocks, reduced them to mere pebbles, which disturbances can raise their heads in front of him?

There were two marble ledges from the middle of which passed out boat. The depth of water could not be told by elephants but submarines. To witness these two ledges, one has to ride the boat. Every person that goes there, betting his life witnesses the marble rocks swinging in the arms of the sky. And their black, white, blue and yellow colours. The boatmen are skilled, capable, but has no boat ever got submerged in the vast water stream? After taking in the beauty of nature, after swimming in the lap of death, will Rekha not say to me, that these rocks are better than us? At least they stay together for centuries.

When our boat was in the middle of two close rock mountains, once the mind wandered to think of the worst- what if the boat topples? Probably this memory is also a conflict of two mountains that are close yet far. One that didn't get expressed and got lost in that restricted environment. The mountains are also emotional. Their sentiments reside in their silence that cannot be read with the eyes of reality, but that of sight of principles. Because principles are related to imagination. The basis of imagination is the emotional ground for reality.

The words don't die. The Ahilyas become the stony rocks. One night's unknown sin, becomes the suffering of lifetime. The songs of these marble rocks have reduced to mere words permeated in the rocks in this conspiracy.

We were returning. Standing on the everlasting stairs of a historical temple, turned and looked once again with silent eyes, towards the Bedhghat who had filled the courage in a reluctant life. It had given the message to flow invariably, to be as strong as the rocks and taught the lesson of being as selfless as nature.

'What are you thinking, Raju?' Mukherjee Dada snorted and rubbed his nose while asking.

'Nothing, Dada..... Tell me this; is my conclusion for today wrong? The truth of bread cannot be wronged and nature's truth can also be not forgotten. If nature makes a human poet, then the bread continues to keep him a human.'

'Are you hungry? The waterfall is indeed a waterfall, not a hotel. Where did the question of bread come from?' Dada asked, surprised, spreading a smile.

'It's time to get up from the lap of nature and hold the finger of reality.... The same state of the heart again, the same tales.'

'Life is remembered to be forgotten.'

'Wow, sir, you have become a poet too.' Dubey ji said, praising Dada.

'Becoming a poet is a big thing, but after witnessing the clouds lifting from the froth of the waterfall can make anyone a poet.' I offered my defence for the rhyme.

The internal quarrels between some people had made it a scene from the nineteen forty two. I used my moral strength to calm them as well as gave a speech, 'aren't you ashamed of doing such indecent acts inside the office? Four illiterates might spend their lives in the same place but all you educated people couldn't spend 8 hours together with love. You forgot that you have a part in the national property. Who will bear the brunt of these broken chairs? Who will pay for them?' I was going to my chair with suspicion, when I even said, 'using chairs.'

'Raju Sahab, why are you getting angry? When it is

possible to use shoes in parliament, then it is no big deal to use chairs in this office?' One colleague said lightening the mood.

Everyone laughed.

The same day a peon from the General section of the office brought me a sealed envelope. The confirmation of the receipt of that envelope was to be given by signing in the peon book. After thinking for a moment turning around the envelope examining it, I returned it to the peon saying 'I will not accept a sealed envelope. I should know what kind of an object I'm signing a receipt for in the peon book.'

Peon took the envelope in his hand but started begging, 'sir, at least care for my job. If you don't want to take it, then write down the reason for not accepting in this book. Otherwise, Sahab will think I did not come to you.'

I did not see any problem in it and wrote down as I had said. The peon returned. Everyone in the section started asking 'what was it, Raju?' One went on and said, without even hearing my answer, 'brother, leaders are conversing with officers through letters only. They talk with the people in lower positions.'

After some time, the section officer called. When I reached his office, he told me to take a seat as well as asked me to take the envelope. I told him the same thing as I told the peon. He was hurt. On using his cordial relations with me, I tried to explain to me the vanity of my denial to accept the envelope.

'If it will be worth my acceptance, I promise you I will definitely take it. If you really want to give it to me, and then first read the letter to me.' I said while giving the solution to my problem. He went on and read it to me, in order to not stretch the matter.

In the Letter, it was asked from Raju, UDS, why shouldn't he be suspended and handed over to the police for the crime of indiscipline, giving provocative speeches in Khamaria and taking actions against the chaos inside the office? The answer was asked to be given within an hour. I said to the officer, 'the one who gave the speech in Khamaria, he wasn't Raju, UDS. He was Raju, the general secretary. Every general secretary has the right to prepare his class for the struggles. Since Raju, UDS, didn't give any speech anywhere, so he shouldn't accept this. As far as indiscipline or sabotage is considered, I do. Not know of any such incident.' On saying this, I left the room ignoring the officer's letter.

The talk of handing over to the police seemed like a cycle of unexpected events. I went to my seat from there, picked my spectacles and taking my bicycle from outside left the office without telling anyone. I was surely thinking that sabotage mentioned must be the fight today in the section. But i did not do that either. It was my first time to indulge in indiscipline in leaving the office without notifying anyone.

It did not seem right to go home, so I went to a friend. There was no need for hiding anything there. It was a colleague, Darpan Babu. One of those people, for whom even I could do anything and even wouldn't back out from making an impossible thing possible. Thinking, he lives alone as well, I should spend the night there. It was not just the matter of spending the night but I also had to think and find a way to save myself. Thinking that I haven't got any date of suspension yet, or received any confirmed news about the case handed over to police, I decide to send an application by a registered post for a week's leave, attaching a medical certificate of a personal illness. I returned home in the morning. On asking, I got to know that no one had come to ask for me, although four kind friends keep coming. I breathed a sigh of relief. Thinking that it would be appropriate to face the crisis by staying at home, I considered the idea of living outside as cowardice.

Darpan Babu was responsible for getting the legitimate news and informing me. After the meal, I lied down with a newspaper. When your own problems are overwhelming, sit with the problems of the world, the state of mind will be closer to the far, outside environment and farther from your personal troubles. Newspaper is a mere tool to pass time, the true meaning lies inside. But for long could the mind be amused by the outside. If Rekha would have been here at this time, the burden would be less and if Saavri would have been here, I would get distracted for some time. But in their places, were suspension and news from the police, opened pages filled with tears of woes of the world, an empty room and I was engrossed in thoughts.

The news from the office will arrive by the evening, what should be done for amusement till then? How to pass time? There were books, matinee shows, but my mind was not ready to wander in that direction. At that time, the idea of writing a letter to Rekha came up in my mind. But it would be wrong to put the burden of my concerns on that innocent woman to lighten my mood. Thinking that, I went quite again. Remembering about her health, my thoughts started flowing in another direction.

I started to believe that the heat of my agony can either be dispensed by alcohol or the love of my beloved or wife. Actually, I wasn't worried so much about how I will the next month's expenses be incurred or spending time in jail but the root cause was immoral accusations. Who sabotaged, and who bore the accusations..... The freedom to speak in a democracy means the use of a language that doesn't stir up the sleeping government, doesn't even make it turn around. If your voice cannot shake the stone idols of the belief turned to temples, then your call amounts to nothing. Although in today's Era, some people have acquired the license to freely abuse the government within their capacity.

There were still three hours left for Darpan Babu to arrive. I thought of writing a letter to Saavri at the village address that day. It started with writing a letter to Rekha and ended at Saavri. I remembered that there will be her in-laws as well... And even Rameshwar has gone there to meet his children....... My Letter will create turmoil in her family life... What of somebody comes to know? ..... Till date she has no proof. My letter will be a proof. By shifting the burden of your sorrow to another, you get lighter....but.....Saavri's life will get burdened. She will reduce to a characterless woman in the eyes of her family, husband and her children. With my mother's life in front of me, wouldn't it be selfish to unnecessarily play with somebody's life? It could also happen that assuming that the letter has come from Saavri's home; they do not wish to read it. But a letter from her home is also addressed to Rameshwar, even if it is meant for Saavri....... Then? ....... Let us see, what happens. I might feel lighter after writing a letter to Saavri but I may get overwhelmed if I write to Rekha. One is a saga associated only with emotions; other is the pulse of every breath of the entire life. For a moment, its distance can be reduced, and the mind can be entertained with love....... Rekha is the partner in happiness and sorrow, a companion for whole life and Saavri is just a means of recreation for a distressed and lonely mind. Amusing the mind is one thing, spending the whole life another. Living the entire life can be a mechanical existence, but the torture of moments is resolved by taking a dip in the river's flow and feeling a sense of euphoria.

Writing a letter to Saavri, I put it in a nearby post box already. Now I felt a bit lighter. It was time for Darpan to return as well. He was about to come,

Thinking that I felt some relief. Thinking of what news he would be bringing, I was also more excited.

Darpan Babu arrived. It must be around six thirty in the evening. He wasn't coming directly from the office. He had spent half an hour in a hotel drinking a cup of tea. He must get a cup of tea on coming back home. He knew that even for tea I have to rely on a hotel.

After making him sit, I looked at him with eager eyes. I was thinking of asking, when he started himself, 'brother in your section. Everyone knew everything. After you left, Bade Sahab's peon had come to call you. I asked everyone around, everyone called you innocent in the matter of sabotage. I even heard that your officer also refuted the charge on you to Bade Sahab. Although you have been suspended and transferred. Probably by tomorrow, you will receive a letter to this effect through a registered post. If possible you should be at your home when it arrives. Receiving it, taking legal advice and giving a fitting response. The people of the office will pay your entire salary. Not only this, some people are ready to support you financially in case of lawsuits. The president of the union also expressed his resistance in front of the officers, calling the whole incident political. Possibly, some people might come with me from the office to meet you.' Darpan made tobacco pressing some in his mouth gave me some.

'Did you not get any information on the police matter?' I asked to know another thing.

'Brother, it is impossible to know anything in this

regard. How can I know such a secretive thing?' He said while relaxing the wrinkles of helplessness on his forehead

'It's fine. I will move out of Allahabad tomorrow itself. I will return after a week. I answered.

I would feel disgusted to complete half my salary through donations. Yes, but if my colleagues help me in the case, I will not deny. I understand, presently, I do not need to take money to feed my family. Those people who live by killing their conscience take the money like this. Or those men who are unable to keep their spirit alive. Such times also come, but I want to live with self respect till my last breath.....I would not be troubled in living a month in debt.'

'But do you want to go out to assemble money? If I bring money on my name from Cooperative and give you, will it still be against your self-respect?' Darpan questioned.

'You are one of those partners through whom I can do anything but I want to go out for two to four days so that I can alert the people of the units and tell Rekha to act with patience.' I answered.

'I did not understand what you said, but yes, if you are bored then go to Kannauj. I will try to arrange money.' After saying that, Darpan Babu stood up to leave. I also expressed my desire to go outside with him. He waited until I closed the outside door.

It was ten in the night when I returned from the hotel after dinner. When the body lay on the bed tired, that time wakes up from their sleep questions in search of answers. I was lying on the side. I wasn't able to understand myself the need of going outs and alerting other units? It is a question of my suspension, going to Rekha to search for ways to prove that baseless, would be useless. Yes, my agony could disappear amidst the chirping of the children for a day or so. I should definitely go to the office and meet my section officer and supporters. A path originates from a place that is left untouched.

The storm that blew for one day cleared the sky but spread dust on all land and houses. The earth and the houses were all getting dusted. Now again, everything was new and more organized. In my mind, suspension and informing the police seemed like mere actions taken on an officer crammed with the pre-requisites.

I did not understand how Bade Sahab felt the need for a police case in this matter. Fighting, sabotaging, everything happened inside the office and that too was an internal conflict among a few people, not a call for a union movement....... Then was it just a threat? Unofficial matters are not handled through written and read words.

In the end I decide to accept the upcoming registered post. Whether it is a creeper or a snake, I will. Only get to know by going closer. My mind was filled with many connotations and immaterial arguments. My mind got cumbersome and my eyes were closing. I wasn't aware, when I fell asleep.

Saavri had come to her in-laws' village after years. In every sense, it was no less than a hospital. She birthed all her children here. She was also satisfied here, Rameshwar too was relaxed and even her parents in law thanked God, and praised their fates, singing greetings on the arrival of a new child at their door. They believed it would grow their dynasty and is the fruit of the virtues of their previous births.

Last time when Saavri had a child, people family planning advised an operation. They roamed around the house. Once his father-in-law got in an argument with the family planning worker at the door. Then the old man thundered, ' if a child would have been a disease managed by a human, then my brother would not have died without a child. Still many people crave to see the face of even a single child. You have me with this drama of family planning. It is our ancestors' blessing that our courtyard will. Once again resonate with the chirps...... brother, the one who has a mouth, he only provided the food. If it had been up to the man, he would not have allowed anyone to live. God wakes us up hungry but doesn't make us sleep hungry. Go, find another house, and don't dare to come to our house again.'

'Whatever you say, Dada ji might be true. But in recent times, the increasing population is not good for our country. The purpose of life is just mere feeding the children day and. night to raise them. Arranging proper education and managing necessary resources should also be done. Government therefore wants family planning so that every person could live life happily.' The worker tried to explain to the old man.

'I do not want to hear your opinion. We earn to feed them, but the stomachs of your government ache. If you want to stop the population from increasing, then why don't you go to Kallan Miyan. He has two wives, and has altogether eleven children. You despise our fifth child only...... go from here, do not be seen here again...... a contractor for happiness and success.'

The old man was now angry.

The worker's job was in danger. He has to complete a fixed amount of quota each month, failing which he wouldn't fare well. His salary will be halted in absence of fulfilment of the quota. He still didn't leave the old man's door. He continued the conversation and said, 'Dada ji, Muslim religion does not accept restriction on children. That is why there is no question of going to Kallan Miyan. If an officer gets to know or someone complains about my visit to their house, my job will get endangered.' Helplessness was clearly visible on his face. 'Yes, so say that you have come to castrate Hindus. Muslims are your government's son in law. Increase their population to make a new Pakistan. And pull us all out and send us to the black waters. Apparently, British emperors tell us we came from Central Asia. The system of government should be the same for everyone, whether he is a Hindu or a Muslim. When Hindu Muslim discrimination is being done in family planning as well, then God save this secular government, and the country's economic condition. Why are Hindus responsible for all evils, victim to all laws?' 'Dada, you said it right but I can't help it, it's a government order that we will have to obey.' The worker, realizing that it was a gone case, resolved to leave with the thought of looking for another household. When he was leaving, Saavri's father in law said this as well, 'go to the ministers' homes and teach them the lesson on family planning. Here no one will ruin their dynasty over ten rupees. Tell me sir, if after the operation one needs a child then he would go to a Muslim...... Going against nature, to explore, for science, for humans, might be a sign of success but burdening the people for it with a political perspective is entirely a mistake. Its consequences will be bad. This is all America's trick. It's a scientific method of eliminating Hindus from the world...... Ok, tell me, what has it done?

Dada ji, you are offended. I have 5children at this young age. I do not earn enough to even raise two children properly. When the fifth child was about to come, I had hot myself operated. Although your accusation that I see in the light of politics seems right to me. But I would also like to add another worry to this. Slow poisoning, that is giving poison to Hindus to gradually in a few centuries an attempt to wipe it from. the map of castes.' The family planning worker felt newness in Saavri's father-in-law's statement on Muslims that he stopped. Realizing similarity in opinion, the old man asked the worker to sit on the bed. He was also a retired headmaster.

'OK, brother. Now that you have said so much, listen to my thoughts as well. You will agree that at this time Christianity is the most developed religion in the world. After which, there is Islam, and on the third position is Buddhism and on fourth is our Hindu religion. My ranking of religions is based on the area count of the followers of that religion. Christians want every religion to blend with them. Religious conversion facilitates forgetting the pride of casteism. Hindus became Christians, Muslims too, but with the change in religion, forget the glorious sagas of the purans and the bloodshed by ancestors. The caste calling family planning useful for India wants to conquer the world. If the government would see the hypocrisy being sown in the name of family planning, then it would be better, beneficial......... Yes, tell me one more thing, the Muslim religion bars them, can the Hindus not add such a rule in their religion?' in order to gauge the effect of his statements, Headmaster Sahab stopped at this and looked at his face carefully.

'I had not thought about this. We can surely add. But that is when our Shankaracharya gets time from reciting the former Shankaracharya. He will look towards the declining human population when he gets time from looking at the protection of cows. Our lord believes in the medicine of God, only after drinking it, can he talk about benefiting humanity. At the time of the primitive Shankaracharya, there would have been discussion on what is god. Today, there is no need to concentrate on God's name or form, but of creating a new morale for humans. It is possible that this era will be outlived by Sanatan dharma. Though in the changing times, it is also felt sometimes that after many centuries the Hindus have become history. Three fourth of it will get converted to a branch of Christianity and one fourth of it will accept Islam. Though the current castes flourished in the name of religion, the people of those centuries were connected to the name of religion, not caste.' The worker explained the same thing differently.

'So should we call that time closer when Hindus, in the name of family planning, reduce to the population of a state? In order to emboss our back faces for the future generations, should we start getting our tubes tied from today? I will say, brother, work at some other place. Why put your eleven lakh population of Hindus the last men, in order to earn some bread?' Headmaster Sahab smiled and expressed his win.

'Dada, the job is not important. I have cleared M.A., for one seventy rupees I have to hear the nonsense from all of you. I roam around looking for asaami. The stomach is a sinner, Dada ji.' Saying this, he joined his hands and left. Saavri's father-in-law did the same with whom he interacted for a while, with enthusiasm, but on getting up even said, 'It shouldn't be that our future grave is being dug by the present. Present is lived so that the future can become history. History shouldn't get lost, remember that.'

He also said, climbing down, 'The present age is also ached with meaning, so family planning is required. The future will suffer for money, so these castes will get destroyed. Yes, the present is surely lived in self hatred. In the end, we have to live like a human, what is to be done with religions, what to give to castes? But I accept that family planning is the result of only this age's financial condition. Those families, whether Hindu or Muslim, should come under the aegis family planning, that are weak in this vision. In any case, a small family is a happy family. But if the government doesn't bring any specific caste on the basis of religion, then you should boycott this in the name of religious discrimination, you should revolt.'

It seemed like the conversation would get reignited, after coming to a close, but the headmaster Sahab turned around and said, 'Humans have erected their own enemies by making machines. This is the end of humanity. Limiting a family to husband, wife and children is also a result of this mechanical age.'

Both of them left in different directions.

Saavri was inside the house. Rameshwar had also come. He had gone to the village to buy a few things from the market. The children were paying something among themselves. Saavri's children were more afraid of their uncles than her brother-in-laws. Children are familiar with love and appreciation. It so happens that they run away from those who put serious relations on them, keep expectations and teach them conduct and courtesy. Do something and get something is the rule. Nemesis of relationships alone is not accepted anywhere.

The familiar house of Saavri. Here she came down as a bride, henna on her hands, vermillion in her hair partition, anklet in feet, red dress in hands and wearing toe rings in her feet. This was the initiation of her second life. Here resides, the empires of her first emotional night of her youth. The room where she was still sitting mending old torn clothes, it is this temple where she for the first time had a solitary conversation with the lord of her life, surrendered and achieved redemption. But now she was upset, because she lived with a smile on her face. Now she quivers even in entering and exiting this room. When her children call someone uncle, her eyes lift with excitement and then resign with disappointment. The children had come after a long time; they found this home to be unique. They couldn't settle into a new house. There was a connection of the old to the new.

The postman called Saavri's name from outside. On hearing her name in his voice, she was surprised. Her father in law wasn't outside. He had picked up a stick and just left. There was no one else either. Only her mother in law was there inside. No idea whether her mother's law heard the postman calling her daughter in law's name. She ran outside..... Is it a letter from my brother?.... He always posts in his name.....probably.... She ran, till then the postman had delivered letters to ten houses. One of her children wanted to come outside and see who called, seeing an envelope lying there, stood up and tried to open it. In an attempt to open it, it got torn. The letter inside was ripped in two. Saavri leapt and took the letter away from him. She arranged the pieces and read the address. On noticing that in the name of the sender, it was written Raju, she scanned around the place and hid it in her blouse.

She did not have enough alone time to join the pieces and read the letter. Two days passed. She became more upset. One night she took out the letter and kept it again at a place where I wasn't allowed. She decided to read it in the bathroom on the terrace. She took a lit candle.

Since the evening, she had published the news of her upset stomach. Rameshwar turned eight in the night after having plenty of conversations. At the time of dinner, seeing the frail body and pale face of Saavri in the light of the candle, he asked, 'what happened? Since I have time, you are upset. What has happened to you? Do you have fever? Pain?'

Saavri said without lifting her head, 'no problem. My body gets feeble and I don't why, I do not like anything.'

Both were quiet.

He pulled her towards the bed lovingly. She got pulled like a corpse. Like when a predator walks with a wounded deer and the way the deer looks at the predator, leave me, devil, the same way Saavri for the first time in her life looked at that man with whom she had started a new life. In the arms of the works, she got nurtured like a creeper. She was remembering something a friend said, Saavri, do not ever stop your husband. The woman, who cannot satisfy her husband, loses him. She shrank in her husband's chest. He pressed his lips on Saavri's pale cheeks. In the act of hugging her, a piece of crumpled paper fell from her blouse. He picked it up and asked, 'what is this?' Saavri said, 'give it to me, it is someone's heritage. It will leave tomorrow morning.' She took it from his hand. Her husband thought, I can always see what's inside that crumpled paper, but yes, this time will pass.

Saavri did not expect to return without hearing anything from her husband. She wasn't even fit enough to give him what he wanted. She thought she could only love him this much. He cannot become Raju. Isn't this called faithfulness? I protected him only. My heart used to flutter to get embraced in Raju arms, but this very definition of faithfulness has always murdered all my desires.

In the courtyard, outside the room, scattered moon rays danced. That night with its light crimson clouds, cold breeze and penetrating moonlight created the atmosphere for a wife's predilection to be shattered.

Saavri carefully pressed the crumpled paper in her palm, walled outside. The client of social rights was tired. A romantic exercise floated in the eyes of Rameshwar. He closed his eyes and lived the epitaph of his lifelong entertainment. Saavri was leaping towards the terrace. When the matchstick hit the box, fire was produced. The letter was much torn. On reading it, she couldn't control herself and with every line the cluster of tears on her cheeks increased. She read it many times even when her eyes were welling up and tears blocked her vision.

'Saavri!'

'Sometimes I used to have fun with you, I am missing that now. You remember when while trying to free your hand, you would double up and get flushed in my arms. My lips.... You shied away with your flushed cheeks. You fluttered like the leaf of the peepal tree and smiled. The letter may end up anywhere, but if it finds you, then read it with the understanding that Raju is leaving to possibly never return. To light up the fire of memories those were doused in your heart. I am leaving Saavri. I wasn't required to go there now. But the decision makers hold the opposite opinion. There is a warrant in my name.'

I have a warrant in my name..... She started fainting...... What did Raju do? He couldn't have ever...... He loves her deeply... Then, what does he think of me? Can a man love two different women to the same extent?...... Why does he have a warrant in his name? He doesn't lie, not even involved in any crime. What did he do? Wealth.....murder, no, that's not possible. He is a very calm and practical person. Surely..... Someone would have given his name out of animosity. Rekha must be dying crying. She is a goddess. God, take my life.... My Raju..... yes, nothing will happen to him. He will definitely be left innocent. I should have seen him once. He saw me even slightly upset, he would instantly ask, what happened Saavri, why are you sad? Be like a flowering lotus. I want to see you happy. I love you, not your body. Yes, I have sinned....a sin. Not under the definitions of Vedas, trapped in the temptation of petty morality, I sinned by hearing Raju's first expression through ears of disobedience. With whose love the lamp of my life was burning, I could not offer him everything. He taught me how to live...... But I have a warrant in my name....Raju.

She yelled. The candle rolled down on the joined pieces of the letter. Everything had lit up. The entire house jolted with Saavri's shriek. Even her husband ran towards the terrace hearing the shriek. She was sobbing on the inside and the darkness of the doused candle spread outside.

Sensing some noise outside, she got up and wiped her tears walking out. Everyone was asking, what happened. Did she get scared? Nobody got scared here till date. Her mother in law said wiping off the blot on her ancestral legacy. Wiping her tears, without looking at anyone, quietly, washing her hands walked inside her room. She didn't answer any one's questions and talked with her tears quietly.

The mother in law was saying, 'since the time she has come here, she doesn't talk to anyone, doesn't sit with a group of women. She is always upset. God knows what disease she has.'

The neighbour said, sister, 'she must be suffering from seizure. These seem like the symptoms of a seizure.'

'Who knows why she is unhappy? She is innocent. She never answers back. Even Rameshwar has kept her nicely.'

'But what was she doing this late on the terrace?'

'What do you go for?' Everyone laughed. Saavri's husband very fondly rubbed her forehead. Rameshwar asked many times with love but she kept quiet like a picture. The tears stopped too. Every rainfall clears the roads. Roads have also been noticed to drown. Every flow ceases.

Rameshwar was not able to understand anything. He thought she might have got scared or maybe this house has some problem. He decided to take her to an exorcist. But... But she screamed calling someone's name. Maybe she has got a letter from her home.

She was thinking..... I Wish I was free like a bird. But

she hadn't got Raju for her entire life. The one who cannot be mine, why is he making me cry? My husband also loves me...... the grains earned with his money is in my veins. Filling my hair partition with the vermillion of his name, I smiled for the first time in my life...... How can I forget the day when for the first time in my life he embraced in his big arms the abundant Ganga of my expectations? Shiva.... Has Shiva's Parvati played the game of love with another man? Hide it? But....the question of one too many does not satisfy but elongates the life of the thirst.

Saavri was flowing in the river of thoughts, uneasy in her restlessness. Her parents in law and Rameshwar tried every possible way to understand but their mind didn't work. 'Whose name did she take? Did she receive a torn letter from her home?' Her mother in law was also thinking the same.

Saavri was quiet. The relaxation of every vein was apparent. She looked at her husband with a look that has emotions, not expressions. Now she had started patting his hand. He also looked at the change in her health, as the river soared.

When the memory of someone arises along with tears, it is an omen in the life of remembrance. Every bud rose in the garden of the heart lives to wilt. Yes, blossoming and wilting after spreading fragrance depends on the bud's nature. Every arrow hurts differently.

Saavri was emotional. Her face was the face of a woman lost in emotions. Her eyes did not have an invitation, but the mascara of wait. Eyes like that of a female deer that cried inside the lids itself, talked less, and said more. Tears, the ultimate vengeance of the eye, did not tire, and gave new energy to fill up the emptiness.

He asked Saavri, 'whose name did you cry out?'

Saavri glanced at her husband's face, pondered, and said, 'Raju.'

'Why, what happened to him? He is a sincere man. Why have you received a letter?'

'It is done. Now the last step is left.'

'How do you have known all this? Do you exchange letters?'

'Not exchanged, he sent a letter for the first and last

time.'

'Where is it, show me?'

'It is no more.'

'What happened? Did you tear it?'

'No, burned it.'

'Why, what was written in it?'

'Nothing much was written. There is a warrant in my name. This is my first and last letter.

'That's it.'

'Warrant? What did he do, it must be mentioned. You are a strange woman, the poor man wrote you to us with love and you burned the letter itself. Tell us the entire details of the letter. Was it just this much?' This is no answer.

'Whatever more was there in it, doesn't concern you.'

'Was it a love letter addressed to you?'

'Yes.'

'Err...what... Yes? Evil woman, do you know what you're saying?'

'I know. But I request you to not question me anymore.'

'Understood. So that Raju  is a wicked man. A father to many sons but who loves another woman. That is why he didn't inform even when his wife and kids got sick. I will break his bones. I will definitely go. He is a learned vagabond, that is why he has been given a warrant. A wooden piece in water will come to the surface for sure......'

Saavri got furious. Interrupting Rameshwar, she said 'what right do you have to insult Raju's character? What did he do to you?'

'What is his fault when your own is unfaithful? Come on tell me correctly, otherwise I will beat you black and blue. You argue with me. He shivered in anger. He held Saavri's braid tightly.'

'You have the sole right to beat me. You do not even need a reason for that. I only want to know why you are furious over him, in front of whom your head always bows. He did not steal from you, did not flee with your woman, and did not incur any loss on you. Why are you cursing him is what I want to know.' She was shivering.

Her entire body was glowing in bitterness. Her

statement had shocked Rameshwar. The reason wasn't clear, the idea of apprehension was inspiring. He was depending on calm and serious words in answering. 'When you have accepted that the love letter was for you, should I ask how many nights have you spent with him? Shameless. That is why you don't like here in the village. Why didn't you tell you need someone else in old age? Go away from here. I think of the children, otherwise a woman like you should be shot down.'

He stood up furiously and walked. Saavri was questioned, not to cry and be quiet but to give an answer.

'He did not use your right on my body. It still belongs to you. I know you will consider it this truth false. The thing is that both of us within our limits had started loving each other immensely. The time the needle in the second of the clock takes to move further, we spent only that much time, but you......' And she went quiet.

'You think if Raju had the chance, he would have protected you to talk to me like that? A woman can do everything.' He stood pressing his teeth.

'Yes, she is rightful of doing anything a man can do. She is not only a body surrounded by boundaries, but a body possessing a heart and a mind as well, in which all the desires reside that do in a man.' Saavri said these words with trembling lips.

He was quiet. He had realised for the first time that Raju has influenced her entire personality. Today she is explaining in the same way as she saw Raju debating in a council of intellectuals.

'Oh, so the teacher taught this much to his pupil. Why would not, a watermelon change colour on seeing another watermelon.' Rameshwar said, controlling his anger.

'So tell me, how did I betray you? Why am I mean? Like Saavri wanted her husband to call her innocent today.

Both kept quiet for some time. Saavri looked expectantly towards Rameshwar for an answer. Rameshwar stood up and lingered. At times his fists clenched, at others his eyes flared up like a flickering fire.

He stood up in front of her and started asking questions.

'Who are you to me?'

'Wife.'

'Do you know the responsibilities of a wife?'

'I know. Service, sacrifice and support.'

'And love.'

'Love arises from emotions, it is the part of support or service. Have I not loved you how a wife loves her husband?'

'You have. But then why did you love Raju? Haven't you sinned?'

'No, I haven't sinned. A person cannot love everyone and when he feels that way for a person, he can. Love is not sin or virtue; it is a result of circumstances that has to be seen through. When two persons feel the love in their hearts in the same way and get close to each other in mutual agreement, how can that be a sin?'

'So, emotions and people, both are not at fault. You mean, every married man and woman, satisfied in every way, can feel the pride of love.'

'Contentment does not give rise to love. It rises from the internal discontent.' Saavri argued like learned men.

'Are you not satisfied with me or your life?'

'That's not a fair question. I wasn't worth obtaining more than what you gave me. You had your limits too.'

'And Raju?'

'I learned to live with him. If I wouldn't have met Raju, then this life would have shattered in the darkness of the absence of his light. It anyway has to shatter. Kitchen, broken cot, children's pee, Raju had given a life out of this life.' She was having an unprecedented experience of her boldness and how deep Raju descended in her life.

'If a woman is not faithful to her husband with her body, mind and soul then she will be called wicked only. The man who has cast his magic on your mind, whose words you're trying to adopt in your life, Saavri is a communist and communists only give such arguments. Conduct themselves unethically. Maybe that is why he has a warrant in his name. Government is arresting them rapidly these days. Such people lure innocent women through a glimpse of life that cannot be true in any caste or country. You should forget these things as well as Raju.' Rameshwar said, turning the course of his arguments.

'Who he was or is, I don't know. I only know he loves his wife dearly and never lies. He had also told Rekha about me. Can a man who inspires to free oneself of the chains around one's body that are pressing on his bones, be a communist? If a person who loves and creates a sense of equality, who is in favour of giving men and women equal rights to a particular limit, is a communist then he is better than the hypocritical Saint who commits adultery in the name of bestowing women the promise of children.' Saavri answered.

'Yes, Saavri. These are more horrifying than those saints. If our government, our newspapers would. Not inform us of their deeds, how would we have known what they are. Do you know, these people roam around borrowing the logic of how to declare other's assets their own?'

'Every argument is confirmed by truth. In order to explain the truth in the right way, material used to give arguments is always noticed. If the person who wants to give a life of equality to everyone, doesn't look at a man's stature through his family, caste or location, is a communist, then it cannot mean the same as advertised in newspapers or by the government.' Saavri was trying every possible way to defend her lover in front of her husband. She has learnt all this from her love only.

'Don't babble, I'm not used to debate. I shall write a letter today itself to your home and I shall see Raju soon.' Rameshwar shuddered. Saavri got upset. The anchor of her boat was broken. She was being smashed by the waves. Her husband did not hit her, expel her from the house and did not even say anything while walking away. He did not even turn around to look, that is enough for a woman needs love as well, a love that doesn't wilt with time and not burdened by the tiredness of the day. Love gives pace. It doesn't just agitate.

She wanted to reply to my letter but was being strangled by the line of hatred drawn in his heart.

For some days, lost in thoughts, she continued her duties towards the house, her husband, and children. On seeing the quietness of a cremation night on their mother's face and the children did not dare to speak loudly. Hardened children do not develop.

People kill, file divorce, on discovering their wife's relations with another man but those who remember the question of their children's future, of social dignity and the family's respect, he is unable to murder a wicked woman or divorce her. Only the person drinking the poison knows about it but in case of a murder or divorce, the entire society discovers. Therefore, Rameshwar was silent, like a page in history.

Today completes 15 days. The effect of a single letter was seen on the atmosphere of the whole house. As long as Rameshwar was out; he tried to forget about the house. Here he had become sharp as a satire in his social interactions. On coming to Allahabad, he didn't get any peace, didn't speak to anyone, and didn’t approach Saavri.

Rameshwar started being upset. He did not expect this behaviour from Saavri even in his dreams. He thought very highly of me. He was a supporter of contemporary culture. He believed that until the backs of a woman and man don't bend, they should not get a chance to meet a man in private. Because he believed you cannot trust your own cry.

His health deteriorated.

A man earning one hundred and fifty rupees was a graduate. He was burdened by debt as well as upset with the tragedy occurring in his life. In order to meet the expenses, after his office hours, he had to give tuitions for two hundred and fifty rupees. It was a new place.

He thought in retrospective. The girl I teach, why do my eyes secretly, hiding even from my own self, linger past her saree? Why do I forget my tiredness from a day's long work, conversations between owners and bosses, hunger and thirst, when I step at Kiran’s door? Why does she shiver on being touched with my latent desire? Her behaviour isn't immoral, rude, even then I think to myself, then I'll say like Saavri did on spending a day with Kiran I live my entire day.

He was teaching Kiran for a year. Now she is eighteen years old.

She has started studying late. Now she has reached a higher secondary. Her father was a potato seller. It was a small family. There were two kids, Kiran and Prabha. The monthly income was around a thousand rupees. Lifestyle was ordinary.

He gradually began forgetting the anger and hatred that arose from the mere memory of Saavri in Kiran's memory. Kiran and Saavri, were a product of the multiplication by Raju himself and Saavri's logic.

Rameshwar lying alone on his bed thought, when a country woman like Saavri who hasn't even seen cinema to say, seen any show, read glitzy novels, could slip then where will one get a woman like Sita who even after living for years with prosperous man like Ravana, worshipped Ram only. Old people say it rightly, a woman is a heap of straw, and it can get scorched in little heat. She did not even remember that she is someone's wife, mother to some kids. If when the kids mature and get to know about their mother having an illegitimate affair with another man, then will she receive the respect of a mother? A woman has two responsibilities, subsistence with her husband and loyalty to her sons. She handled them both. She hid everything from me as well as the kids. It is amazing how no one witnessed this love story going on for so many days. A woman can do everything. Those which cannot be hidden by anyone else, she can hide it from the world for her entire life. Upon hiding all human secrets of nature in woman, when the creator himself went silent then a man is an ordinary being of the great artist.

He was now feeling less sleepy. Since he had returned from the village, he has only been seen furious. While teaching Kiran, he kept in mind that he is a teacher. But when she looked at Rameshwar with her big eyes strewn in the thread of kohl grasping her scarf, asked a question, he shuddered involuntarily, calming down and answering her question. Kiran would flinch her eyes, listening to the master with her head lowered.

Kiran couldn't resist today and asked a question from. His master, 'Why are the arms of restraint so feeble that they become anxious to spread in their worst state?'

Firstly, Rameshwar shivered from his thumb to hair on his head then on seeing her lowered head, eager ears and hands scribbling unreasonably, he gathered courage and asked, 'In which lesson, did you study this?' His heart was beating.

For the first time, Kiran had fixed her eyes on

Rameshwar's face and looked at him with the intention of understanding the chaos behind the answer to her question and the simplicity behind the question in the form of an answer. Rameshwar's eyes were on the book lying below that said, Kiran Verma, first year.

There was utter silence between the two.

'I haven't read this in a book, but often read it on your face, just asking its meaning from you today.' Kiran answered Rameshwar's question. The ground beneath Rameshwar's feet slid. He was still like a patient of paralysis. Shivered inside like a patient of muteness. He did not expect an answer like that from Kiran. But on being quiet he would have lost the dignity of a teacher, the respect of a mature father, so he gathered courage and challenged her answer, like a serious teacher, 'Your immoral answer is sharper than your previous question. That had the tone of a distracted lady and this is the attitude of an undisciplined girl. You have no right to read my face. A student read books, not their teacher's face. That too, you are a girl, from a respected family. What made you read my face?'

Kiran got hurt by the tone of his answer. She thought of answering at first, then giving it a thought, she only said, 'I apologize for the language of my answer. But I definitely want the teacher to not shudder on seeing the student, stay calm.' And she began gathering her books. Her fair cheeks were getting ripe like the slices of pomegranate. She lowered her head, hearing the heart beating. While leaving, Rameshwar only said this much to her, 'write the essay and whatever has been done, learn it..... For coming to learn a student shouldn't dress up and should come simply. A teacher is a man, not an angel....'

Kiran didn't even nod in reply. Rameshwar walked away.

The next day, he sent a letter to Kiran's father saying my wife will be giving birth to our child and I'm going to my village for a month. Hire another teacher so that Kiran doesn't suffer any loss in her studies. She is intelligent, but she needs a qualified teacher at this time. I will take the salary after returning, Kiran also hoped so. But Rameshwar was upset, sad, filled with guilt. He hated his weakness.

Saavri gave birth to a son. On hearing the news, Rameshwar had a thought, who is the father of the child? He started thinking, creation of nature is only known to a woman, and a man can only approve it with a stamp.

It was the first time when Rameshwar wasn't present while Saavri gave birth. She wanted to give the child's father the decorated piece of his gift. She wanted to say to him, 'He is a creation of your muscle only, play with him, my partner.' But Rameshwar wasn't there. Just the long conversations of that particular night. The family members and neighbours were worried about Rameshwar not being present. His absence was a subject of discussion. Saavri thought what would I have lost if I hadn't told him? He wouldn't have figured out ever. Nobody could have deciphered from Raju's conduct. He used to lose control sometimes but that too when we were alone. I swung the axe on my own feet. It is. Not important for him to every truth of my life. Everyone has secrets, that they only keep to themselves.

**P**rofessor Raju was searching for a diary in an old box. He had a habit for a few days of writing about special events in a diary. The truths that a person does not accept in front of anyone, he writes them in the pages of a dairy. A diary is self validation, and also directions for the future. A man unfolds his heart in such a way, that even God cannot find fraud in it. It makes the heart feel lighter.

There were things like that in the old diary as well. He was suspended from the office and there were newspapers, magazines, books and silence at home. Excerpts of Guru's meeting in the evening, and pondering about the entire day in the night.

There was only thinking in his life. Interpretation of what he said and analysis of what others said was a routine now. So, he started saying.... A man cannot find peace even after leaving the world if he is taking a river of sorrow inside. That is why I envy those who abandon their household lives and adopt the saffron colour like saints. The atmosphere outside affects that of inside. But if someone gets upset indulging in the worldly sorrows, then he suffocates, melts. Either a great man can be an introvert or a mad person. For both of them, the world even after residing in water is like a lotus. They reside with the four walls of the heart at the door of memories. This is a living death. One, who is away from the society while living in it, is dead for the society. Professor Sahab continued searching. But where he expected, he didn't get it there. Due to which he started throwing the pages here and there exasperated and finally found it. Withdrawing it, looking at it carefully, turning it over and sitting on the bed, I read. It said, Yashpal, listen carefully, I don't know at which word the story may die.

I am detached. Also learned to tilt and slide from end to another like a plastic monkey balancing on one needle of the cycle, with the help of spring. I wasn't, but now I have. It is a mystery how many meters of situation and transcendence constitutes the distance between the heart and the hand. Initiation of the communication process is probably every breath's intention. Whatever it may be, I am away from worries today.

Probably entirely wrong. I think that cot lying in the courtyard, where the tired sunshine rests and frantic moonshine cries as well. Shattered threads of the cot, the body aches that left the tightness of its ropes loose. When there is no worry in the heart, what is the detachment for? Why the distance from letting go?

All of them met together in my dream. Projecting in the four directions, like the four legs of the cot. Deena, Shivshankar and Shakkan. We looked at each other, as if we have seen each other before, but don't remember. A diseased rose was seen in everyone's eyes.

Deena, my partner in the time of basic school, a pro at gulli-danda, wrestling and paisa-pichuk. Shivshankar was a kite flyer. Shakkan, an argumentative person and a trader in his ways.

Deena used to sit at his uncle's shop of tobacco. Shivshankar was a teacher at a school, and Shakkan was the manager at a garage. It wasn't a dream. It was a film's trailer. All of them had pride in their eyes, and I had pain in mine.

The happiness of satisfaction and the sorrow of loss.

The night's dream, a newsreel , converted to chaos in the day. It gets known after 2 decimal places.

There was a letter from Razia...... 'I used to think, you will shatter the courage of conflicts. The crashing waves can cut you into the Bay of Bengal,

The pebbles of Narmada cannot be drifted away.

Now the ribs of hope have emerged. Razia is outspoken.

In '42 you dislodged the electric poles, cut the telephone wires. Actually you are not clever. If you had been, you would have shown that degree and become something. My uncle's son, who only had a knife graze through the ear, even he has become an expert in having the courage to look out. He was not like you, self possessed, dependent on luck. Now I know, you are born to live with boundaries.

Razia. After all, you are a woman. Happiness spreads around from whose lap, whose eyes capture the sadness. A sensitive creation of the woman's world. Just think when the masculinity of a man dies, he doesn't even remain a woman.

Razia's letter brought back inspired pages selected from the book of time and rotting dampness. A new version of life got introduced. Life, flowing, was stuck in the stagnancy.

I am also feeling lighter today. Instead of gulping down sips of liquor, I feel like clinking those bottles. After drinking my steps will be enchanted, on clicking the bottles the silence of the room will shudder. I want the silence to die yelling. That's when there will be peace.

If I drink, only my mouth will smell, if I sprinkle, then the floor, the walls, all this, will fill with the odour that till now, only I smelled with the handkerchief on my mouth. Razia has shaken me, my mind has insulted me, the mirror has also disowned.

If I were a painter, then I would have made such a painting today in which there would be a forest of Babul trees, drier than grass, a ground filled with leaves and a new sunshine sitting on every branch. But I am, a defeated gambler, who doesn't have a new tongue, or ground for a new resolution, establishing a new trust.

Razia challenged, 'If somebody feeds you, then also

you'll eat with inhibition. This is not sincerity, but a feeling of inferiority. Get yourself out of this weakness. One who can snatch and eat, does not die hungry.'

She says it right. I wanted that the world will itself evaluate. But no, one who has to sell himself should go to those in power. Every earning is business.

Fame is also an achievement of some business. A product is priced on the basis of its publicity, not on its value.

And sex has died fasting for it. One who considers his own mind dead, what will he aspire for? When a single lamp longs to twinkle, in that case the talk of one to many, isn't it a Hypothesis?

Every night for me is married. Youth filled with the fragrance of a ripe mango, muscular arms like string of jasmine, luscious hair is my sustenance for every night. I am. Not alone, Razia.

Razia, my childhood friend, who I met during summer vacation, is not anyone's wife or mother of any kid. She is not anyone's culmination even in imagination. Seeing whom Mauje Naseem shies away, and the group for clouds envies. What is the need of a wedding, in which beauty diminishes, curses grow like a child. The body is beautified for carrying only one corpse.

Don't mind me. Every belief in human life is not eternal; it is borne out of circumstances. Age passing like milestones gives awareness to every traveller, and when it sinks in the depths of our breath, it lives by recognition.

I haven't been wiped off, but definitely tired.

Probably like a lover, for the light, death seems like life to you. A beautiful life. Wish me the life that doesn't pass buzzing around a lamp like a firefly. That breaks the rock interrupting the flow of the waterfall. I didn't expect you to evaluate me like a foggy unit.

After a pause, Professor Sahab said,

'Razia who was sealed in the diary had started descending my thoughts. He wanted to come out of the room being afraid of his own words. The sequence of the narrative was the same.'

I had to inform Rekha as well. I had arranged money from a special friend on Going out. There wasn't a thing to worry about. Because I expected to be freed as innocent in the court of inquiry. When I was moving out of the house, I suddenly saw Bade climbing down from the rickshaw. So I was worriedly thinking, why did Rekha come, without any information? But I don't know why, after a moment, my heat filled with delight.

Mummy and papa are coming. Bade looked at me and said. Our eyes met and smiled. I took the box in my hand. Opening the door of the house, I smiled and asked, 'Madam, you arrived without even informing.' She also answered by spreading a smile; 'I thought I should go informed to check if it hasn't been owned by somebody else.'

'You have taken a leave from the school.' I asked Rekha. 'Yes, when I received your letter, I panicked. When I see you in a problem, I get worried being alone. It is important for a wife to be with her husband during testing times. It is her religion. I didn't have money, the job was new, so I had to wait till I received the salary and I have left the kids there. I also stopped at Kanpur to see my mother. I wished I had wings and could fly to you.' She was in my vicinity, I was relieved of worries. She gradually hid her face in my chest and asked 'Where is Saavri?'

'She has given birth to a son, and is in the village.' I said cupping her face with my hand.

She had brought food with her. Although I wasn't hungry at all, sitting with Rekha to eat was soul relieving so we all had dinner together.

This time Rekha met on a domestic level with a man with whom she didn't have to be shy, or formal. Surendra used to work in my office. He didn't visit our home often but on hearing about Rekha coming from Darpan he himself came. For the first time. He was a man, but in terms of talking, romanticism, he could put to shame any other woman. The women had started envying him. He has been fond of dancing since childhood. This interest made him more beautiful and more fun loving than a prostitute despite all kinds of men. No man looked at him with the correct eye. He used to tell everyone, if I were a girl, I would have settled with a man, you would have been left sighing.

Dark complexion, body like Italian tea. Twelve inch hero. Lips had simplicity, the redness of paan, and sometimes the natural colour of lipstick, left parted hair combed upwards. Kajal is as thin as a nylon thread in his eyes. Surendra was Meenakshi. The motion of eyebrows, postures of an actress, that had now become natural to him, didn't cease. He mimicked Lata's very well. He danced well on twist songs but also had interest in classical dances like Bharatnatyam. There was a skill in his coughing. I have even seen instances like the Time when he even coughed standing behind a man then that man instantly turned around expecting a young woman and would be astonished to see a man standing there. He would doubt what he experienced through his eyes and ears. Once Surendra with innocence filled eyes, with a mesmerizing stare smiled with a glee looking down and then slowly clearing his throat behind to defeat the motion of no confidence in the eyes and ears brought by the heart of the next person. When a person inspired by him, would get eager to give him the love like a lover, he would laugh at his foolish expectation, find a way to rescue himself by declining his wish smiling. He was accustomed to withstand such situations. Habitual of coming out of traps that he deliberately got caught in. A person out of the house of Mascara. Impressed by the imagination of Beatnik poet Johnsburg's male wife, countless people wish to be Beatnik seeing him..... He wasn't like he propounded through his actions. But who accepted this? Who wanted to know? Being a man, Surendra, who lived the style of a woman, was raised like a girl since childhood, grew up among girls.

The melodrama is his voice that even surprised Rekha when they first met. Seeing the innocence like a child in his eyes, conversations with women and hearing friendly talks from him, made Rekha fall for him. He called her Didi, the kids called him Bhai Sahab. He formed a connection with the first meeting itself. When he came, Rekha's tiredness would turn into the freshness of a flower. Kids listened to songs from him, Rekha asked him. To dance. The whole house would turn into an entertainment club.

Surendra was a subject at Freud's laboratory. Love was his religion and habitual of flourishing in the heat of the kisses of love. Both of which look Good in solitude, not in society. He was extremely fond of watching movies. He knew several movie dialogues and the art of bringing them up at the right time. His neck, eyes and eyebrows were unstable in the same way as the fishes in a pond. He wasn't even fond of eating paan.

Upon eating a paan, his thin eyes would put even the rose Bengal dye to shame. He was also prohibited by his family to eat paan. This wasn't Lakshman Rekha. Although he was from a Christian family, but without telling, no Hindu family would call him Christian. He could establish oneness with the feelings of any Hindu family, be it Janmashtami or Deepawali. He respects them. But not the ways of worship.

It was twelve in the night. I was tossing around. Rekha was also aware of the situation entirely. After putting the young son to sleep, she came to my bed and lied down. Pressing my forehead, she said, 'open the window, it's full moon night today. Let the moonshine lie between us.' She was smiling.

I opened the window. The children of the few grey clouds in the sky teased the group of moon rays and obstructed their way. Both of us saw the moon exiting and entering their trap many times. My state of mind was changing. In the milky light, the pink lipstick dot on her forehead didn't shine but was clearly visible. Her chest rested on the pillow with the help of her elbow bathing in the moonlight. The vermillion in the partition of her ordinarily combed hair was clearly visible. The fake pearl on her pierced nose and the embossed mole on her nose were also visible clearly in the moonlight in the dark room.

Rekha suddenly turning her eyes from outside said, 'Why are you staring like you are seeing me for the first time?' She broke into a smile. 'A moment doesn't take birth twice, every moment takes birth for the first time. You tell me, have you seen the new moon for the first time? But why do we feel newness in the heart?' I said.

'Probably because we think so. The waves of the mind are borne out of the outer darkness but the mind can look at it in the colour it wants. The eyes of mind don't remain the same always. Currently our eyes are longing to talk to the moon.' Rekha turned around. 'You are right. If anything is needed even after food, it's love. I remember you in the time of difficulty, not God.' I smiled and embraced her.

Moonlight was lying between the two of us. We didn't realize when it stood up and sneaked out.

Rameshwar had come to the village after many months. He had come to terms with the conflict going on for so many days. He hated me but didn't express it. He thought nobody knew yet, on talking about it, everyone would know. It will be a Slander. Raju's honour may remain even after being destroyed, but Saavri and my lives will be hell. So he was quiet drinking the poison like Shankara.

His mother asked why he hadn't come for so many days. He said it's the job of a miser, you don't get leaves every day. He could explain everybody but there wasn't a need to explain Saavri. On getting the news of Saavri's son, when her mother-in-law beat a plate of flowers, said happily, one eyed daughter has been given birth. That time, Saavri wiped her eyes, hiding them from the babysitter. She had cried in solitude while feeding her child. There was Rameshwar in her heart... Even in her lap lay Rameshwar's form. The face of the son was exactly like his father's face. She was satisfied seeing that. She felt proud and loved the living proof of her faithfulness.

It was the day of Karwa Chauth. Rameshwar had reached the village on the same day. Saavri was fasting. On many occasions throughout the stay, Saavri tried to apologize to Rameshwar, but was scared. Rameshwar also breathed a sigh of relief seeing the kid in his mother's lap. Now he wanted to take back the words he said to Saavri. Many times he wished to embrace Saavri in silence, but there was no lone time during the day. He eagerly waited for the night to draw. Both waited for the night.

Saavri wouldn't even drink water without offering it to the moon, Rameshwar knew that. He thought of buying some sweets from the market. Today, a cup of sweets would be sufficient as a treaty.

In the Hindu culture, the day of moon worship was the day of praying for the children and husband and......

Saavri dressed up and went to the terrace to offer to the moon. Today the smiling moon of the fourth, easy going clouds in the sky of the month of Kartika and the liquid like candy. She probably hadn't seen the moon so fittingly before. Even the moon has its scars. It didn't leave Guru's wife as well. But the reason for offering this moon in our culture. Worshipping the scars? A liar being worshipped? A gem which is being worshipped even after being scarred? An emotion which is an inspiration even after being foul?

When Saavri was climbing stairs, she felt as if someone pulled the end of her saree. She turned around but no one was there. She remembered, she stood there dressed up for the worship of the moon. When Raju saw, he said, 'I wish! There was a photographer today.' And then I said, 'Who is better than you?' He had pulled the end of my saree while I was climbing up the stairs. Additionally, he did not even let me go for the prayer without a touch. He had said, 'let me worship my moon first, then you can worship yours.' That day, did he see Rekha's face in mine? He had been remembering her since the morning. He had said, 'before the moon, I have the right on Saavri.' And I blushed, flushing with blood.

Did he used to search for Rekha in me? Yes, probably. I have seen him talking to Rekha. He ran like the Gardner of a garden and Rekha flew away like a butterfly. Actually he longed for love. He didn't limit himself to a river to quench his thirst. Why did he give me so much love that I thrived. He knew that Saavri wouldn't be his neighbour for always. Even then why did he pull me this closer to himself? How did he manage to be a true lover as well as a loyal husband?

Actor? No, but probably yes. An actor can perform two acts simultaneously without a photographer as well. If their acts did not associate with their characters' conversation. So did Raju act? It wasn't original, but an imitation. He had wanted the body in addition to the mind. But when I had started loving him from my heart, then why did I cease at the limits of my body? ....... I wish! I was Rekha.

The worship of the Moon ended. Saavri rested his head on her husband's feet. Usually, she knew he touched his feet after the prayer. Probably today, there wasn't just blessing, but also a request to respect the refugee.

Rameshwar lifted her forehead and put it on his chest. There weren't tears in Saavri's eyes, but a dampness saluting the new agreement. She didn't say anything. Her eyes welled up with tears. On the other side, he wasn't satisfied with not talking to Saavri and putting to flames the happiness of the house. He was burning inside, he had loved Saavri, he was fascinated by her qualities. Today, the accused and indifferent silence of so many days wanted to flow thundering on the rocks like a stupefied waterfall.

Saavri pressed to her husband's chest, stood in a way like it was the first quiver of the wedding night. Saavri was glad about this dedication filled with gestures of some shyness and dedication.

The sound of Rameshwar's heartbeat had conveyed his apology to her ears. Be it Saavri's mind, or Rameshwar accepting her embracing her tightly in his arms, nothing is everlasting, not even the prick of love. Gradually the moon of the fourth began to grow.

Both were silent. Tonight was not the night of communicating through words. It was that of forgetting the words said earlier. The time of the product of repentance. A night of the troubled weather to get a new birth, of forgetting the past and making history in their lives.

Handling Saavri with great affection, Rameshwar sat on the bed. Making her lie down on his lap started caressing her hair. Saavri lingered her finger on the edge of his vest. Rameshwar's eyes were fixed on Saavri's cheeks like the light of a lamp and a few pearls had settled on her eyelashes. It was the season of threading the pearls of happiness. The vibrations she got today were unparalleled. She hadn't experienced a calming and, at the same time, exciting pleasure.

'Take this sweet. You've been fasting all day.'

Rameshwar said, keeping the bowl in her hand. She talked meaningfully with Rameshwar's eyes once. 'Why did you bring this? What was the use of the expenditure?' Saavri said, breaking the threads of the bowl.

'Sweets are given on the night which is the first night of their married life. I don't remember any of the previous nights. This is my first night. A night of sweets........' Rameshwar pulled Saavri towards himself while answering. Placing his lips on Saavri's ears, he said 'tonight is the night of karwa chauth. This day will be celebrated next year as the day of our first union.'

Saavri was filled with the shyness of the first day of puberty. She considered it the first night amongst the countless nights spent as part of the married life till date. She was entering the life of new vibrations. She was thinking, this is what I had succumbed to Raju's arms for. This desire of woman makes her wander........... If this night would have arrived in my life before today, then was it possible to smile in the tone of the memories of Raju...... it is karwa chauth. Raju had said, on a similar night while I was returning from the terrace wearing lehnga, nose ring, bracelet in the upper arm and silver jewellery in my middle parting of my hair, today, I am anxious to gain you and Rameshwar would also want you on this day. He is the one who'll get you. I am like a passenger you met on the train; I can be a guest or get down at my station. Today's night is more intoxicating than a full moon night. On a full. Moon night, only the moonshine is decorated, today the moon of the earth gets decorated too. My appearance wasn't that good, that he put me at the top of such a high mountain. Rekha is beautiful. Such words won't be an exaggeration for her. I was Rekha for her, despite him calling home Saavri. But I didn't consider him in Rameshwar place ever.......... He will have to forget. The co-passengers on a journey can be a means to pass time, not partner for life. The sustenance of life is the work of one, not many.

Rameshwar fed imarti to her with his own hand. She was not accustomed to such affection. At first she was surprised, then smiled and took a bite out of the rest of it in Rameshwar's mouth.

Rameshwar was thinking to me about today's

intoxicating night. Saavri was still wearing the clothes for offering prayers. Saavri, with a red dot on her forehead, vermillion as a sign of marriage, looked as if the bees picked up the bride from the stool and sent her to meet her groom. In the race of time, the wilting youth was filled with the delicacy. He also had a question in his mind; does a woman want expression of mind more than lust? Is the expression of ornate inferiority impure? Is the birth of art necessary to live? Only the enhanced version of the true copy is acceptable to human sensation......... I could have echoed the previous nights with the songs of intoxication...... probably not........ If a man doesn't bathe a woman's heart in uncontrollable affection, then willingly or unwillingly, she could get foreign. He was starting to believe that today's night was the night of Raju's exile.

Half the night passed in expressions of submission and the other half in the tenderness of submission. The next day was spent in contemplation, in the exhaustion of the body. The body was exhausted, but the face was lit up. Like the bowing weighted bud of marigold. Rameshwar had slept in the afternoon. In the anticipation of the coming nights, forgetting the tiredness from the previous nights.

Although Saavri had returned from the village, she wasn't the same Saavri who I had bid goodbye. The birth of a child is the mother's new birth. So she had come taking a new birth. The unfamiliar behaviour of her eyes had intimated me of my limits. Rekha was still here. This time she wanted to go only after hearing the decision on my job. She was assured that I didn't harm anyone, so nothing bad would happen to me as well. The kids were called as well through Karan so that they don't have to live alone. Because of all of them living with me, one month passed rapidly like one week.

A wife, like Kaikayi, can put her finger on the broken wheel in the battleground, and can also take her husband's life.

A woman, belonging to any religion, race, caste, is more devoted than a man. She continues to believe in rituals, the authority of God, and the laws of the regulator. Yes, women of France satisfying their lust don't fall in this category. Like the waves, they put their arms on the shoulders of waves, in search of bees, and consider their youth meaningful in getting lost in the ebb of the tide. I don't talk of those women. A man can be an atheist, disturb the entire world with his arguments against the guarded belief in God but is unable to change his wife's religious beliefs. This is where Charvaka lost, where Marx accepted failure, and where I have failed too. Rekha herself read the mythological story of Satyanarayana every full moon's night. Even today, she makes offerings to Bajrangbali every Tuesday. I have come a long way from such acts of worship. I have chased away the weapon bearers of belief with the stick of my arguments. With the assurance of carrying my corpse on my own shoulders, I have accepted the last truth of 'Ram Ram Satya Hai'. This is the intoxication of rationalism that rides and destroys the rituals of Ashoka garden. Later the stereotypes are set to fire.

It was the day of the court of enquiry. Rekha has been busy in her prayers since morning. Since it wasn't the night of the full moon, so had prayed to Goddess Durga. After giving me Prasad, making me taste curd and peda, she was stubborn about sending me since the morning. When I was leaving for the office, she had kept a bucket full of water at the eastward door of my exit. She had told the sons, when dad will leave, say dahi macchli.

All of them were ready as per their mother's instructions, to perform their respective roles. She had quietly kept petals of the flower that was offered to the goddess. She had promised in her heart to organize an unending Ramayana path on winning the case and I, considering them her faith, sometimes smiled, sometimes got annoyed, but didn't insist. I believe that God is a thing of faith and the right of faith is personal. Considering creating obstacles in someone's freedom, coercing someone with your beliefs as an injustice, I kept quiet. It was a life of settlement for the person in your family who cannot accept this outside. I believe there is greater inner strength in atheism. Whereas a religious person believes in the inspiration and support of an unforeseen, supernatural power. One wants to live closely with the Creator, while living with humans. The others also considered him responsible for humanity. One believes in himself, the other in invisible authority.

I considered the good fortune line she made, meaningless. Not because I didn't believe in it, but those things were now baseless signs for me that is it. We have prayed to and respected Good fortune for the past centuries to invoke belief in the unconscious sphincters of our consciousness, so that The intention that we leave the house with, gets fulfilled. I am used to injecting strength in my conscience with my determination, not on these bases. Therefore, I do. Not consider them significant. Although bad omens affect the minds of people inadvertently, in the form of psychological processes of the brain. That is why enjoying Rekha's rituals for good omen and taking strength from my determination I walked in the search for the direction of unknown decision.

Rekha was depending on luck, located on the mercy of God. I don't deny the saying that the fate of a person is written at the time of his creation. Those situations continue writing your luck, that become your own after being disowned, called foreign even after being your own. A story grows with the sequence of events, not in order to achieve the end but with the belief to get along sitting on the shoulder of time. The end of man's fate is unknown like the last flame of the crest of the evening of stories.

On reaching the office, my colleagues welcome me with great enthusiasm. The news of the court of enquiry spread in the entire city. There was discussion among the officers. An officer had come from outside for the enquiry. Court of inquiry was to take place in Bade Sahab's room outside Srivastava Sahab, our Bade Sahab and to assist Officer Ramanujan Sahab from the general section had arrived.

The court proceeding started.

'Mr Raju, did you give a provocative speech at Khamaria?' Srivastava Sahab posed the question. 'To provoke whom?' I questioned in reply.

'The people of the staff.'

'Why did I provoke them, please throw light on that?'

'You provoked the group of people present against the department. You inspired them to instil indiscipline.' Srivastava Sahab said with a slight bend in his eyebrows.

'Yes, I provoked them. But not against the department, or with the intention of indiscipline. I provoked them to fight for their demands, inspired them to suffer to end unethical orders and acts. Is awakening the latent consciousness a deed against the spirit of the Indian constitution?'

Our officer from the general section Mr Ramanujan was noting down our questions and answers.

'So you do not accept that you have done anything against the code of conduct of the government employees.'

'The question of accepting or not accepting arises where there is a trespass. As a staff leader I have the fundamental right to enliven the spirits of my colleagues, the right to freedom of expression. In this context, I consider your allegations inconsistent as well as baseless. If a staff leader in a democratic country, for his demands, for protection of his interests, incites his colleagues, what injustice does he do? Has the government given us, the freedom to strengthen our organizations, the right to present our demands in front of the government through organizations, only as the assurance of a prostitute?' I ran my eyes across everyone as I said my statement. Our Bade Sahab was smiling within his lips, Srivastava Sahab was burning inside his spectacles, and Ramanujan Sahab, running his eyes across us and sometimes at the mimics of the debate, was furious inside. Bade Sahab wanted to inform Srivastava Sahab, who was senior to Bade Sahab, through his smile that look, how brutal he is, how brave. If it was easy, I would have mended it, you didn't have to come.

'Well, acceptance or nonacceptance, both depend on the society more than the person.' Srivastava Sahab said, expressing dissatisfaction.

'Your questions were baseless. Neither did you put forward any statement of my speech, nor presented any proof against what I said. As a rule, I shouldn't have answered improperly that is an abstract allegation but keeping in mind the use of national wealth in your commute, I didn't say this earlier. If you want to ask any further questions then talk in the prescribed format only. Only then we can expect to reach a decision. Otherwise both of us would contempt the value of the nation's time, against which a similar court of enquiry shouldn't sit for you, where you are charged why was the time wasted not considering the national interests.' I was smiling at my argument. Everyone broke into laughter in the last sentence. Probably the fire of revenge would have deepened inside.

'Mr Raju, there should only be answers to the questions in the court of enquiry, not speech.' Our Bade Sahab said gravely. I did not realize the need for a debate only said, 'be assured, only answers will be given for questions.'

Srivastava Sahab glancing at the file in his hand, turned towards me to ask the next question.

'So, tell me, inside the office, during the office hours, the damage you have done to the national property by creating a ruckus, telling people to break furniture or breaking it yourself, what do you want to say about that?' Srivastava Sahab looked at me expecting an answer.

'In your question and in the letter that was given to me to prove my innocence, there is no mention about the date of the incident and why is my involvement assumed in it? In the absence of both, this question is nothing more than erecting a building in air to my understanding. Although I am not related, directly or indirectly, to any such event in which the intention of your question is implied.' My answer made Bade Sahab's face become pale. He immediately rang the bell and called the superintendent of the general section.

He was scolded for getting the incomplete draft of the letter signed. He only said this much in defence, the day this letter was sent to Mr Raju, the incident was of the same day. Maybe that's why the date was missed. Saying that, he stood there hanging down his neck like a culprit. Srivastava Sahab saw the date on the memo and said, 'the incident is of 11-11-65. Now tell us, who should be punished for the damage done to the chairs and table on that day?'

'This question points to a different direction than the previous question. In the earlier question, you accused me and in this one, you are asking me the name of the culprit. In this situation, it will be better if you sequence your questions first. Because the latter question clearly states that you have accepted, at least, in your conscience, that I'm not the culprit. Now as far as the subject of punishment is considered, it will be better if you call and question the superintendent of that section.' Srivastava Sahab was shocked to hear my answer.

He wasn't expecting that he would have to face court arguments. He was a direct IDAS officer. Our Sahab had become a king from Babu, but Srivastava Sahab had taken birth as a high level officer in the department.

The superintendent was called. Facing Bade Sahab and the officer that had come from outside, is facing death for the superintendent of our department. A ghost resides in him. He keeps telling him, you are a superintendent from the clergy, if the influence of the officer's even slightly reverses, then the next promotion would be cancelled. Your dream of a gazetted officer would be smashed. Straining eyes for years of study for subordinate accounts service, consumed in code, manual and taking complaints from wife, friends, and relatives, the revenge for that neglect will all go into ashes. Now the officer is your lord. Keep worshipping him.

Our superintendent sir, before walking, looked at his clothes with such eyes that no critical entity of any genre would go unescaped. On entering the room, he bowed to Paramhansa Swami Radhakrishna in his heart. Even the air occupying the room wouldn't know who entered, the silence of the room wouldn't be disturbed, and with that intention superintendent N P Ghosh entered the room.

Just near the entrance at some distance there was a stand curtain ahead in the left hand corner. A large table to the north side of that curtain, a shelf beside it and chairs around. And on one. Of those revolving chairs was seated, Srivastava Sahab, on his left our Bade Sahab, Ramanujan Sahab and I were sitting opposite to them. The superintendent sir wished everyone in English on entering. Probably an Indian salutation pecks our nation's officers.

Srivastava Sahab asked him to take a seat. Ghosh Sahab very obediently followed his order. When he was seated, Srivastava Sahab asked him, 'Mr. Ghosh, were chairs broken in your section on 11-11-65?'

Ghosh Sahab's face ashened. If he says yes, then will be asked what action did you take, and he says no, the question will be how did the chairs then. It was death both ways. With some thought he answered, 'I, sir, I was with Sahab at that time.'

'On returning when you saw the vandalism, you must

have found out who was responsible for damaging the national property? Did you find out who was responsible for that act?' This question from Srivastava Sahab was more serious. If he would take someone's name in front of me, then fear of defamation and he would hide, then Sahab would get angry. Along with this, he also knew that Bade Sahab had accused me. The poor man's situation was grave. It was possible that if I wouldn't have been there, he would have become a government witness but my presence was a deterrent for him. Gathering courage, he answered, 'somebody blames someone, somebody blamed some other, and I cannot, without having witnessed it, doubt a specific person.' It was a very clean answer. Srivastava Sahab smiled at Ghosh Sahab's compulsive explanation. 'Alright, tell me, when you returned to the section, what was Mr Raju doing?' Srivastava Sahab asked.

'At that time, he was rebuking some people.' Mr Ghosh answered.

'Why was he rebuking?'

'Some of those people had had a fight, and threw chairs at each other.'

'You can go now.' Srivastava Sahab said to Mr Ghosh.

'Mr Raju, who were the people who broke the chairs and spread commotion?' Srivastava Sahab got serious.

'I understand that the court of inquiry is to investigate the allegations on me, not to investigate the incident of 11-11-65. I consider this question to be outside the limits of this court. I should. Not be compelled to answer such questions that are outside the limits of the court.' I answered.

'So this means that you do not wish to answer this question.' Srivastava Sahab asked.

'Yes, it will be appropriate to understand that. I answered.

'So now you can leave.' Srivastava Sahab said.

When I stood up to leave, Bade Sahab smiled and said, 'you advocate well.'

'That is the beauty of your sight. Every question had to be answered.' I said pausing for a moment. When I came out of Bade Sahab's room, there was a good enough gathering at some distance. It was a trial of the general secretary, it wasn't a minor news. As soon as I stepped outside, I got surrounded by people. I smiled naturally and kept moving, waiting to get far from the room.

'What happened? This was the question.' I recited all the dialogues. After that incident, a new feeling of reverence was seen sprouting in the people.

Bade Sahab had got hurt from inside. The supporters who wished for the Bade Sahab's growth began envying.

Rekha's full bucket, dahi pede and the children saying dahi machhli became meaningful. After a month, the petition with the allegations against me may get withdrawn. Might receive the salary for a suspended period and my special influence on the officers may be seen.

Everything had changed. The environment of the house, office and that of the boundaries of friendship. It was the same Allahabad, same office, same office, same Rekha, Saavri and me. But it was like some connecting hinge was broken between us. Rekha lived close. Mother taking the pride of her decision had departed the world. Saavri wasn't anything more than the other neighbours. Guru's circle had disintegrated. I had got bored with the Union. Inflation had broken our back. Sons had reached high level job positions. Month's salary was mortgaged. The only thing remaining was the ultimate weapon of untouchable self respect. How, in what way, this was unknown.

I was standing, waiting for the bus from Katra to Johnson Ganj. In Allahabad, the bus routes were limited, as compared to other cities. The buses ran on a few selected roads. There was no sign of the bus. Although, except to Kanpur and Delhi, I usually prefer travelling to all the places by rickshaw or scooter. Who will waste the time waiting for government services? The wait for government buses requires a long period of time like the judgement on civil suits. You need ample time to enjoy the ride in these buses. But in the scope of the city's growing with time and in the decreasing dimensions with the Era, there are countless who, in order to traverse the distance in the shortest interval of time, take the help of these social means. Cyclists take their help, as well as the scooter riders, all are subjected to time so they want to live the time.

That moment also came when I saw the bus approaching. Not just that, it was better because all the passengers had to de-board there. From here, it had to load new passengers to go to the same place, where I wanted to go. In order to get a seat in the bus, the tricks I learned in my childhood to buy tickets for the third class of Motimahal Talkies, I used the same practice. A brother who was holding the rod at the entrance door of the bus with his strong hands, I entered ducking beneath his arm. Because of a few elbows being hit, the people at the back got annoyed and pushed the crowd forward, sending me inside the bus. I was panting, from my clothes to my hair, everything got disorganized. Not only mine, people who wanted to climb the bus hurriedly and grab a seat had the same condition. Even then by the time I entered the bus, all the ladies had taken the seats. I wandered my eyes here and there and holding the rod at the roof of the bus, stood there silently.

The Indian women, who talk about being given equal rights, travel in the general coach in the trains, but even if a single man is seen in the female coach, then they get offended. If women can willingly travel alongside men in trains or buses, then they should and a man doesn't have the right to travel on a seat or coach meant for women, even if it's vacant. Women don't want equal but special rights. They want to be in control. A woman eager to obtain the historical power of matriarchal clans begins to associate the matter of getting alienated with merely sitting next to a man and gets afraid of getting alienated. Does a man experience a new pleasure in getting alienated? Is the meaning of alienation only applicable in a particular case? Is this fear in women also a former of her eternal shame?

There only one passenger was sitting on the single women's seat. But who will say, sister, please let me sit. If the sister slapped the brother being a man on his frail face with heated statements, then what will happen?

Everyone was standing, I was also. Meanwhile, a gentleman from the office who was standing at the gate shouted, Raju Sahab, pay for me as well, the conductor doesn't have change for 10 rupees.

By that time, the sound of the word 'Raju' repeated in

a surprised tone in a female voice surprised me. I don't know whether the people around heard it too. My eyes circled all the women sitting on the right side once. I didn't understand. There was a fear of looking at an unknown woman with great concentration. That is when I heard a clear voice from the left side, 'Sit down, there's a vacant seat.' This time all eyes together turned to the left.

It took me a while to recognize the female passenger. It was Razia. I was meeting her after about ten years. On seeing her suddenly, I uttered, 'Razia'......you.......How are you here?' She gestured to me to sit, not giving an answer. Razia was in her full swing. A pink saree on fair complexion, with matching blouse, an English haircut, a pink purse in her hand and lipstick on her lips. Everyone stared at Razia, but with an even greater envy looked at me. I didn't care about anyone and sat beside her. The women sitting around looked at us with surprise. Someone must have seen, but who did we care about?

I asked as soon as I sat, 'when did you come to Allahabad?'

'It has been two days.' Razia said carefully, tucking to a side.

'Two days. Didn't you remember our house?' I said in a sarcastic tone.

'You should say that when I would have had your address.' Razia answered smiling.

The ears of all the people, not eyes, were concentrated at our conversation, monitoring it.

'How did you come here?' I asked out of curiosity.

'Where is Rekha?' She questioned me without answering my question.

'She is here. Everyone is here. Come on, come with me to our house first, then you can go wherever you're going to.' I said excitedly requesting her. Meanwhile, the bus halted, I stood up, and Razia stood up as well. When we were getting down, the conductor said, 'Of these two, the man took a ticket for Johnson Ganj and the woman for Naini. Why did they get down here?' Some lewd passenger said, 'They must be old friends. One Hindu, the other Muslim.'

People laughed. The women sitting around looked at

each other and smiled.

We got down near Purshottamdas Tandon Park. It was the pink winter day of November. It was just half past five in the evening but the darkness was descending on the roads. The electricity poles erected on the footpath will begin to cast shadows of the passersby soon; such was the essence of that beautiful night. I looked nicely at Razia from the head to toe. She was wearing black bangles on one arm and a watch on the other.

We continued to cross the road, busy in ourselves, vigilant of the passing vehicles.

Razia's age would be 35 years at that time. But no one would be willing to accept her to be more than 25 for the first time in my life today we were walking alongside the road. Till that day, I hadn't walked with any other woman other than Rekha like that. There used to be a constant reminder, about what somebody who knows us, thinks about seeing us. There was a shiver in the heart, uncertainty on the face. Razia had no such feeling in her heart.

I was looking at Razia's body wrapped tightly in that hazy darkness. Although Razia was walking with her bowed, she had seen the madness in my eyes through the corner of her eyes. She instantly looked at me and said smiling, 'what are you looking at? Haven't you seen me before?' I did get taken by surprise, but it was as if that question squeezed all the hesitation. I also answered with a brave smile, 'although I saw once a year, but you never looked so beautiful.'

'What happened today then? I look beautiful to you at a time when the hairs on your temples, in your beard have started greying and I'm standing on the last leg of my youth. Where were these eyes before today?' There was a hint of an indication to the time before an unknown history. I got into some thinking. Has Razia cautioned me about my old age with a civil indication? But her inner happiness resting on her cheeks had cleared the way of the bottleneck of doubts. I got lost in the memories of the long lost childhood.

Razia was a girl from an educated and progressive Muslim family. Her father had studied in London. Probably Razia would have also gone there to study if he wouldn't have died untimely. Her mother hadn't married again in order to keep his love and memories alive. Although her elder brother in law was fascinated by her beauty. He also wanted her to be his wife but Razia's mother didn't give birth to the idea of rebuilding the ruins of her marital life into a palace. Though at that time she must not have been more than 35-36 years of age. Razia's father was ICS. At the time of his death, he was the Collector of Agra. Razia's mother used to get a pension. Also, the income of the property purchased by her husband was also around thousand rupees per month. Incentives were extra. There was a good bank balance as well in the name of Razia.

Realizing my quietness, Razia thought I felt bad. She shook me with her hand and said, 'your habit of feeling bad didn't go.' On saying this, she smiled. On waking up from the memories of Razia's past, I got lost in the present light. I gained; don't know what, in getting lost.

No, there is no question of hanging my face. You have met me after so many years today, and that too, outside the four walls of the house. I had got lost in the times where you once met me. How do you like this first meeting of ours alone?' I said. I hadn't talked to Razia before today, in a romantic mood. Though, we were habitual of talking about every kind of thing. But today, contexts as well as meaning both were alive.

She looked at me with slight seriousness. And then again in a calm tone, halting for a moment, answered my question. 'I am surprised that you are asking me about the meaning of the words of today's weather?..... Did Rekha make you understand the language of solitary meeting?' She said, spreading a bright sheet of smile on her lips. 'Although I knew Rekha before as well, the polishing is her gift. I also added difference to her meaning.'

We had reached the Royal Hotel while strolling. She turned towards the hotel and said, 'I'm staying here. Come, let's sit here and talk. You have met me after years and that too with new references.' Having said this, she looked at my face carefully. Today we were probably in a new reference indeed.

The meaning of 'With new references' was left as a question.

There was one bed in the room. Sofa set, dressing table, tea table, I rolled on the sofa carelessly.

'Yes Razia, tell me how you came here. I started the conversation from.' Where it had been left.

'Do you not know, I had done IPS. I am in the intelligence department. I have come here for some government work.' She answered.

'I would have known if you would have sent a letter even in this regard. Then you are also like your father. So, for how long will you stay?'

'No idea. We have such work whose time of completion we ourselves don't know. Well, keep it to yourself, I've come. In search for Pakistani agents. Allahabad is a decent hub for Pakistani agents.' I looked at Razia's face carefully once. I started remembering the days when I used to get to meet her during summer vacation. She used to come to her uncle's house and I used to go to Bareilly to visit my uncle. Like her father, her maternal uncle was well off. We both were unaware of the bitterness of life and seriousness of age. We used to play together. When she got used to putting a drape over her vest and I used my 7 o'clock razor to shave my beard, our meetings ended. The memories had begun to be forgotten, but used to get fresh on receiving Razia's letters. At that time, she had to traverse the roads of Bareilly in a mask. Though, even after getting mature, she used to meet me, even if it's only for a while. A woman expects initiation from a man and the man gets afraid. Because of his pathetic condition. One day, I don't know why, she had said only this much, I wish I was also Hindu....

'Yes, so how will you find out?' I asked her a question that was appropriate for the fulfilment of curiosity and knowledge. But due to official formality, it was unethical.

'Some Muslims living here, in order to prove their allegiance to Pakistan, are laying dynamite under the ground of our motherland. I kept an eye on them by being one of them. Some Hindu rich people who trade the band of patriotism under the influence of their money, I live amongst them. Tell me about yourself, Raju. I am betraying the traitorous deeds of my community.' Razia got serious.

'The same clerkship, what else is written in this poor

man's fate.' I had also poured out the fun of my personality in the manner of my saying. ........ I furthered the conversation saying, 'well, it's a strange thing, fathers and grandfather are buried in India, they are dying to make their own for Pakistan. There is no question of the materialisation of the history of Hindu or Muslim kings now, then why are such people dying for the welfare of Pakistan. The Hindus that are in Pakistan should show their loyalty for Pakistan, and the Muslims living here, for India. The community that isn't loyal to its country doesn't prosper. Whether Shankaracharya comes or Mohammed Sahab, there cannot be creation of states on the basis of castes. When the world is coming together in the boundaries of ideas, the people of our country are getting divided into castes.'

'You say rightly. But those who don't understand and even after declining and so many restrictions, continue, there's a mystery behind it. They earn meaning by trading nationalism. Some earn from trade, some from service, they get rich by wearing masks. Whether China climbs over the country, or Pakistan, these big shots have to earn four bucks by taking advantage of the situation. The goods will be sold to those, who will pay such an amount. The country can die of hunger, but they need to export rice to China. How will the people of the country give so much money? Aircrafts from other countries will fire bombs on our country, they don't care about that. They will even convey secret news to the enemy if there is a hope of getting paid.'

'In a society of capitalist civilization, patriotism, nationalism, it is not necessary that everything is a business. I have had bitter experiences. I will say to the extent that every country's Muslim is a mere offspring of its primitive people. How can the colour of blood flowing in the veins change with the change of religion? It should sloganeer of unity at the ground of sublime humanity rather than under the flag of Islam. The sons of Muhammad only had given the slogan of 'all are one in the eyes of god' in the world. They should recite this slogan, but not in the name of Islam but in the name of the unity of humanity.' Razia expressed her heart's foulness. At that time, she, like a skilled politician, was resolving the provinces originating from Allahabad.

Razia's statements were topical. Their series could be increased, but turning away from the dullness of politics, I felt like saying or hearing something that unfolds our private lives. Every moment is. Not a moment for thinking about the country. I started looking outside. The curtain of the room was partially drawn. The wind blew fast outside. Razia sometimes maintained her flowing saree over her chest, sometimes looking for the answers to some serious questions in my eyes. And that too swam on the eyelids of her eyes.

'Did you not marry?' I said plucking on the silent lotus petals, Razia kept looking at me.

'No?'

'Why?'

'I didn't feel its necessity.' Razia answered, looking down at her feet covered by the saree.

'Why? Is marriage only a necessity? Not a social obligation?' I was a bit surprised by her answer.

'For a woman, there are only two images of a man, one is satisfying sexual desire and other is a means of providing financial support. A woman is dependent on a man for financial reasons only, in the other; the man is himself dependent on the woman. I'm earning to live life......' and Razia's eyes shot up.

'I couldn't imagine a woman who could explain, so bravely, such a sensitive topic. Such a clear oration and tears in eyes?'

'But Razia, a man isn't just a necessity but her completion. In the same way as a woman for a man. Why don't you understand this?' I found Razia's argument unconvincing.

Razia looked at me for a moment and smiled. Now she was holding the end of her saree in a relaxed manner. 'I understand Raju, I understand everything you're trying to say. But the objective of completion isn't just fulfilled by getting fastened to a peg.' Razia said.

'Pardon me Razia. I felt like talking extra clearly today. The objective of completion gets fulfilled when a woman embraces another person. A prostitute can present this argument for completion.' My answer didn't put Razia to shame, she got furious. Then calmed down.

She started talking in a serious tone.

'A domestic relationship of man and a woman that you are referring to, is usually nothing more than pieces of flesh. We often choose proportionality between bodies over thoughts. They buy someone's life and body with dowry. I had a beating heart along with a body. I also wanted to burn like a devoted lamp crest in the courtyard of my lover...... When I didn't find a groom of my choice, then what is the meaning of a married life?......... The hunger for body is the nomad of the road, quenches thirst, doesn't revolve around the well. I believe..... Is not the goal of life.' She probably couldn't say further. Her throat was full.

There was an uproar in my heart..... Did Razia also love someone like me? I loved Asha but on finding Rekha I forgot her. She could also forget the lord of her heart...... but she never told me even the title of her love story. Now the cultural influence of the question and answer had abandoned hesitation, reluctance and shame. I asked, 'I discovered today that there is a story as well. Who did you love? Who is that merciless man whose detached bud from the branch of hope was sometimes offered to God, sometimes tasted dust.' I looked at her eagerly and asked.

I felt some inner excitement in asking this question, getting transmitted and that wanted it to be assimilated. Razia was silent. I also didn't have the courage to stress on the question being answered. It was her personal matter. How rightful was I to know it? I didn't know even that.

The eyes with which she looked at me, had hatred, apology and affection. The way she looked changed every second. My eyes, for some reason, couldn't meet her eyes. After some time, she herself said, 'that man couldn't break the fingers of the outcast society. He could face death, bring a revolution but was a coward. He was so engrossed in achieving his dreams that he started loving in an unfavourable environment. He had not won over culture. He wanted to break the barriers but not for himself. He wanted to create a new world, but not for himself. He waited to return to his house of culture after having done everything...... he was a very good man. He gives trust, also wants trust. Doesn't hurt anyone. He could keep me happy. If I would have got him, Razia wouldn't be as you are seeing now. Her bun would also have been braided with jasmine flowers; vermillion in her hair would wash the river of the heaven. In every meeting, he only said this much through his unsaid words, Razia you are my ideological complement. When I halt, you give me the pace. He never peaked into my eyes. I wasn't a flutter for him, I remained sandalwood. Probably even today.....' She suddenly stopped while talking. Her melancholic love affair tickled me. The sadness of a blissful heart got prevalent.

'Though I want to know the name of that phantom, but even if you don't tell me, the use of vermillion indicates that he must be some young Hindu man?' I said.

'He was Hindu, additionally Brahmin, a whole 20 years old. That great Saint of possibilities was also unaware of my heart's determination. I love him very much, Raju. Till date, this very moment........ But he, on understanding the heartbeat of the entire world, couldn't hear my heart's voice. I also wanted to settle down, be a mother, wanted to grow like a creeper in his courtyard but...... but he never understood, and I never said.' Razia got quiet and looked at the handkerchief peeking out of my coat's pocket. I don't why but I began remembering some relaxed, frightening incidents with the Razia of the past. Today those signs got meaningful. The feelings were getting a context.

'If you loved him so much, why didn't you tell him? Probably that Saint would have revolted. He could have turned down the world for you. Who knows, his seriousness would have grown its possibilities on getting you. It may be that he would be thinking that you're a Muslim, and didn't want to become Hindu.' I started gauging her reaction.

She said looking in my eyes, 'Probably.'

'Is it not possible now?' I asked.

'Sometimes you talk like a child, Raju. He must be 35-36 years of age. He is someone's vermillion and father to some kids. When I couldn't say it authoritatively why would I want him by default now? I am a woman, I cannot take away another woman's man.' She was now getting closer to a smile.

'Who cares if he couldn't be your life partner, would you not accept living with him?' I kept on questioning, purposeless, spontaneously some. Juices started flowing in the dullness of the heart.

'You only answer that.' She looked at me and said. I lost my mind. I couldn't understand. What I did understand, I couldn't believe it........ If I'm the person whose memory left her to roam like a nomad, then..... But no, I cannot be. If I would have been, I would have disowned all Relations, accepting Razia. Razia had a brain, beauty, advancement, everything that I always wanted. Razia is worth having...... I got lost in such thoughts. Suddenly the light of her eyes spread on my face. I said, if I would have been in that person's place, I would have revolted against the repressiveness of the society. Razia was enough for me. I wouldn't have required the support of the whole world. I spread trust with eyes filled with love on the pleats of her saree that waved on her woollen blouse.

Really. She stood up from my opposite and sat beside me. I shivered, she was shivering. I gathered her in my arms. The hearts of both of them were beating. A heart beat that probably didn't happen even while meeting Rekha or Roopa. There hadn't been such times of meeting Asha and Saavri.

We both were quiet. My fingers were playing with her cropped hair. I was. Now sitting on the bed. She was lying with her eyes closed keeping her head on my thighs. Her fingers tangled with the buttons of my coat. She slowly got up and began hiding her head in my chest. I rolled on the bed. She said, 'Raju, what I'm getting today, I probably would have got it fifteen years back if you would have just asked, Razia, when will you marry?' I merely smiled in answer. My heart was lost in the crowd of new questions. I was staggering like the rose lying untouched in the waves.

What's Rekha's value in my life? I was thinking..... She is a devoted wife, what else? I shuddered. I got confused.... Her intellectual level is not as evolved as Razia; her beauty cannot agonize like that of Razia. She who cannot induce vibration in her husband's core, what is the enjoyment of a life with her? ..... But.... But she is as beloved to me as my breath. She has suffered the sun and shade of life with me, spread squeals in my deserted courtyard........ Razia could also have done it.... No, never, Razia would have lived more like a friend than a wife. A wife doesn't claim her equality in front of her husband, a girl friend can. So... I only wanted a wife, also a partner to accompany me outside the house. Rekha endures the heat of the house; Razia would have helped in the battles outside as well... Razia was rubbing my palm.

'So what do you instruct for the life ahead? .... Today I begin my life in a new direction.' She asked, embracing me.

'Instruction? I'm looking for a way not to order. You are somewhere, I am somewhere else, and how will we tread this difficult road of a long life? There is Rekha as well.' I said placing my lips on her lips.

'We will keep meeting. I will keep coming, you wouldn't have to suffer. It will be difficult to live without a job; otherwise I would have done that. I will keep helping you in your family obligations. But we will have to hide all this from Rekha. On knowing it, she will dissolve and die. I only want to steal a few moments from her life. You be hers, I only want the right to call you mine as well. Tell me, do you accept me tonight? Razia was looking at me with pleading eyes. I was unsure. On one side was only the fulfilment of bodily hunger and on the side was lifelong companionship. How do I keep two swords in the one sheath?

'Razia I am pleased with your wait, meditation and sacrifice. I mistook myself as a deity because of your prayer of love, I don't have the strength to reject you. But.....' I stopped mid sentence.

'But what? Why did you stop talking?' Razia asked eagerly.

'But if you got pregnant then......'

'That will not happen. I don't want to be a mother now. A woman who does not wish to be a mother can be saved in the scientific age. It is not an age of faith in God but an age of trusting science.' She was talking like she didn't care at all about the fire. She didn't want to care about the future in getting lost in the present. Though she also kept in mind that she was an IPS officer. A respectable woman.

'Then why do you want to accept the unsocial life of a vice wife? Will it not be an injustice to two women at the same time?' I was now trying to get out of the trap of acceptance that I had forced her to spread. Intellectual stimulation had caused a problem. I was constantly thinking... Rekha... my nun wife.

'Do you want to define my future today itself? .... I

forgot in the conversation that you've been here for such a long time. It has also gotten colder. I didn't even ask for a cup of tea.' With that, her hand touched a button on the bed. She sat in front of the dressing table, setting her clothes.

The chauffeur came and saluted her. Razia only asked me, 'it must be okay to drink it in the winter sometimes isn't it?' And without waiting for an answer, said, 'Two pegs of black and white.' The chauffeur bowed and promised with his eyes to return.

I was getting trapped. It was like she didn't want to understand anything now. Was she so hungry for so long? She also drinks alcohol. Such women in a country like India would be called prostitutes, what else? But her government position is such that a man at that position cannot remain a good man. Now that women have also come to these high positions then can they be saved? I hadn't ever touched liquor with my lips with a woman, what will I do today? All my moral strength diminished at the moment when I took Razia in my arms. This death of hesitation and shame was very beautiful. I started thinking about Saavri. There I wasn't hesitant, here Razia is fearless. There, I was a man, here she is the man.

By the time the chauffeur brought two pegs of black and white whiskey on a tray, Razia had adorned herself in a new way. The chauffeur was probably aware, so he brought a packet of cigarettes, matchbox, snacks, everything and kept it. On keeping it, when he began leaving, Razia said, 'some police officers will be coming soon, tell them I'll meet them tomorrow, I'm busy. Do not allow anyone to come upstairs.' And while talking to him, said to me, 'I don't even have two minutes of solitude in this job.' I sat there smiling like that character of a drama that is bound to play his role.

'Why did you take this job? This is suitable for men.' I asked her.

'Even in this area, a woman completes a man.' She came smiling and sat beside me. To tempt me with the fragrance of her hair. She picked up a peg and touched it to my lips. I shivered. But the lips couldn't remain closed. Even they wanted to experience this. In which a beautiful woman with her arms around his neck makes them drink alcohol and that too who is not easily available like a prostitute to others.

In some time, all the hesitation drowned in the melted cubes, I forgot everything. Razia was on my lap, and I was putting the glass of alcohol to her mouth.

The clock had struck nine in the night. Nine of a winter night and that too on the roads of Allahabad, what else is there except for silence. It isn't a city of workers, servants, that keeps working. Day and night continuously. I wanted to return to that place that was on the other side of the beliefs of the earth. It was like Razia's eyes kept singing songs..

The translation of every sentence of every sight is remaining.

The history of every door of union is remaining.

Stop for now....

Somebody's sense of thirst diminishes,

You may go.

But my mood had retreated. I had come out of the room. The wind outside today seemed more intoxicating than yesterday's. It floated in a moment, with the black clouds. The body was light, eyes colourful and the heart was heavy. The way to repentance was obstructed. Razia was standing with her head leaning on my shoulder. Her hair reached my chest. She wasn't on earth. She wasn't in front of her hotel room. She was somewhere beyond the sky, somewhere in the search of sweet truth in heaven. Her hoarse voice repeated the saying by Hayaat,

'These tears scattered like the deck of cards

Looks like someone losing the chance.'

I said to her waking her up from the trance, 'Razia I will go now. Rekha must be worried. I started walking without waiting for her answer.' She looked at me opening her eyes, handling her scattered hair, 'you want to go, go. Someone else has the right on you....... Wish this night had come 15 years ago.' I kept walking, she stood there bidding goodbye with her silent eyes.

I told the rickshaw puller to stop at a paan shop. The rickshaw stopped near Niranjan cinema, I had the paan, and then got lost in thoughts.

What will Rekha think if she detects the smell of liquor? I will fall so hard in her eyes. She will start hating me. And what if she gets to know that..... No, never, I'll hide this from her. I've never hidden anything from. Her, but this has to be. She is a sincere woman. What if considering herself a hindrance between me and Razia she.....no she'll never do that. A woman cares about her children as well, not just her husband.... But..... She will be a living dead. She'll look at me with hateful eyes. She'll spit on me, calling me a Casanova. It will be appropriate; I have done wrong to her. I wiped the vermillion of her head on someone else's head.

The rickshaw stopped outside the garage, I gave the money and walked rapidly inside. Save my eyes, so that nobody gets to know that I've drank alcohol. Drinking is fine in a few good meetings in years. It had its own limited memories, but they were vibrant.

I tried a lot to be saved but Chhote Guru collided with me. He leapt and said, 'how are you Raju? Where are you heading? You don't get seen around.' I answered without even looking there, 'Chhote Guru, I'm in a little hurry. We'll meet tomorrow morning.'

I started feeling nauseous. I entered inside somehow; Rekha and the kids were all sleeping. She was about to say anything on seeing me but I started puking at the basin itself. On seeing me puking, she leapt forward and started rubbing my back. Sent Bade to fetch water, and told Chhote to take care of Neena. I was getting better. Razia's love drink was getting expelled. After gargling with the water from a jug, without anything to anyone, I headed straight to my room and laid down on the bed. Rekha came after me. Bade had opened the basin's pipe.

'How are you?' Rekha asked in a worried tone. She probably didn't want to accept anything unpleasant under the guise of seriousness.

'I am fine now.' On saying this much, I pulled her towards me. She slowly said, 'everyone is here,' and sat near me. 'What did you eat? Where were you?' Rekha asked.

'I hadn't eaten anything. I got nauseous when I got down from the rickshaw here.' I held her hand on my chest and slowly petted it. 'I had met an old friend. He stays outside; I had stayed with him only.' On saying this, I started getting up carefully. She started untying my shoes. Told Bade to bring a lungi.

I didn't eat any food. Rekha had fed everyone. She brought some warm milk for me. I told her to keep the milk there. Everyone had lied down. Rekha caressed my forehead, sitting near me, while I was engrossed in my thoughts. On thinking that I'm sick, she brought a dose of a homeopathic medicine Ipecac from the neighbour.

I summoned sleep to get rid of the suffocation. We don't know when we dozed off together.

Razia didn't see Rekha. Rekha couldn't even hear Razia's name. Razia had even left. I got informed through mail about her reaching Lucknow the next day. A peon of the police had come to the office to deliver a sealed envelope. The people in the office were surprised, what's going on?

In it, it was written,

'I'm returning. You've got mail. I'll write a Letter.

Yours only

Razia.'

I pulled it out while having nearly kept it in the inside pocket of my coat. I tore it into pieces and threw in the dustbin. With 'yours only' it was as if a needle pierced in my eye. I felt like taking off the burden on the paper. After getting an envelope from the peon, I started writing a letter to Razia.

'My Razia for a night

I got the paper you sent. Reading 'yours only' made me anxious. Forgive me Razia, I cannot be yours. Although our Hindu religion believes in rebirth, I don't. So that birth is right this is in an eternal sense with historicity. I don't consider her in my desire for rebirth who I have no relation with in this life. Even after believing that only form changes, the philosophy of a scientist can be fulfilled, but the patio of the world of love doesn't shine in that form. I don't want to deceive my heart with the idea of rebirth. I don't expect to meet you in the next birth as well, even if that happens, I don't assure you.

I had lived my entire life in a moment with you. Now I

don't want to distort the past moments by reliving it in future. I'm the vermillion of someone's hair partition; you are the lamp burning at the footpath. Restriction is my responsibility, and violates your right to freedom. Your thirst has been nomadic and desire has been married as well. Us living together is not possible in the periphery of impossibility.

I cannot betray Rekha, I cannot deceive myself. I cannot keep you in the dark. I am no more unattainable to you, and you are no more a stranger to me. Let's return to our boundaries.

Rest on the doomsday.

Yours fictitious

Raju'

In order for it to reach Razia soon, I put it in the station post box while returning from the office. I started looking a little grim. Rekha asked that day, 'What's the matter. You seem disturbed since a few days.'

I displayed a natural grin and said, 'There's nothing like that. Yes, here in the office there's some extra work so I get tired. Maybe that's why you think so.' Saying this, I took Neena from her lap. I started loving her. I don't know why Rekha stood in the window in my vision while combing her hair.

It was the holiday of the second Saturday of the month. I was reading a newspaper sitting on the cot under the sun. Even Rekha on finishing all household chores, putting radio's Vividh Bharati program on low volume sat beside me with Neena. My mind again got surrounded by questions. I sensed Surendra coming from outside. Rekha got up and sat down. Keeping the newspaper aside, I looked towards the door. As soon as he entered, he said, 'Good morning Bhai Sahab, good morning didi.' And hopped down and sat beside me. Rekha said to him, "whether it's morning or afternoon, you always say good morning.' She also smiled. Surendra laughed. 'It's because we're meeting for the first time today.' He said looking at me sideways.

I said annoyed with his look, 'It would have been better if you were a girl. Somebody would have settled down. I don't like the looks you give.'

'If I were a girl, then you wouldn't stand a chance. You have got such a lovely wife like didi. Why are you thinking of turning me into a girl? Look didi, this is how he always talks to me. You only tell, if I were a girl, my father would have to suffer so much to get my hands yellow.' Surendra said, showing the innocence of a child. Rekha was laughing, Surendra is a strange man.

He snatched the newspaper from my hand and kept it away. He said, 'I was getting bored at home so I came here. Now you are boring us with your face hanging like a sack. Didi is here, I am here and you are glued to the newspaper.'

'There is a time for this well...... Yes, what happened?' I said rolling one eye towards Rekha. Rekha left smiling. Surendra started saying, 'You made didi leave, and the poor woman blushed. You have no rein on your tongue.'

Rekha on keeping some water to heat for tea had quickly come back. She had no one calling her didi in this life. Seeing Surendra, and with his talks, she used to feel lighter. Whenever he came, he got involved in whatever she was doing. Rekha stopped him but he calmed her by giving such answers. That she just smiles and couldn't say further. Why would I lie, talking with him in isolation, even my fatigue would get relieved. The agility like children, shy sarcastic comments like a fun loving girl, the look of the eyes that tempts like a prostitute were Surendra's characteristics. He was the male dancer playing the role of a female.

The kids were also listening to him sing. The radio was turned off. Rekha said to him, Surendra, sing this song, nobody is ours in this crowded world. He quickly gave an answer, looking at me while turning his flexible hands, whether you have anybody or not, Surendra is yours. You don't care about such selfish people. Who gets mad without even saying anything and when he speaks, then he talks rubbish? Rekha said laughing; 'his and your arguments are like reprimands of the mother in law.' Rekha had this to say but for a moment Surendra's face ashened. He started thinking to himself, didi also think of me wrongly like others.

In order to lighten my mind, I told Rekha and Surendra to listen carefully; I started the conversation at the end of a story. I said, 'Surendra, it's a story, I'll tell you it's a summary. All of you give your opinion on its ending. A Muslim girl loved a Hindu boy dearly. But she didn't tell. Him how she felt due to shyness. And the boy didn't understand without him being told.......' Interrupting me in the middle, Surendra said, 'it must have been some handsome guy like you.' 'Keep quiet. It's not right to interrupt in between.' I scolded him, hiding my facial expressions. Saying, 'Ok', he also started acting eager to know the summary of the story. Rekha wasn't paying attention. I continued, after telling her to pay attention. 'One day that woman meets that Hindu boy suddenly. That day the girl tells her beloved why she spent her whole life unmarried. Even today, she wants to be with that guy, even after knowing that he's not only a husband but also a father. Even After spending fifteen years of her youth alone, she wants to have him in some or the other form. The guy also gets unstable on realizing her sacrifice and patience. She is extraordinarily beautiful, educated and has a high level job. The girl even goes on to say that she will support him in his current financial matters as well. The guy slips only for her youth and wants to compensate for not being able to be her husband by being a friend. Now tell me, how should the story end?'

Rekha listened to the story closely. She said, 'if that girl is respectable, then she shouldn't try to get that man. Because the value of a woman is not from a partner. Even the guy should control his sensual greed. He should realise the importance of a wife. Though a partner wife brought to give financial support will one day, get the bride who came after taking the seven vows, out of the house and destroy that guy's life. A good natured wife is not easy to get, women who wait for so long are also less. I laud the sacrifice of that woman but if the story ends in encouraging the practice of a vice wife, then I'll regard it as the downfall of the protagonist.'

'But didi, whatever you said is related to want; art is directly related to what is.' Surendra said supporting the art form like an artist.

'But we don't know the end. Even then as an ordinary woman, I can say this much that Looking at what can be helpful in the growth of a society, should also be important for the artist.' Rekha presented her view on the morality of the story.

'But Rekha, if the woman doesn't get the man even after narrating her story. And in this situation on revealing her hearts secret if she attempts suicide on getting ashamed on not getting accepted for it, will be the protagonist do justice to that woman?' I said enjoying the argument.

'A woman is not property, in whose account the number of partners increases with each generation or who can have more than one owner. A woman gets born for a single man, not for many.' Rekha said.

'But here, the question is not of a woman, but of a man.

Can a man under different circumstances not love two women? Is the woman who gets the protagonist of that story without any prayer greater than the woman who spent her nights of youth mortgaging someone's memories under her pillow?' I asked Rekha.

'I'll answer that. If a man only wants to keep himself in the middle of two women, because one is his social obligation, that is his wife and the other has occupied his heart, then I'll say that even a woman should have the right to keep two men under different circumstances.' Surendra indirectly supported Rekha's ideas.

'You people want to solve such an interesting and serious issue on the basis of sentiments. You must know Surendra, earlier in the primitive era, there were matriarchal clans. They didn't have one husband. Both man and woman had the option of fulfilling their physical contention anywhere. There was no society, no rules. But today, a woman is dependent on a man as his companion. A man can keep two wives approved by the society but a woman cannot keep two society approved husbands. The society makes the rules considering the physical inequalities, dispositions and utilities of a man and a woman. A woman is the creator, a man's mere helper. One person being part of attaining reproduction facilitates the system. Of responsibilities. But with two women together, a man doesn't have to face that dilemma.' I explained.

'There is a description of Panchali in our Hindu mythology. You are really wrong to say that a woman cannot have two husbands.' Rekha said.

'And that resulted in Arjuna's Brahmanash life. It was proved against the system.' I said answering her.

'Do both the situations not prove that a man only considers a woman as an object of reverence? And faith, respect, are all hypocritical adjectives for her?' Surendra said looking towards my face.

'Indulgence is the core of the universe, utilizing its tool. A woman carries that burden of life that a man cannot, so she is faithful. She helps the man in giving birth to new ideals, so she is respected. This can also be said in reference to men as well that he is not just a creature of sensual longing but more than that.' I said, explaining Surendra.

'Yes, you will stubbornly keep saying your point. Have you ever listened to anyone?' Surendra said in a feminine pose. Seeing her feminine pose, even Rekha laughed, and I did too.

'Where is that story, let me read it. Let me see what the protagonist says in what circumstances. Have you completed it?' Rekha asked.

'Kant had taken me to a story seminar one day. A writer had read a piece of his novel there. As much as I heard, I told you. The end will. Only be known after reading it.' I said.

Surendra stared at me and said, 'I had come relaxed. You kept someone else's burden on me. Your protagonist and that girl can go to hell, what do we have to do with it? Right, didi?'

Rekha affirmed.

Tea was prepared again and this time there were snacks as well.

I had gone to the office after two days' leave. I got two envelopes there. Neither had the name of the sender. I turned them over and checked. The handwriting wasn't unfamiliar but still seemed unfamiliar. While. Opening the letter, I realised that it's Razia's handwriting. On opening it, my doubt got clarified. The letter was from Lucknow.

'The man of my dreams,

You accepted me, I lived up. The helplessness of the job distanced us untimely, I'm not at fault. I hope you haven't made any incorrect opinion about me, so I wrote this letter as soon as possible. The work that I came for there is completed. I will soon come again for some government work. I'll write to you. If you get a chance, meet me, I'll wait.

I felt regretful that I couldn't meet the children leaving. I'll give you the work of getting my kids woollen suits made. I hope you will deliver my things to my kids. The cloth will be of Rekha's choice, take her along. Then get a photograph clicked with Rekha and the kids and Send it to me through a registered post.

Rest, in your memory and wait-

Yours only

Razia'

Attached a check

The envelope dropped from my hand. Razia's letter wasn't less intimate than that from Rekha. But her sending a check of one thousand rupees touched my self-respect. She was displaying her riches already. This thing revolved in my mind. I also got reminded of Razia's promise of fulfilling her family obligations. This is probably its evidence only.

Razia wouldn't be a financial burden. When this thought came to mind, my mind would convince me.

Keeping that letter in my pocket, I opened the other letter. She probably would have written this letter after receiving my letter. Her language was entirely different.

'My found, and lost,

Whom I found even after losing, lived in his fantasies, I'm not used to losing him even after finding him only for a few moments. I don't desire to falsify your beliefs. I'm not pure like Rekha but whatever I am, is in your absence, whatever I'll be, will be in your absence.

I only want you to be happy. I don't want to expand your periphery of 'possible'. Don't be afraid of me even on the doomsday-

We are not those who will claim of blood to you
Even if God asks us, we will deny it.

I know how to keep. You had described fulfilment of unmarried desire as the quality of a prostitute. I agreed to be even a prostitute for you. I don't know what I saw in you that I didn't see in any other man till date.

When I come, I'll meet. Would that be possible at least? She who didn't believe in bowing, considered it cowardice, the same Razia salutes you.

Yours only
Razia'

I started fainting. For what reason is a woman who is at a position of IPS, willing to give up her self respect for a clerk like me? I'm not worth her in any way.

That day, I didn't feel good at the office. I returned home early. Seeing me come early, Rekha asked, 'how are you early today?'

'Just like that, I got bored, so came.'

I was just as happy on the outside as I usually was.

Razia' s check was crushing my heart repeatedly. After a lot of. Conflict I finally decided that I should at least return the check. But I shouldn't write anything that scathes Razia's heart in any way. Her every sentence is devoted, every line is prayer. She does not feel refused even after my rejection. She doesn't want to be punished for giving her an assurance and then taking it back. She doesn't hate me.

I sat down to write a letter to Razia. After gathering all my thoughts.

'Dear Razia,

I got both your letters together on Monday. I am. Returning the check sent with the first letter, don't misunderstand the reason. When nothing of the past holds up, then what is the use of this check? If ever I'll need money, I'll write to you. When you are given so much hope, let the opportunity arrive as well.

If you visit Allahabad, come to our house for sure. Rest later.

Yours

Raju'

The next day Rekha asked, 'yesterday there was a check in the coat's pocket, did you submit it?' I was taken aback. 'No, I returned it to the person who had given it.' On saying this, I looked at Rekha with smiling eyes. She paused for a moment, and then said, 'whose was it? Why did it come? Why did you return it?' The situation was getting tense. Probably when the coat was sent for dry wash, she had taken out the papers from the pocket and saw the two letters. Read the letters. I was in the situation of getting caught red handed. But I was calm.

'They were letters from Razia and the check was sent by her also. The reason she sent it was clear in that letter, you should understand yourself why I returned it.'

'Who is Razia? She's a Muslim girl, no?'

'Yes, she's Muslim. She is a childhood friend who I met sometimes during the summer vacation at uncle's city Bareilly.'

'Which night was it when you accepted her? Before our marriage or after it?'

'The night I puked on returning home, that was the night.' I was used to giving right answers to questions, and did the same.

'Was this part of that novel which you were telling about in front of Surendra?'

'Yes.'

'You had tried to know my opinion indirectly. Have you ever thought that there's a woman whose husband, although loves him, from time to time he falls in love with other naked, girls, women willingly or unwillingly, then in that case what will be the end of that woman's life? Do you, in the spirit of retaliation, want to leave me a pimp myself?' Rekha was serious, but still calm.

'Knowing your opinion was necessary. A woman caught in such circumstances can become a pimp, but becoming something in retaliation is one thing, and naturally is another. You can be whatever you want to be, it depends on your personal situation. It's the scientific judgement of circumstances. The place I have been giving you in my life, I will continue giving it until every possible situation. I didn't betray you, didn't hide anything from you, and didn't disregard you. And what did I even do? Only to entertain myself, talk to someone lovingly for some time. I agree that I don't have any such moral code that I can use to give myself a good character, if the meaning of character only gets corrupted by ecstatic union.' I got quiet.

'The man who talks lovingly for some time may be a great man, but he'll be called greedy for physical pleasure and characterless.' Rekha said in a serious tone bowing her head.

'She doesn't want to stand on the patio of my life, but needs a space to stand near the outer door. As soon as I received her letter, I sent my letter of disapproval. She isn't a woman who wants to trap me. She is a superintendent in the police department. You have even read her other letter. Is the woman who spent her entire life waiting for me only evil because she wants a piece of your marital monopoly? Am I bad because I want to give her the fruit of her long unknown prayer? Don't worry; she is also a practitioner of my unacceptance. She doesn't wish to take away your rights, a compromise cannot be denied.' I got up and walked.

'I am not a lawyer who will keep giving arguments for another argument. I am a wife, in order to save my rights; I can even start an unexpected revolt. It's every married woman's birthright that she doesn't allow her husband to meet other unmarried, married, or professional women. You want to have Razia through arguments? Domestic life is not a trading institution whose shares get sold. Where there is a possibility of compromise.' Rekha answered.

I peeked into Rekha's eyes. In her crest, craters were seen like the images obtained from the moon, a suffocating gas was floating, the lava overflowing from the volcanoes spreading from the eyes, the flames of a revolt originated in the garden of determination were producing blood beds. I accepted everything except bowing down to a woman, bowing down to Rekha.

'You know this that I'm myself a rebel. I have always crushed the arrogance of the obstacles faced. You are my wife; if for your rights you can create the premise for a strong revolt then even I for the realization of the natural appetite of men can revolt. Razia can satisfy my mental and ideological hunger that you can just entertain. Anyone can carry the burden of this household. You are free to revolt.'

Rekha's eyes welled up. She spread her wet eyelids towards me and only said, 'bring Razia. I have endured you till date, now her...' The clouds rained on her lips, she got lost in tears.

Today I didn't convince her. Her tears were incapable of touching my heart today.

'If possible, give me back my peace. I can even leave your way forever but what do I do, these kids wouldn't let me die..... When I spent my entire life trying to see you happy then I don't wish to tie this unhappiness to my grave.' Rekha wiping her tears, holding my shirt from the arm drew me closer to her.

A wife's revolt can be suppressed, her suffering cannot be ridiculed. The woman has heated up like iron in revolting and in the tone of solstice can melt even the Himalayas. A man breaks the thorns on getting entangled in them but on getting surrounded by flower buds, pats them and appeals to their importance. He suffers in both the situations.

'Don't get emotional, Rekha. History doesn't get erased by anything, the future isn't the legacy of one's desires and the present has to be lived even if you don't wish to'. Saying that, changing clothes, I took my bicycle and left for outside.

Saavri was standing there. The children with their minds were analyzing the circumstances looking from afar at the rotating spikes in the wheels of the bicycle. There was only annoyance of unrest in my mind, turning over questions of buried dreams. Rekha kept looking at the boat with the broken anchor drifting afar into the west.

Time can heal wounds.......

After this, neither I remember what else Professor Sahab said, nor do I have the ability to write it.